CADUCEUS

ALLIE GREY

CONTENTS

TRIGGER WARNINGS

Death

Graphic sexual scenes (Breath play, light bondage, cockwarming, anal sex, knife play (minimal, no injuries)

To all the girls who read Hades and Persephone retellings and thought, why isn't there more Charon?
And to Victoria, who was the first to ask, will your books have any smut?

Charon! O gentle Charon! let me woo thee – Robert Herrick

CHAPTER ONE

Anastacia believed in gods and deities. The sight in front of her was all the proof she needed.

She had only been standing on the riverbank edge for mere moments, but that was almost enough to force her to mutter a prayer for safety. The water below was dark and treacherous, promising that anyone who fell in would drown painfully, its victims dragged through the froth and crushed against large, barely-hidden rocks as they were raced away. Further downstream, hidden from view, the Acheron eventually boiled and steamed, the fire of the Phlegethon River replacing it until its final descent into Tartarus.

The Acheron's water appeared black this far beneath the earth, its roiling anger and yawning depths nothing like its clear counterpart near her home. *That* water was fresh and inviting with a joyful soul, the lifeblood of her fishing village by the sea. This water, however, had been transformed during its journey below. Perhaps it was poisoned the deeper into the earth it went, or maybe only stripped of its niceties; those were only reserved for the living. After all, below, there was no need for calm water, no one to be polite to, no children to teach how to swim, and no hungry bellies to fill.

No, in the underworld, there were only souls to deter from wandering.

And the Acheron did its job.

Misery, it was called—as if the souls trapped here in the underworld could feel, as if they experienced the same fear she did when she stared into the river's howling depths. They were lucky; only the living could know the abject terror this water held. The dead needn't fear the water—they could not feel emotion or pain. Not here, not on the riverbank of waiting.

Here, they only lingered, their souls suspended in a place of un-awareness, until Charon came to collect them. Even then, they would only regain their memories and personalities briefly before being fer-ried to Hades and judged.

There were stories about what happened after that, but Anastacia didn't dwell on those.

She believed only in what she had seen with her own two eyes. She had told too many lies, created too many tales, and started too many rumors to put any stock into words without proof.

Anastacia stepped away from the bank, leaving the water behind and melding into the crowd of dead souls. Their eyes were vacant, unseeing, though they still walked as though they had somewhere to be. She supposed some habits, like the unnecessary rising and falling of their chests, were so deeply ingrained that not even death could steal them.

The underworld was bleak—at least, this side of the riverbank was. Only rocky cliffs lacking vegetation and a sandy shore with shuffled footprints that never disappeared.

The dead were lucky they could not see. Their first glimpse into the underworld would be depressing indeed.

It wasn't difficult for Anastacia to blend in with the other aimless souls who waited for their turn with the Ferryman, her short stature keeping her concealed. The farther away from the river she walked, the denser the crowd became—not many walked close to the Acheron, as if they inherently knew that to fall in was to disappear, forced to wait for years until Charon retrieved them from wherever they floated to.

She ducked away from a lumbering man, impatiently scanning the faces of every soul she passed. Her jaw clenched with every additional unfamiliar person, irritation making her muscles tighten. Anastacia didn't mind the company of the dead; some days, she preferred it to that of the living. However, today was not one of those days.

Today, Anastacia was there for a reason—a woman. A mother of three, young and beautiful, with a husband who loved her enough to defy the gods to retrieve her. Not enough to do it himself, of course, but that was wise. He had no skills to offer the gods in return. He was not Heracles, strong enough to win her back, nor was he Orpheus with his lyre to charm his way across the river.

But he was smart enough to find Anastacia, and that was all he needed to be.

Because Anastacia might not be strong, nor was she musically inclined, but she was certainly skilled.

Her eyes finally paused on a familiar face, the same one she had seen in the world above, though there it had been painted with death. The woman's face rested as she wandered among the others, vacant and empty. She would stay that way, unanimated, until Anastacia touched her skin to skin, giving her soul something to tether itself to.

Satisfaction eased the tightness in her chest. The woman's husband had followed Ophelia's directions, delaying his wife's funeral rites, keeping his obol from her eyes, mouth, or hands. Her lack of coin meant she would haunt the riverbank for one hundred years before the Ferryman retrieved her, unless Anastacia interfered.

Anastacia's eyes traveled back to the river, ensuring it was as empty as she believed it to be. Charon had already left with his boat of souls and wouldn't return again today.

By the time he came tomorrow, he wouldn't notice a random woman missing from his bank.

She knew that better than most.

Anastacia weaved through the souls and toward her target, careful not to touch any skin. She avoided them easily, their movements slow and lacking purpose. Her feet were as silent on the ground as theirs were, blending in as though she belonged. At the last moment before she reached the woman, Anastacia shifted, grabbing her staff from where she had it tucked artfully into the belt of her peplos. She pressed the staff against the woman's back, using it to push her lightly through the others without making a scene. Although she didn't believe the gods monitored the riverbank while Charon was gone, she also didn't want to draw more attention to her actions than necessary.

Some souls did not appreciate being woken in this state, their minds uncomprehending of time without a tether, without someone alive to help keep them conscious. The act of their thoughts returning, the knowledge of their past life and death with it, was jarring. It was better to allow the woman to stay in her liminal state for as long as she could. It was a mercy.

Anastacia artfully herded the woman out of the center of souls without touching her, using her own body as a guide until they exited the mass. Free of the others, it was likely safe to tether themselves together now, but she glanced one more time over her shoulder. Her eyes scanned for the familiar build of the Ferryman, searching for his broad, cloaked shoulders. She waited to hear the skiff pole that he used to fight the currents, the sound of his boat cutting through the angry waves of the river, but the Acheron was silent.

He had disappeared into the darkness beyond.

Charon had always been a captivating deity, his striking, rugged face shadowed even in a world without sun. His eyes were dark, intelligent, knowing.

How he presented to the other souls, she wasn't sure. Some men and women quaked with fear at his face or flinched with disgust. Others cried in awe or knelt with rapture. To her, he had always appeared as a handsome man. If Anastacia saw him in her village, she would think him a typical seaman, though far more beautiful than those she grew up with. His crooked nose looked like it had been broken too many times and his tan skin was an olive color that caught even the smallest rays of light in the darkest areas of the underworld. He was the only bright thing on the river, the only piece of life that survived.

It was always strange to see him belong so seamlessly in a place so different from him. A lifeless, plain riverbank contrasting with a virile, captivating deity. For years, Anastacia had watched the way he interacted with the souls he ferried, and a man that full of contradiction could not be empty like the entrance to the underworld.

Kind to some and cruel to others, patient with those who needed it and rough with those who didn't. She once saw him carry an old woman onto his skiff like a child, cradled in his arms like a toddler he was bringing to bed. Then, she once witnessed him use his skiff pole to throw a resisting man into the river, holding him down as he flailed before fishing him out unceremoniously and depositing him on the boat.

Despite her searching, her mind almost creating a mirage of him over the water with her focus, she saw neither hide nor hair of him.

With the reassurance that Charon was gone, her actions unnoticed by the deity, she palmed her staff hard enough that her fingers went white, a smile creeping onto her face. *This* was the moment she remembered what it was to be alive, to cherish the world above and fight for it over anything else.

This was the moment Anastacia felt like a goddess.

Her hand reached out to touch the mother kindly, the skin warm against Anastacia's fingertips, though somehow the texture always reminded her more of soft dirt than flesh. Like if she dug her nails in, the woman would fall apart underneath her grip, like she was malleable and the shape of her soul was only held together by muscle memory instead of tendons and bone. At the contact, awareness came back to the woman's gaze slowly and then all at once as she gasped.

Anastacia covered the woman's mouth before she could speak, shushing her. "You will trust me if you want to see your children and husband again. Say nothing. Do not scream."

Against her hand, the woman stiffened, her eyes filling with fear before she nodded. Did she remember her death? Were her last moments replaying in her head as she wondered how close to eternity she currently stood?

Anastacia lowered her hand, peeking over her shoulder one more time out of habit to see if she could catch a glimpse of her Ferryman. Disappointment warred with relief at his absence before she shook her head and began walking away from the safety of the crowd. She pulled the woman with her, keeping her arm in her grasp the entire time. She couldn't risk letting their tether fade yet, not this close to the bank.

It would be all too easy for the woman to return to her place of waiting, for Anastacia to lose her again with the others. Better to keep contact as they hurried across the barren ground and to the cliffs surrounding the entrance to the underworld.

There was no conversation as Anastacia navigated their way to her trail, discreetly blending into the cavernous walls. They didn't have the luxury of taking the well-worn path that stories were told about, the famed stairs Orpheus had walked with Eurydice. No, Anastacia had been forced to make her own way, hidden and treacherous, all narrow ledges and steep inclines.

But the souls were already dead, and Anastacia was too sure-footed to lose her balance. There may not have been any gods on her side, none that guided or cared for her, but she didn't need a god's favor. Had lived her entire life without it and done just fine.

Anastacia and the woman ascended, hands dirty from the places they had to dig their fingers in and climb, the stones worn from Anastacia's palms, fitting like gloves. It wasn't a difficult climb for the soul, though Anastacia always minded herself. To fall from such a height would be disastrous, enough that even without a fear of heights, she was always careful not to stare down for too long.

When they were high enough off the ground to take a break, a ledge widening before the trail tunneled into the mountain walls and led to the world above, Anastacia sat and allowed her legs to dangle over the edge. With every passing moment that she left the woman without a reassuring touch, the light in her eyes faded, her body becoming listless once more. She would not walk off the ledge, would not risk harm to her soul, but nor was she a mother any longer.

Just another empty vessel waiting to cross to the other side.

Still, Anastacia always took a few minutes to stare at the view from the ledge with every journey she took, watching the Acheron River descend from the world far above her. It was a sight to behold, the waterfall cascading off the side of a cliff, billowing as it battered itself into the miserable entity below.

The sound was more muffled than it should have been, though everything on this side of the riverbank was. Hollow, unalive. The Acheron continued from the waterfall, joined by the Cocytus River which sprung from the ground somewhere beyond. The color of the water was dark through the gray rock, a dismal sight even as it was magnificent in its representation.

Anastacia swallowed a prayer for retrieving the mother without any issue, unwilling to risk the gods hearing it even if she didn't believe they would listen. She didn't want to invoke them—didn't want their attention or the pressure that came with it.

Others used their prayers so frivolously, so easily, as if for tradition and habit's sake rather than because they meant for the gods to answer.

Anastacia's words were never so casual because she knew better than most. One should never invoke the gods unless one wanted them to interfere.

Yes, she thought again. Anastacia believed in the gods and deities. Not because she was told to, not because she feared retribution or punishment.

No, she believed because she had fallen in love with one.

CHAPTER TWO

T he world above looked no different than when she had left it, aside from the sun having progressed through the sky. Time always seemed to pass differently in the underworld, though Anastacia couldn't articulate if it felt faster or slower.

When there was no reason to live, there was no reason to keep time.

The underworld had no sun or stars, no waxing and waning moon to help its inhabitants orient themselves. It was still a beautiful place, awe-inspiring and captivating, but there was no mistaking it for Gaia. It was a world of the dead.

The woman still didn't speak as they walked down the mountainside, the entrance to the underworld disappearing beneath them with finality. Anastacia didn't mind the silence—it was easier when she didn't have to answer questions. She loved rescuing souls, the feeling of stealing them from the gods, but interacting with them was never her strong suit.

Her feet were silent as she descended, naturally avoiding anything that might make noise even though it was unnecessary. No mortals walked these cliffsides; the mountain was too treacherous to risk without cause. Perhaps they would come if they knew what she had found there, but she doubted it. Sane mortals didn't want to go to the underworld any earlier than they were forced to.

Her village was indistinguishable below the thick brush and terrain, but the sea to the east was a sight like no other, more beautiful with the dramatic contrast of the dark cave behind her. Anastacia would never forget the first time she discovered it, the way she sat above the world for hours as the sun set, its flames dancing over the water like a cascade of ruby jewels.

She ran her hands habitually down her staff as she finally broke skin contact with the woman, trusting her to follow on her own with some amount of awareness now that they were far enough away from the pull of the underworld. The feeling of the grooves and carvings against her fingertips settled her, even though she had each one memorized. No longer than her forearm, it was strong and sturdy.

Caduceus, it was called.

There were others like it, some meant to be used as a staff while others were impractical imitations, crafted with gold or silver, intricate artwork painstakingly decorating the smooth metal. Others were carved from wood or painted on pottery.

All were shoddy imitations of Hermes' staff, in Anastacia's opinion.

Anastacia's staff was better than theirs. It was not golden, not flashy or gaudy. It did not draw attention to itself. No, like Anastacia, it was rather plain. A simple ivory, the bone well-worn from the many nights spent with her hands running over it.

Hermes used his staff to guide the newly dead to Charon's riverbank, to gain access to the underworld.

It was only fitting that she used it to bring them back.

Anastacia paused as voices reached her ears, putting her hand up to stop the woman from walking forward. No one else would see her if she continued without Anastacia, but she preferred to keep the souls behind her. It made her uncomfortable to look upon them once they had exited the underworld—she didn't like the longing on their faces, the yearning for life as they followed her through the mountainside and realized they were no longer a part of it.

It was tragic. It was the look of someone coming to terms with their death, the realization that the world had continued without them.

Luckily, by the time they came to terms with their reality, Anastacia was already guiding their souls back into their bodies.

She relaxed when she recognized Ophelia's calm, warm voice. As always, her friend's tone was peaceful and confident. She was different than Anastacia, both in her ethereal beauty and her natural softness. She drew eyes in every setting, her blonde hair unique enough that poems had been written about her loveliness.

Born to stand out, attention and power followed Ophelia like a puppy desperate for attention. She was a tree with roots cascading through the ground, proud and solid no matter what tried to move her, providing shade and shelter to those who asked.

Anastacia, on the other hand, was the current deep within the river. The one that didn't make waves on the surface but gave strength to those who braved it.

Despite their differences, they were the same at the core of their beings—both committing atrocities against the will of the gods. If they had been blessed, their actions would be justified, sanctioned, and revered. They would not have to hide or make promises under moonless skies with whispered words and threats of silence.

But neither woman had been blessed. Whatever power they had, they had ripped from a world that didn't want to give it to them. Perhaps the gods might have admired their strength and tenacity if they hadn't made their living by defying the natural way of the world, but Anastacia didn't worry. The gods had never seen her, even when she wanted them to.

She put her staff securely in her belt, slipping her hand into the sewn-in linen of her peplos, feeling the coin settled deeply within. Then, Anastacia broke from the foliage.

Ophelia glanced up at the noise of her sandals crunching against the ground, standing from where she had perched over the woman's newly healed body. A man waited behind her with shifting eyes and tense shoulders. Anastacia was surprised he didn't dart away as she revealed herself, the flinch accompanying his averted eyes the only tell that he knew what she had done, who she carried with her.

The man swallowed hard when his eyes finally landed on her. "Did you find her?"

Anastacia raised her eyebrow as a smirk teased her face. "I'm insulted you'd even ask."

She knelt beside the woman's body, examining it. Fresh, no mottling, skin still warm to the touch, though she had died during the night prior due to childbirth complications. Ophelia had arrived too late to help her while she was still breathing, but her gifts extended past those for the living.

It wasn't something they did often. Anastacia would only risk retrieving those who she felt the fight within. If a soul was ready, it was ready. *This* woman's soul, however, was not finished with the world. She had felt it the moment they arrived at her body—the way the woman had railed against death with a vendetta.

Hermes had to argue with this one.

Ophelia had healed her body while Anastacia was below, but she could do nothing to return the woman to life with her soul still in the underworld. They were not necromancers, not witches who meddled with the bodies but left the soul wandering. No, this was true resurrection.

The man stepped forward as if to interrupt Anastacia as she viewed the woman's body, but Ophelia put her hand out to stop him. There was no sound aside from the birds chirping above, the wind traveling calmly through the trees. The sun was warm on her skin, baking into her back as she beckoned the soul behind her forward.

The woman knelt over her physical body, eyes wide and filling with tears, a cruel mirror of what she had lost, what Hermes had pulled her soul away from after Death had severed her ties to the world.

Anastacia did the opposite of the messenger god, however. She held the woman's hands, one real and one intangible. Then she closed her eyes, focused on the staff against the skin of her back, and brought their hands together.

There was a moment of tension, of a bubble about to burst, the second before a knife broke skin where it merely indented. Then, the soul disappeared from Anastacia's sight, only air where she once waited.

The woman on the ground gasped as she woke, her brown eyes flying open as a coughing fit overtook her. Her hands scrabbled at the dirt, fingertips digging into the soil as her body seized. She was as a new babe, birthed into a foreign, unrecognizable world. Even though she hadn't been gone for even a day, her soul understood what her body did not.

She had died.

Her return was a bitter victory.

The woman began sobbing, her husband running forward and collapsing next to her until he gathered her into his arms, kissing her cheeks as he muttered incoherent thanks. Ophelia stepped forward and touched his shoulder. "Do not mention the gods when you speak of this," she instructed.

His teary eyes glanced up to stare at her, wide and hopeful. "Of course, we will not speak of it at all, " he said. "I don't know how I could ever repay you."

Ophelia raised a bag of coin as though the paltry amount of money was worth the wrath of the gods they would face if caught. "You already have."

Anastacia stood and cleared her throat, interrupting. "She will need time to adjust. Don't go home until she's feeling normal, and mind who you tell of her endeavor. Not everyone can come back from death, nor should they. Your wife was an exception, not a rule. Do not make me regret this."

"I won't," he said as his hand skimmed down his wife's jaw. "You have my word." His eyes darted to a golden ring, coated in blood and herbs, and placed on a makeshift altar.

Before he could consider further, Anastacia shook her head. "That was your price. You chose to sacrifice it to gain back your wife. It's as good as gone to you now. You shouldn't try to retrieve it, or the magic may try to retrieve her," she inclined her head towards the woman.

He nodded shakily. "I will not touch it, then."

With his promises ringing in her ears, Anastacia walked home with Ophelia next to her, quiet as they listened to the birdsong trilling above them. She looked at the blue sky, reminding herself *this* was the world she belonged to, even if it wasn't always the one she longed for.

The colors of the underworld didn't appear with the same vividness, no pastel sunsets or blue, cloudy skies. Nothing but a cavern so high that it was invisible from below, no sunlight to touch her skin or birds to sing to her. Perhaps in Elysium things looked different, but she had never made it to the land of eternal peace, and the riverbank was not a place for beauty.

Ophelia gave Anastacia time to return to herself as a living being, not speaking or questioning how retrieving the soul had gone. Their friendship was so seamless that she knew when not to press. The journey to the underworld was always easy for Anastacia.

The one back to the living, less so.

They lived with one another on the outskirts of their village in a nice but tiny home, away from any accidental visitors. Ophelia was widely known as a healer, a woman who brewed tonics and birthed children, one with an unnatural gift for fixing injuries. In quieter circles, rumors that she worshipped the witch goddess, Hecate, ran rampant. They claimed she was kin to the witches Circe and Medea, but with a soft spot for her human friends.

However they spoke of Ophelia, they spoke of Anastacia not at all. Ophelia's quiet friend, quick to smirk and quicker to disappear, she simply helped Ophelia gather herbs and items. In her free time, she listened to news of people who needed help and others who needed humbling. Her soul-stealing habit wasn't mentioned, those who knew of her face and skills clever enough to keep their mouths shut.

By the time they got home, Anastacia had begun to feel like one of the living again. *Human. I am human,* she reminded herself with every step she took from the underworld.

From Charon.

Her shoulders had loosened, her eyes growing heavy. A horse knickered in their stable, impatient to be fed, and three chickens ran out of their coop, angry squawking flowing from their beaks. The ocean waves crashed against their soft, pearly beach in the distance, and she tried to shake off the feeling that she didn't belong there.

Ophelia and Anastacia fell into their routine, feeding the animals who had been neglected in their absence. After they'd finished, they ducked inside where Ophelia brewed tea, handing Anastacia a warm cup as she leaned against their table. "How was it?"

Anastacia shrugged. "Uneventful. Unchanging." Her hand traveled, unbidden, to her hip. She stopped herself from dipping her fingers within the folded fabric and pulled away before Ophelia noticed the slip. "How was the healing?"

"Simple, though we need more herbs and a new knife," she grimaced as her hand unfurled, revealing a large cut in her palm. Anastacia's lip curled, and she turned away. The deep, self-inflicted gash was a necessary but gruesome part of the process she didn't enjoy watching, though Ophelia always healed herself quickly.

Anastacia and Ophelia had perfected their ritual over time, Hetate the only goddess Ophelia invoked while healing. Ophelia possessed more of the witch goddess's power than anyone else Anastacia had ever met, and whether out of love for Ophelia or amusement at their heretic behaviors, Hetate had never interfered with their lives.

"I can go find some tomorrow," Anastacia offered, her mind darting back to the herbs and ritual knife. There were plenty sold at vendors that no one would miss. Ophelia nodded her head gratefully. It would be a long time before they risked performing another ritual, but those items couldn't be replaced without planning and were not always easy to find in a hurry.

Exhaustion tugged at her body, her bones begging to return to the earth. Her shoulders felt too heavy in her body, too sluggish. Anastacia had been up since the prior morning, her visit to the underworld leaving no time for rest.

She left Ophelia to her work, stepping heavily to her room until she collapsed into bed and finally slept.

CHAPTER THREE

Anastacia *was* going to get the herbs. She had just taken a detour. A very slight, very minor detour.

Inside her village's inn, in the room of a wealthy guest.

Which currently happened to be unoccupied.

Perhaps Anastacia should have abided by kinder laws and controlled her impulses, but she hadn't been able to stop herself when a couple exited the inn, graced in gold and jewels, the glint catching her eye even from a distance.

The woman's necklace was a work of art, immaculately designed and inlaid with flawless gemstones. Anastacia was walking down the street, her head down, when the woman bumped into her as though she had expected Anastacia to feel her presence and dodge. She might have been able to deny herself after the first time their eyes met, but after the collision, she was drawn to her like a shark to blood.

Her hands had simply reacted, fingers rising deftly to unclasp the beautiful artwork and slip it into her peplos. The sewn swatches of fabric lining her belt hid a myriad of items when she needed it to, and the necklace settled there easily as she brought her hands to the woman's hair, ruffling it under the guise of righting her appearance. Anastacia apologized profusely, though the woman was so incensed that she had only waved her off and continued on her way.

Anastacia had paused in the road, watching the woman's back.

Then she broke into their room, picking the lock until she could sneak in and rifle through their belongings. She had already returned the necklace, throwing it casually on the bed. She hadn't meant to steal it—not really. It was only admiration for its beauty that made her fingers itch to hold it, only for a moment.

The red ruby ring on the nightstand, however... *that* she wanted to steal.

Inlaid in a gold setting, it fit her finger perfectly. Snug enough that it wouldn't slip, loose enough that it didn't feel restrictive. She settled herself on the bed, her hand turning in the air in front of her as her eyes traced the jewel on her finger.

Graceful, she thought. Elegant. She wondered if it held any sentimental value, if it could be her thank you gift for returning the necklace. Would the woman even notice it was missing? Surely, Anastacia would appreciate it far more than the woman had. After all, the rich lady clearly had so many jewels she could hardly keep track of them.

She sighed and averted her eyes, her fingers working easily to remove the ring and set it back in its place before she blew out another breath, vaulting off the bed. She ran a finger along the edge of a sword to test whether it was as sharp as it looked, placed her hand on a discarded peplos to feel the silk against her skin, thumbed through a small pile of letters, reading words that meant nothing to her.

Finally, she pursed her lips and turned back towards the door. Anastacia was procrastinating and she knew it, but stealing herbs was boring. There was no challenge, no reward to stare at in awe, no keepsake to hide in her room.

Her eyes roamed lazily until they landed on a polished copper mirror. Her reflection stared back at her, dark brown hair and honey brown eyes, a straight nose set in olive skin.

Pretty enough, she supposed. If one ignored the glint in her eye, the grace in her muscles, and the balance with which she held her body, she was average. Easily forgettable. Not a great quality for a woman, but a fantastic one for a thief.

Anastacia looked away from the mirror and hopped rudely over the bed, the sheets musing underneath her feet. Her hand swiped against the table as she landed, eyes firmly on the exit until she stepped outside. No one watched as she locked the door before sliding her tools back into the hidden folds within her clothing.

If she wasn't careful, they might jingle against one another.

But Anastacia was always careful.

***

The herb vendor was always too friendly, the poor man. Lonely, eager to speak, aging with no other skills besides a green thumb. Anastacia often considered her conversation to be payment for the herbs, even if he never knew the correct amount she took.

With the stolen items carefully tucked in her clothing, she hurried home. The clouds rolling in promised a thunderstorm, rare but not unexpected. She'd appreciate the relief from the unseasonably sweltering weather, though the color of the sky made her anxious. The wind blowing in from the sea was violent and sudden, the waves angry on the horizon.

Any smart fishermen would already be heading inland, eager to get off the water before their boats capsized. The sea here was typically calm, a playful and mischievous entity unlike on some coastlines. Today, though, it was livid.

Anastacia turned her sights towards home, unconcerned. She hardly stepped foot in the ocean, let alone traveled deeply enough within that she couldn't easily touch the ground. The rain and wind might rage against the walls of her home, but she wouldn't be taken down in the sea.

Would never risk the feeling or water flooding her lungs, of gasping and inhaling salt, the burn in her chest as she tried to gag it away only to find it replaced with more water.

By the time Anastacia returned to Ophelia, the sky had broken open like a monster with its maw gaping. Although it was early evening, the sun had been swallowed. In the dim light of their home, Ophelia sat, cooing at the newest stray dog she had rescued a few weeks prior. He was an old, skinny creature who had looked so unhealthy when Ophelia first brought him home that Anastacia thought him dead.

She collected dogs like Anastacia collected jewels, though she claimed it was to keep her in good standing with Hecate. She thought it was more likely Ophelia didn't know how to see a creature suffer.

Over the many years together, she had seen Ophelia nurse plenty of animals through a long life and into a peaceful death. She smiled softly at the imagery of Charon ferrying over a skiff full of the furry creatures, their bodies swaying next to one another as he navigated the Acheron. Would he let them lick his palms or shove them away? Could Charon grin if it wasn't to comfort a soul who needed it, did he know how to smile for himself?

Anastacia fell asleep that night thinking of him, the knocking of the trees outside her room sounding similar to his skiff pole against his boat. She dreamt of nothing.

***

The storm had been out of season, surprising those stranded in the water who had misread the wrath in its approach. Already, Ophelia had filled her bags with tonics and salves to distribute among the injured. Anastacia trailed behind her, nothing more than a pack slave as she led their horse, saddled with bags filled to the brim with clay and medical instruments. The dog, clearly as in love with Ophelia as everyone became, meandered alongside her.

They traveled inland, down roads that had already dried in the morning heat. Anastacia was whistling happily, enjoying the relief from the heat that the storm had delivered, when she heard the un-mistakable sound of horse hooves pounding against the ground. She tugged her horse to the side of the road, Ophelia pausing for a moment before doing the same.

Anastacia expected the man to ride past, so she was surprised when he saw them and raised a hand, shouting incoherently. He stopped abruptly, his sides heaving as he tried to catch his breath and speak at the same time. She vaguely recognized him, though she wasn't sure from where.

"Need help," he spat out quickly as he collected himself. "A boy went with his father yesterday, fishing in the sea. They didn't see the signs of the storm and waited too long to return to shore. They capsized, and the boy hit his head hard. By the time his father got him home, he was unconscious."

Ophelia was calm as she listened, though her eyes were shrewd. "Has he already passed?"

The man glanced around him as if even speaking the words out loud would be blasphemy. "Yes."

"How long has it been?"

"No more than a few hours. They notified me only recently, and I came to get you." His eyes flashed to Anastacia before they looked away again. "Please, you must help them. He is only a boy."

Boys died all the time, but she bit her tongue against the harsh words. It wouldn't hurt to try. Ophelia stepped back, eyes darting to Anastacia. If she said no, Ophelia would respect her decision. Her friend may know about healing the body, dead and alive alike, but the underworld was Anastacia's domain.

Anastacia nodded, holding her hand out. "Lead the way. I will see if there is anything to be done."

Their steps had purpose, sandals kicking up dust while they jogged as quickly as they could without breaking any of the valuables they carried. It wasn't a long distance to the neighboring village, though enough time had passed that Anastacia knew Ophelia needed to treat the body soon to preserve it.

The home was what she would expect from someone in the middle class, nice but unmemorable. A horse rested out front, eyes dozing and head low. Anastacia tied her mount next to it and then hesitated at the door. "Did you tell the family we were coming?"

The man shook his head. "I didn't want to get their hopes up."

Anastacia swallowed her irritation. She would have preferred to know how open the family was to defying their gods before they knew her face. Their offer was a risk—they had to be selective of who they pitched their services to. If too many learned of the possibility of cheating death, one of two things would happen.

One, she and Ophelia would be swarmed with those trying to save their loved ones, or two, they would be killed or exiled for tempting the gods' wrath.

Still, she knocked politely before stepping into the home. The air was solemn, laying heavily against her skin. A wooden table sat in the center of the room with an intricately decorated urn set upon it, a woman painting the clay pot even as her hair ran loosely into her red-rimmed eyes. Her face was set in a grimace, shoulders hunched.

Grief leaked off her, infecting the home.

The boy had been set on a bed in the corner of the room, his eyes closed, his body covered in blankets pulled to his neck and tucked tightly around him. His father sat on the floor beside him, one hand buried in his son's hair.

Ophelia cleared her throat, drawing both of their gazes until she gestured for the father to join her. At his hesitance, she waved her hand once more, her ingrained patience warring with irritation. If they were going to help, the parents wouldn't have much time to think. They had waited dangerously long already.

Anastacia passed him as he rose, questions on his lips that she ignored. He could speak with Ophelia—Anastacia didn't have time to waste, stepping close to the boy to assess him. She lowered the blanket, her eyes looking beyond the boy's body. Already, she could feel the echo of life left behind, the way his laughter filled these walls. She placed a thumb on his lips, the corners still slightly upturned even in death, as though he had smiled so much in his few years that not even his soul's absence could remove it from his face.

She raised her hand to his eyes, opening one and then the other. There was no lividity in his body yet, but there would be soon. Anastacia took a deep breath and opened his mouth.

She had to smother her gasp, her fingers plucking the coin from underneath his tongue as her head whipped around. She rushed toward the table, placing the coin on top.

"Put that back!" his mother sobbed, her entire body caving forward as she reached for the obol, interrupting whatever Ophelia was explaining. "It is his passage, he will wander without it!"

"You get the obol or you get your son. You cannot have both. Choose," Anastacia snapped. The woman looked at her husband, the desperation on their faces plain. "I need to go if you want him back. Even now, I'm not sure it will be possible."

If the boy had already given his payment to Charon, he would be long gone by the time she arrived. She could not—would not—cross the river to find him, no matter how young or sweet he was.

"Eutimio. We want Eutimio," the father finally said.

Anastacia ran then, trusting Ophelia to find what she needed on her own. Their horse was still ladened with items, so she grabbed the reins of the dozing animal instead, untying him before vaulting onto his back and pressing her heels into his sides urgently.

They ran like death was on their heels, and in a way, it was. She forced the creature forward unfairly, aiming him up her mountain when she would normally tether him at the base. She didn't have the time, and would have to hope the poor animal didn't twist its leg.

She didn't thank the gods when she reached the hidden entrance to the underworld, didn't waste her time looking at the beautiful view behind her as she ducked into the darkness ahead. Anastacia went blind immediately, the contrast in lighting so different that it would take longer than she was willing to wait for her eyes to adjust. She paused for only a moment to take her sandals off, her bare feet quieter and with better balance.

Then, Anastacia placed her hand against the wall and began her descent.

It was quick. Despite the rocky trail, the steep cliffside, and the dim lighting, she knew this place like the back of her hand. It was etched into her soul, every part of her belonging here even if she didn't want it to. Mortals were not meant to visit death like Anastacia did, teasing it with fleeting touches and almost kisses.

When she broke into the open side of the cavern, Charon's hulking mass was revealed, his bare chest on display beneath his tunic. He was muscular, his body rippling as he balanced on the river's edge, assessing those Hermes had brought him.

Those without a coin would go to Anastacia's riverbank, while those with one would be allowed on the skiff. She didn't know what kind of magic worked in the underworld, but his boat was never the same size. Sometimes small enough to fit one person alone with him, sometimes so large it seemed it could carry the entire riverbank if he wished.

Anastacia was lucky today. The storm must have killed many because it was crowded, souls patiently waiting to see the Ferryman. It was clear they didn't see him the same way Anastacia did, their demeanor changing the moment he approached and their mind returned. Most shied away, futile and cowardly.

She ignored the men and women, searching from above for Eutimio. It was harder because of his small size, his head hidden within the group. It would be a boon later, though—easier to sneak around with a boy than a man.

Already, Anastacia knew she should back out. Make her excuses to the family and apologize, tell them he had already given his payment to the Ferryman.

But then she spotted him, and her resolve strengthened. He was not so close that it was over, that it was impossible to retrieve him. If she were quick, if she were perfect...

Anastacia vaulted down the rest of the pathway, cursing quietly when her foot caught on a rock, a sharp sting warning her she had cut herself open, blood immediately causing sand to coat her skin. She ignored it, weaving through the surrounding bodies, careful not to touch anyone lest they look at her. She didn't want to draw any attention, wanted to get in and out without Charon knowing the difference.

She might enjoy looking at him, but she didn't want him to look at her—not now. Not when there was so much at stake.

Anastacia slid behind the boy, only needing a moment as she bumped him with her clothed shoulder. Her fingers grabbed his wrist and slid down until she pried his palm open, relieving him of his coin before she was gone again, ducking into the crowd.

A moment of impulse overtook her as she ran, perhaps her joy at her success, and her hand caught on the not-sun of the underworld before she could think twice. Then, she disappeared within the throng of souls.

Once hidden, she took a moment to push her hair back and eye the boy. His head swung around as he gained enough awareness to know he was missing something he needed. She winced when the boy raised his hands to his face, rolling them in front of him, his fingers twitching at their emptiness. "Mom?" he said, confused. He spoke loudly enough that Charon's head raised.

She melted backwards farther, controlling her breathing as she twirled the cold obol through her fingers. Her eyes stayed locked on the Ferryman as she did her best to calm herself.

Charon straightened at the boy's confusion, his eyes scanning the riverbank. Anastacia told herself to move, tried to take a step to blend in deeper with those meandering around her, but she was trapped by the knowledge that she was close enough to Charon for her to hear his words, frozen by his sharp jawline that could have been chiseled from marble. His crooked nose created a small shadow, an imperfection that turned him into art.

Her heart raced despite her attempt to slow it, crawling into her throat at his stoic perusal. She swore she could smell his scent—water, salt and earth. Perhaps it was her imagination or maybe it was the scent of the river itself, misting her with spray while she waited so close to its edge.

Charon stayed calm as he stood aside to let the people in front of the boy pass onto the skiff politely. Then, he bent down on one knee. Even kneeling, he was large, towering over the child. She couldn't hear their exchange, but the boy raised his hands and waved them before patting his torso as if looking for his bag. Searching for his missing coin, held safely in her fingertips.

Charon put a hand on Eutimio's head kindly, ruffling his hair before directing him to the bank. His smile looked sincere and unconcerned. Anastacia had seen some souls wait for only days until their families performed proper funeral rights for them, an obol appearing in their hands to pay their way.

Some waited the entire hundred years for Charon to collect them.

It didn't matter. Not really. Time passed strangely for the souls in this purgatory; they didn't know the difference.

Eutimio didn't argue or fight, only pausing to look one last time at his empty hands before he stepped away from the skiff. Charon moved on, continuing his job. Still, Anastacia stayed away, waiting patiently. She recognized the cunning in his eyes and didn't trust that he had forgotten his suspicion, that brief niggling at the back of his mind that made him search the riverbank when he heard Eutimio speak.

It wasn't until Charon pushed his skiff off the bank that she allowed herself to approach the boy, her hand gently reaching for him once more, her other hand brushing unconsciously against the staff in her belt, an impossible habit to break. This time, she allowed her hand to remain within his and watched his awareness return.

"Your parents sent me," she whispered, putting a finger against her lips to warn him. "Follow me but stay quiet. I'll get you home."

He nodded, his face so small and innocent, the mind of a child malleable enough that he did not fear or question her. A sudden relief overwhelmed her—she had almost missed him. Had almost lost him to the underworld beyond. Did he understand how close he had come to a permanent death?

She squeezed his hand in comfort before bringing him into the shadows with her, their footsteps quiet on the soft ground of the riverbank. They began ascending, her foot aching with every press of her injury. It had gotten bearable in her stillness, but as she moved, she could feel the heat of blood squish between her toes.

She ignored the pain, focused only on getting into the world above. She didn't know how much time had passed, but it had certainly been hours. She wouldn't calm until the boy was far away, untouchable from those within the earth.

It wasn't until she and Eutimio had walked high enough that she could overlook the river that she turned around. She expected the same thing she always saw—the empty water below her, Charon's skiff invisible in the darkness. But that was not the vision that awaited her.

Instead, Charon floated in the middle of the Acheron, his pole shaking against its raging force. His face was turned toward her, his chin tilted up as he stared. There was nowhere else for her to disappear, and though she and Eutimio were pressed against the cavern walls, hidden within shadows, she felt it in her bones.

It was not the first time Charon had seen her.

But it was the first time he noticed.

CHAPTER FOUR

C haron's curiosity had been piqued when he noticed a flash of red in the corner of his eye—there, then gone. It was uncommon for anything to move that fast on the riverbank, to be shiny enough to cause a reflection.

Then the boy spoke, the sound ringing unusually in the air. He should not have been able to mutter even one word, should have been stuck in that strange space that souls existed in when they had no tether, no body to contain them and no living being for them to ground to.

One change might be attributed to chance, but two could not. Something was different, *off*.

So, when the boy reached him, Charon had examined him carefully. But the boy was not special. There was no reason he should have found consciousness on his own, no blessing from a god or goddess, no unique blood in his veins.

It was then that his interest had been truly deepened, his eyes scanning the riverbank, which looked no different than normal. He had ferried millions of souls in his eternal life, and never had it altered—until today, a change in a world that was usually so steadfast. Death did not evolve, nor did souls. Death was the end, the moment something became locked into stone. Charon had never seen true change, not from the gods, nor from mortals.

Years passed, and they both stayed the same.

Yet he felt something at the base of his spine as he stood there, looking at the coinless boy. For one so young to lack funeral rites was rare, but Charon still directed him to the undulating mass on the side of the river. It might be years before Charon saw him again, though it always felt like only moments to him.

He had never experienced time the way others described it. Even Hades and Persephone could not explain the feeling to him, the difference between a second and a century. But as he averted his eyes from the boy, the first thing that had caught his attention since the artist with the lyre, he kept his ears alert and his gaze careful.

Charon waited so long that he began to think he was wrong, that he had imagined the flash of color, the boys voice. The rest of the souls obeyed without question, his skiff shifting with their weight as they boarded and stood patiently. He scanned the riverbank one last time before using his pole to push off the ground and into the roiling waters.

He compensated automatically, his legs moving with the motion as he angled his body. Charon looked forward, focusing on the Acheron. He had never capsized, never fallen into the water accidentally, but it would be possible if he were careless.

Still, he felt something.

Wrong wasn't quite the word he was searching for—it was a taste at the back of his tongue that he almost recognized, a smell in the air that he had picked out before but never fully acknowledged.

Charon opened his mouth and took a deep breath, letting the scent coat his tongue. It was light, almost undetectable. It was so similar to the world around him that he understood why he had never given it attention in the past. It was sage.

But sage did not grow on this part of the bank.

Once again, he turned. Nothing but the dim lighting of the cavern greeted him until—there. Another flash of red, the glint of something shiny, a reflection within a jewel. He hadn't expected to find anything on the cavern wall, an area that had been untouched and untended for as long as he had existed. He had never needed to look up before. There was only one set of stairs into the underworld, and it had only ever been traveled by Hermes and his souls, Heracles, and Orpheus.

And yet, once he saw the woman's outline, he couldn't believe she had escaped him for that long. Long enough to scale the rocky face halfway, hidden in the dark shadows above. Charon might not have noticed her at all save for the blood-colored ruby on her finger, gaudy compared to the linen peplos she wore.

Charon had noticed jewelry on souls in the past, but usually it blended naturally, their clothing representing their wealth in its fabric, just as in their jewelry. Even then, those did not shine like this, had been paled by death and their crossing into the underworld. All beauty became obsolete here, inconsequential, an afterthought. All on the riverbank was dull.

Which only meant one thing, he thought as he watched her step onto a ledge that he wasn't sure even a goat could successfully balance on.

It meant she was not dead.

He tilted his head curiously, watching the boy's soul trail behind her, his hand occasionally snaking out to grab hers. Charon couldn't see her expression, but her body language showed her discomfort at his touch.

He placed his pole in the river, lodging it deeply into the rocks below and pausing their movement. The souls on board did not question
or scream in apprehension as he stopped them in the current of the
Acheron, where to fall would be to disappear for years.

He was patient, waiting until she stopped high enough above that
her view would be all encompassing. Perhaps Charon should have
been angered, but he only felt impressed. Aside from the ring, she
blended so well into the world around her that she might as well be
invisible.

He considered notifying Hades, but the thought fled as she glanced
down, looking for him the same way he looked for her. She stumbled
back as their eyes met, and even from here, he saw her mouth drop
open in surprise.

Now that she had looked at him, it was easier for Charon to pick
out the details of her face. The strong nose, the full lips, the olive
skin. If someone were to ask him to paint a typical Grecian woman,
it would have been a copy of her. But Charon's mind grabbed onto
those specific features and burned them into his brain.

Because she would be back.

He might get reprimanded for keeping it from Hades, but he had
been reprimanded before. The last time was many years ago, and it was
for such a brief sentence that Charon hardly remembered that year of
his life as any different than the others. It wasn't until now that Charon
considered Hades' punishment too light, too inconsequential.

Because Charon found out, as he watched the woman turn and
disappear into the wall of the mountain with the boy, that he had not
obeyed for all these years simply because he respected Hades. He had
obeyed because nothing happened that was worth disobeying *for*.

But his wonder was too much. To notify Hades would be to get
the girl taken, punished, or killed. It would take away his ability to

question her himself. To ask how many times she had avoided him, to discover what she was doing in his domain. It would rid him of the first thing that had caught his interest in... he did not know how long.

He waited anxiously to see her again, but she had already disappeared. It could have been minutes ago or hours. It didn't matter. Charon raised a hand toward her anyway.

And smiled.

CHAPTER FIVE

Anastacia felt cold with fear, cursing herself and her impulsiveness. She ran, her hand grasping the boy like he might fall behind, although as he was, he couldn't stumble. Still, in Anastacia's panic, logic had abandoned her.

When she reached the horse, still tied although night had come, she rode him faster than was reasonable. Fast enough that he stumbled on the terrain, but Anastacia swallowed her guilt and pushed him harder like his hooves could outrun the gods.

She did not doubt Charon had seen her. His dark eyes had imprinted on her body, his head tilting curiously at their colliding gazes. Anastacia had made a mistake in touching the boy when he was so close to the Ferryman. She should have let him board the skiff, wished him peace, and explained to his parents that she had arrived too late.

Her risk had gained her Eutimio, but cost her something else.

She waited to be struck down as Ophelia helped her return the boy's soul to his body, as they instructed the family on care and caution. She expected to be confronted while they walked back home, and then again as she tucked herself into bed. Perhaps it would happen while she slept, or she would wake up transformed into a rat or some other sneaky creature.

But none of these things happened, and a week passed. Then another.

And though Anastacia experienced an overwhelming relief, there was also a slight feeling of disappointment. A promise of excitement, of a climax that had never arrived. For some, the passing time might have helped them forget, convinced them that they were lucky and to never attempt such a feat again.

For Anastacia, it did the opposite.

Her confidence in her ability grew once more, even as she tried to temper the satisfaction glowing in her chest. Charon hadn't seen her face well enough to describe or identify her to the gods, or perhaps he simply hadn't cared enough to bother. Once again, she had defied them, had done something no one else could, had looked the Ferryman in the eye and returned to the world of the living.

She also found that as her adrenaline faded, so too did her will to focus on anything other than the underworld. No one else approached her and Ophelia, which was normal, but the knowledge that Charon had seen her face made her eager to descend again. Anastacia's boredom grew with the lack of interesting work, and she couldn't shake the increasing itch at the base of her spine.

When she couldn't distract herself from the feeling any longer, she gave in to it.

She left the horse at home and a note for Ophelia. Her friend would only berate her, tell her not to be so careless. Anastacia knew that while she might nod her head and understand why Ophelia would be so against her visiting the underworld without a specific reason, she wouldn't listen.

Anastacia had taken the time to let her foot heal, the gash still pink and raw but far better than before. Ophelia offered to use her magic on the injury, but Anastacia had turned her down. It was nothing her own body couldn't handle by itself. She did not like to use the gods' gifts when it wasn't necessary.

She scaled the mountain, taking her time. Spring was dissolving into summer, and the weather was hot enough that she had to pause in the shade with her waterskin to stay comfortable. It hadn't stormed since Eutimio's death, the coast hoarding its rain, saving it for deeper water.

Anastacia ran her hand along the cliff just outside of the cave entrance. It was difficult to find, almost impossible if you didn't know it was there. No sane man or woman would traverse this side of the mountain, where one slip would cost your life. Especially not for the view alone, which while breathtaking, wasn't worth never drawing breath again.

Anastacia wasn't sure what people would do if they knew there was access to the underworld from this far above the earth. After all, not many were likely to *want* to visit. It was a dark, gloomy, depressing place.

And yet she couldn't stop herself as she entered once more, making her way down the familiar path. Her eyes automatically scanned the bank and water below as she looked for the outline of the Ferryman. She couldn't articulate whether it was out of habit, or out of a misplaced hope that she would make eye contact with him again from a safe distance.

She had never experienced the rush his gaze invoked before, the way she felt both vulnerable and yet powerful to exist under the nose of a deity like that. Of a male who had been alive since there had been souls to ferry, who had stood strong in his oath to the underworld, who was kind, cruel and inevitable.

She settled onto her perch on the side of the cavern wall, so worn from her feet that they had carved out their own grooves with every time they shifted on the ground.

Charon was not there.

Anastacia let out a breath and sat back on her haunches, her staff digging into her spine. She could go home—*should* go home. But she continued anyway, scaling down the wall until she was on stable ground. Her fingers went to her ring, twirling it around her finger. The movement had become an impulse she had developed in the past few weeks it had sat behind her knuckle.

The bank was neither empty or crowded. The souls waiting for their time to pass automatically stayed near one another, as though from an echo of their life—when to stay with people and create a community was to stay alive.

Charon must have already left to the river for the day. She didn't know what he did on the other side, though there were plenty of stories. She didn't believe them, none ever able to explain how they knew; if they had spoken to the gods, if they had seen it themselves.

Anastacia had never seen another living person down below and she had never met someone who communicated with the gods.

Perhaps they were out there, somewhere, but until she found a story she believed the source of, she did not assume they were correct. After all, Charon had been described as a hideous thing. An old, wrinkled and skinny seaman by some accounts. An evil, hunchbacked skeleton by others.

And they were all wrong.

If Anastacia could find the words, if she thought for even one moment that she could do him justice, she would have described him on paper. She would have talked about his chiseled face, the dark hair and black eyes, his muscles and his strong hands. She might have mentioned how watching him had given her life, had made her yearn, had made her *want*.

Anastacia would have spoken of addiction, of the way she was drawn to him even when she was nowhere near, the way she could watch him do nothing for hours and feel content.

But she did not want to describe his beauty to others. She did not want to share him or the fragile thing she had cultivated in herself when she watched him.

She pursed her lips as she wandered down to solid ground, feeling like one of the dead. The underworld's surrounding bank no longer held the same curiosity for her that it once did. She had explored every area possible on the outskirts of the river, the trip around the underworld taking more time than she was willing to admit she had spent. She had seen as the Acheron turned into the Styx. She had felt the hollowness of the Lethe as she dipped her hand within it and noticed its absence; there was no substance to the river, nothing but a slight cool breeze on her hand as it swirled around her fingertips.

Anastacia had watched the fires of the Phlegethon pour into the depths of the Tartarus, spitting and hissing as it fell, a waterfall like nothing she had ever seen. She had scaled the caverns to try and peek at Elysium, wondering if the blessed fields were all they were claimed to be.

But she had never passed the rivers that guarded Hades' palace. She supposed she could have tried, but the waters that guarded the area were violent and deep. She had only ever seen Charon cross them, and even he disappeared once halfway through the crossing.

Besides the bank, she had only ever stepped foot in Persephone's grove, a quiet and beautiful garden that contained plants she had never seen on Gaia, food she had never dared try. Anastacia had traveled there multiple times. Sometimes, she saw the goddess sitting among the trees and flowers, her rich, golden-brown hair almost glowing in the strange lighting that mimicked the sun but was not.

Anastacia always left a gift behind for her; a seed from above, a piece of fruit, a cutting from one of Ophelia's herbs.

It was her own way of leaving something at an altar to the goddess she respected most. Persephone had a kind spot for mortals; she was the goddess who allowed Eurydice to follow Orpheus, who let Sysiphus return to his wife. She was the goddess of rebirth and life.

If Anastacia was going to garner favor with anyone, *that* would be the goddess to have on her side.

She kicked at a rock, sending it scattering forward. Anastacia could stay down here forever, no need to eat or drink or sleep, suspended in time where her mortal needs did not matter. She would not change so long as she was on the riverbank.

Even cuts were dangerous, as her body would not heal them. She would bleed and bleed and bleed, maybe until there was no blood left within her. Anastacia did not know what would happen then, if she would still live and breathe without a beating heart or if she would meet the Ferryman as a half-soul one day, too drained to hide any longer. She was still staring at her previously injured foot when she realized her mistake.

A thief was always close to being discovered. It was the rule she never let herself forget, one that had haunted her since she was a child. She was *always* a thief, even when she wasn't stealing. That meant it was always dangerous to get caught, even if she carried nothing stolen.

And unfortunately for Anastacia, she always carried something stolen.

Charon's footsteps were quiet. She knew this from studying him, knew that although he was large, he could blend his mass in easily with the world around him. He knew how to walk through the underworld, how to float through the river, how to shift without disturbing the air.

Anastacia had not seen his skiff or his body, and assumed that meant he was gone. He had *never* been far from his skiff, not in all of her years of watching him.

And yet as her eyes landed on his feet, bare like hers, his toes placidly lying against the ground with his heels set equally apart like a warrior, she admitted to herself she must have been wrong.

Because Charon was not on the river.

No, her gaze traveled from his strong calves, past his tunic to his half-bare chest, up to his cunning eyes. Those dark, infinite eyes that had haunted her since the first time she saw them.

The full mouth that she had seen smile for some did not so much as twitch for her.

"Hello, little thief. I wondered when you'd come back to me," he said

It was only instinct that forced her to move, for her mind had turned to stone as if she had stared at Medusa. She was surprised when she blinked and found she had moved away from him, her feet dancing away before he could reach out and grab her.

"Hello, Ferryman," she said. Her voice was confident even as her body did its best to cower. She had imagined this happening before, of course. Had pictured them speaking, wondered what it would be like to have his eyes acknowledge her as more than another soul on his riverbank.

But she always thought it would be on her own terms. This was, decidedly, not.

He took a step, then another, circling her like a shark. She turned her body as he moved, keeping him at her front. Something told her that the moment she gave the Ferryman her back, she would lose whatever game they had begun playing the moment they locked eyes.

"You have quite quick feet, don't you?"

She let the edge of her lip tilt up. "They have not failed me yet."

His head cocked, his gaze traveling down her body. She didn't shift, couldn't fidget, wouldn't allow his silence to make her speak. Finally, he looked behind her. "They have failed you at least once," he commented lightly.

Anastacia frowned. He inclined his head, and though she didn't turn around to see what he gestured at, she knew his eyes had found her trail to his riverbank. "When you cut yourself," he continued. "You could run from me anywhere now, on the earth, within it, and I would know your smell." His eyes darted back down to hers, and even with distance in between them, she had to tilt her head up. "Your taste," he said, and she sucked in a breath as his tongue ran over his bottom lip.

"You wouldn't be able to follow me above," she argued.

"I wouldn't have to. You would come back to me."

"I would not," she said. It was a lie. Already, she had come to him multiple times whether he was aware of it or not. She knew whatever happened, she would visit again.

"Oh, but you absolutely would." He walked towards her so languidly that she forgot she should run, her thief's heart hammering in her chest. Whether from excitement or fear, she wasn't positive.

She arched a brow, tilting her head up farther until he was standing in front of her, easily within reach. "How do you know?"

His hand raised, grabbing a strand of her dark brown hair and rubbing it between his fingers. "Because all mortals come to me, eventually." He began twirling his hand, wrapping her hair around it until the heat of his skin was pressed against the side of her head and neck, so tangled within her that she would not be able to pull away even if she tried. "Whether you run for days, months, years, I am always here. And you will meet me then, no matter what you do."

He leaned in closely, inhaling deeply as his nose ran up the other side of her neck, bumping against her skin until she had no choice but to bend her head to the side. She wondered if he could feel the life fluttering within her at his presence, the way adrenaline was flooding her veins.

"But it seems I won't have to wait that long after all. Not when I have you in my arms already, hmm?"

Her eyes darted down to his lips as they finally curled into a smile. He moved the hand in her hair, rotating her head from side to side slightly as his gaze devoured her. She breathed deeply, his clean, salty scent tickling her nose. For a deity who dwelled within the underworld, he smelled like a man who had spent his life with his skin baking in the sun, water and sand coating his legs.

Anastacia was in a haze, caught between the flash of his teeth as his lips pulled up and the scent of his body. She took a step closer, pressing herself against his chest to see if it felt as solid as his hand did. She had always wondered if Charon would feel like a man or like a soul.

Souls were tangible to her, but they did not feel human.

Charon felt human, like muscle and smooth skin, his calluses rough against her neck as she shifted, his breath real on her face.

"And what would you do with me, Ferryman?" she asked curiously.

"What do men do with thieves on Gaia?"

She cleared her throat. "I suppose it depends on the man. Fines, reimbursement, humiliation..." she trailed off.

He moved his free hand, grasping her palm. He pulled it up until it was between them, her long fingers straight as he stared at them. He thumbed her stolen ruby ring, running the jewel along the pad of his finger. "I've heard of other things, my liar. I've heard of physical punishments. Seen men come to the underworld to be judged without their fingers, their hands," he used his own hand to encircle her wrist tightly, though it did not hurt. "I've seen people who were killed for their indiscretions."

Anastacia watched him touch her hand so threateningly, yet so gently, and she smothered a laugh. It was inappropriate. She was nervous, but she did not believe him. "And will you cut off my fingers? My hand? Take my life?" She wiggled her fingers quickly, her other hand raising to her hair as she pulled her head just slightly away, his fingers staying tangled in her strands but far lower than before.

"No," he finally admitted. "Though, then how could I punish you? How could you reimburse me for what you've taken?"

She raised an eyebrow. "What have I taken?"

He huffed. "The question is not what, but how many."

Her smile flitted over her face before she could stop it. *Many*, she thought.

His expression darkened as though he could read her mind. "How could you possibly reimburse me for souls?"

She grinned at him as she shifted again, testing how strong his grip on her hair was. She absently wondered how fast he could move, how far he could go from the river. Was there a limit? He was too large to scale the cavern walls the same way she did, too bulky to fit in the nooks and crannies she usually hid within.

And he did not know this place as she did.

He knew it as a predator, as the top of the food chain.

But Anastacia knew it as prey, which meant she knew their shared riverbank far more intricately. She pushed her hand just above his, pulling her hair tight with tension. He responded how she expected, stiffening his grasp enough that her head strained, her skin pulling taught.

"What could the Ferryman possibly need?" she asked. "Reimburse-ment implies I could give you something you want, but you are ru-mored to want nothing."

He frowned, but before he could speak, she flicked her wrist hard. The knife within her grip was tiny, sharp, thin, something she kept hidden with her lock picks in case of an emergency. She didn't bother aiming for Charon, unwilling to injure him even if it were possible.

Instead, it ripped quickly through her mass of hair, just above his fist. The strands that she missed ripped out of her head as she pulled away before he could react further than gripping her loose hair harder, as if it were still attached.

She knew if he caught her again, if that vice of a grip landed on her arm, her neck, anything she couldn't easily cut off, she would be in a bind. She would have to hope he brought her to his home and left her alone to discover a way out, and even then... if it was on the wrong side of the river, she would be stranded.

Anastacia could not fight off the Ferryman, but she didn't need to fight if she could be clever. And she would not need to be impulsive if she was careful enough not to get caught again.

She scrambled away, ducking as his other hand darted towards her faster than she had expected. He was used to catching souls who tried to flee from him, fighting those who raged against their fate.

But Anastacia was not a soul.

His hand grappled against the back of her peplos but she fell for-ward, gravity and her momentum tearing the fabric out of his fingers. She swore she could feel another swipe, air movement against the back of her scalp. If she hadn't cut off most of her hair, perhaps he would have had something to grab, but there was nothing.

She sprinted towards the cavern wall, ignoring her usual trail. That would take time to scurry up, and he would be on her before she got high enough to escape his reach. He was tall, his arms long. Not even a squirrel could climb quickly enough to clear his hands.

Anastacia also knew that in a long-distance run, his legs would eat up the ground faster than she could move. It wouldn't need to be that long of a distance either—already, she expected him to catch her at any moment. She couldn't risk turning around, but her ears had homed in on the way his feet hit the ground behind her. They informed her he wasn't far behind at all.

There were no shadows to warn her, nothing but a pause in one of his footsteps that instinctively made her dart to the side as he leapt. Her foot slid against the ground at her change in momentum and she laughed, her heart jumping into her throat as he stumbled slightly past her.

He caught himself, but his mistake cost him. She fled faster, her feet quick as she found the entrance she was looking for. A narrow hole in the cavern wall, a small offshoot of one of the five rivers that flowed through the underworld. Not the Lethe, for it was true water, and not the Phlegethon for it did not burn.

She had used it before to traverse the world below, and though there were plenty of tunnels she hadn't set foot in, this one she trusted.

Anastacia chose one of the narrowest, lowest entrances, one that forced her to lay flat on her belly and scurry through like a snake in the mud. Her cheek touched the water as she ducked her head and pulled.

She had almost made it through when Charon managed to squeeze into the entrance of the tunnel. She couldn't see him, but his hand grabbed her ankle. She was lucky for the water then, for the tight space that forced his body into a contortion that weakened his grip, because with one good tug she pulled free. Her foot slipped through his hand, his fingers digging briefly into the arch before she was able to pull out of his reach.

The cavern opened up just ahead and she continued forward. She could not risk backing out, unsure of how long he would wait there for her. She wasn't sure she'd be able to trust the trail for a long while either, not with his assessing eyes watching for her. There were other ways into the underworld, of course, but none were as straightforward as her pathway.

The one she had painstakingly worn down herself, walking it so many times that it was her skin instead of water that had eroded the earth.

Alas, a thief always knew to have a way out. A *good* thief knew to have multiple. She would be okay whether Charon was waiting for her or not.

When Anastacia made it far enough that she was certain she had escaped, she turned and peeked back through her little escape hole. Charon did not kneel, but she saw his feet and ankles angled towards where she had disappeared. There was a glow emanating from behind him, made more dramatic by the lack of light within her little tunnel.

Once he disappeared, she would be left in the dark.

She could picture the anger in his eyes, the usual blackness bright with emotion. She patted her peplos, her belt, taking stock of her items. She had lost her knife in the scramble, but her staff was still pressed snugly against her back. She swallowed her disappointment. "Would you mind grabbing my knife?" she asked him. There was no need to shout; it was quiet enough in the mountain she was certain he could hear her breathing.

"I've got it right here in my hand. Come out and get it." His frustration was palpable in his words, and she tried to smother her smile, though he could not see it.

"Next time, then," she commented as she stood. Anastacia placed her hand on the wall and turned away from him.

He paused for a moment, likely listening to the sound of her feet as she began her trek into the darkness. "Will there be a next time?" he asked, just as she was sure he had already walked away. His words echoed to her easily through the empty tunnel.

"You said it yourself, didn't you?" she called back. "All mortals come to you eventually."

He didn't respond, but she felt him looking at the wall where she had disappeared. Anastacia could have been imagining it.

But she didn't think she was.

***

"What did you *do?*" Ophelia asked as Anastacia trudged into their home. Her hair was uneven, a massive chunk gone while half was still at its normal length.

Anastacia shrugged. "Help me cut it?" She turned towards their mirror, assessing it realistically. They would have to cut it above her shoulders if she wanted it even. Ophelia gestured for her to sit before picking up the ruined strands and running her fingers through it.

Although it was ridiculous, she almost told her to stop. She liked knowing that the last person who had touched her hair was Charon. Still, she kept her mouth shut as Ophelia began working, watching little bits of her hair fall to the floor. "Who did this?"

"I did," Anastacia answered. Ophelia rolled her eyes.

"What *made* you do this?"

"I made a little mistake and someone got a hold of my hair. It was the quickest way to get out."

"I thought you weren't going to steal near home anymore," her friend said sternly.

"It won't be a problem," she promised.

Ophelia's eyes darted down to Anastacia's ring, though she said nothing. For a time, when she had started stealing souls, it was enough to stop her impulses. Enough to give her satisfaction, to fill that hole in her chest that craved adrenaline, that wanted the feeling of outsmarting everyone in a room.

But eventually, it began to feel like everything else. There was no challenge to it. No one to avoid, no one to run from, no stakes to beat.

Boring.

Today, though... Anastacia smiled as her hair was cut so short that it just barely hit her chin. Today had been anything but boring.

The feeling would last for some time, but then it would go away again. She could touch her hair and remind herself, but even that would grow longer with each passing day, taking away his unintentional mark on her.

She wasn't stupid enough to return soon. But she was desperate enough that she'd certainly go back.

Ophelia watched her warily over the next few weeks as Anastacia busied herself foraging for herbs, fishing, and coming home with the occasional pretty bauble in her hand. While her friend didn't enjoy Anastacia's compulsive need to steal, sometimes nothing more than a loaf of bread or a cheap item, she never commented.

It was always something they could use, never complete junk or trash. Many times, Ophelia needed items to dedicate to Hecate or to use during her rituals. Anastacia made sure she was always contributing, one way or another.

There had not been any deaths recently that prompted them to offer their more secretive services. She knew Charon would be looking for her no matter how long she waited, but even the idea of descending into the underworld made her shiver with a mixture of anxiety and longing.

She might not have the bravery to convince herself to go down on her own without a purpose, but the moment an opportunity presented itself, she knew she wouldn't hesitate.

Some deaths, she and Ophelia respected. They could not, would not, save everyone from the inevitable end. But others, they could not deny. Some souls fought so hard, so valiantly, to stay alive that Anastacia believed they should be rewarded for it. The ones who clung to their bodies, who screamed at the fates as they cut their string. Those who raged at Thanatos as he severed their souls from their earthly vessel, who bit and scratched at Hermes as he carried them away.

Those were the men, women, and children she could not ignore.

She and Ophelia fell back into their routine of healing, ignoring the suspicious whispers of those who disliked or feared their methods. Anastacia kept waiting, some days less patiently than others, to find a soul that fit her requirements. Perhaps she shouldn't have been wishing for someone to die, but they wouldn't be that way for long, she reminded herself.

And then it happened. A man who suffered a medical event. They rushed to him, Ophelia hoping to arrive in time before he passed, but he was gone by the time they arrived. Anastacia felt like she had been so close behind Hermes that his winged shoes ruffled her hair as he fled with the soul.

She wondered if he noticed her presence the same way she felt his. If he recognized her soul, felt the staff she carried. If the blood in her veins called to him.

They were lucky they made it quickly enough to tell the family not to give the man a coin and to delay funeral rites. Anastacia was glad to know she would not have to get that close to Charon again in a rush, wondering how easily he would spot her, if he could really smell her now that he knew her blood. If his tongue had truly tasted something that her body relied on so staunchly.

Ophelia said nothing as Anastacia left the man's home. Perhaps she would have argued if she knew it was Charon who had captured Anastacia and forced her to cut her hair, but Anastacia hadn't said anything for a reason.

She hurried to her mountain, confident enough to use her trail, even if she was unable to sneak back up afterwards. The soul would follow her directions, unable to think for himself when she wasn't around.

Anastacia might not have to change anything at all if she could stop herself from drawing Charon's attention in the first place. After all, he still needed to leave to ferry his souls, needed to rest and sleep.

But she *wanted* to change things.

She wanted to feel his hands, hear his voice, discover if he was witty or sarcastic, if he only smiled as a ruse to help souls trust him or if she could make him laugh. She had watched him from afar, and now that she had seen him up close, nothing else would do.

Anastacia looked at the mouth of her cave, squared her shoulders, and descended.

Chapter Six

Charon had never noticed time passing so acutely. Even when he was busy, he was counting the moments.

Wondering if, while he visited with Hades, the thief was sneaking her way onto his riverbank and taking one of the souls waiting by the Cocytus. The water of wailing. The area of the river where all the souls with no coin waited for their years to pass.

Was she above him now, observing as he sat on his skiff, watching the souls as a shepherd would his flock?

Hades had not questioned his renewed dedication to his position, but Persephone had watched him strangely when he excused himself after ferrying the souls to Hades' palace for judgement. Usually, he waited while the judges—Rhadamanthus, Aeacus, and Minos—deliberated.

Today, like the others in his recent memory, he had left quickly. He did not want to be away from the riverbank, knowing she would come back to him. A different woman might not, might have hedged her bets and been content knowing she had escaped him once. He didn't think his thief would do that. He had looked into her eyes, seen through the window and into her soul.

She would come again, and he would wait. Counting the moments carefully.

The water lapped calmly at the bank where he was moored, rocking him slowly. The day was no different until suddenly, it was. A commotion drew his attention, a soul on the bank speaking angrily. *It had to be her.* His gaze snagged on the group and he rushed over, hoping to find her even if he wasn't sure what he would do when he had her.

The correct thing to do would be to tell Hades.

In fact, he should have told Hades when he first encountered the woman. No, before that. When he first saw her steal the boy and guide him to the surface.

After all, the last time he had betrayed his post, Cerberus and Charon had both paid for his leniency. Cerberus, being carried by Heracles to the world above like a trophy, and Charon, by a year shackled in chains. He kept his chains in his home as a token to the consequences of failing his duty. They had not bothered him terribly, but they still reminded him that while he commanded the river, he was not the god of the underworld.

Even with those thoughts in the back of his mind, he did not call to Hades as he searched for his thief.

The souls calmed, whatever had caused their irritation gone. Charon tried to swallow his disappointment, certain that had been her. Had he merely missed her? Had she truly evaded him once more? Hope convinced him to keep an eye out as he walked back to his skiff, even as his heart sank.

And then he saw it.

A large ring, sitting upon the sturdy wood. It was far bigger than what would fit on a woman's finger. He picked it up, rolling it in his palm as he admired the craftsmanship; a golden band with a black jewel set within. Curious, he slid it gently onto his pointer finger.

He glanced around again, his shoulders straightening. It wasn't until he began looking critically at the cavern walls, the places his thief seemed to hide in best, that he saw her. She leaned against the stone lazily, one foot braced against it, her arms crossed in front of her. She was already watching him, a teasing smile on her face.

He took one step toward her and then another, wondering if she would run away. If he would scare her off too quickly, before he could speak with her. Before he could catch her.

He still had her locks of hair within his home, tied with a string. It was easy for Charon to remember the way it felt within his hands, he had touched it so often. It was the only new thing he had collected since the beginning of his time, since he had created his home here. And now, with the jewelry, he had another new thing.

She did not budge as he approached, though he noticed the way she shifted just a tad to her right, towards the hole he knew he could not reach her through. How fast would he need to lunge to grab her before she disappeared from him again? Her smirk told him he would not be fast enough.

"Do you like it?"

Both of their eyes moved to the ring gracing his finger. "Did you steal it?"

She rolled her eyes. "Who could say?"

"Have you come to steal from me?"

"No," she answered genuinely.

He looked at her peplos, wondering what else she had hidden within it. It was draped artfully over her, tucked into a belt around her waist before the excess fabric was pulled out to hang below it. A pretty cream color, it made her skin appear sun-kissed.

He pulled her knife out from where he had it tucked at his side, the blade flashing as he spun it through his fingers. "I've got something of yours."

She smiled and brought a hand up to her shorn locks. "Many things of mine," she amended.

He raised an eyebrow but held out the knife handle first, the blade cool in his palm. He held it tightly enough that he could feel the edge press into his hand. She laughed but didn't move. "I may have gotten close to you once, Ferryman, but I am not silly enough to do it twice."

"You don't want it back?"

"You can throw it," she shrugged. At his look, she grinned. "I trust your aim. More importantly, I trust my ability to dodge."

He paced to the side, non-threateningly, slowly, wondering if he could chase her the opposite way of her tunnel. He hoped she would start shifting away as he crowded her. "Why are you here, if not to take something from me?"

"I said I didn't want to steal from you, not that I didn't want to take something."

He lifted his chin. She was so much smaller than him, so much quicker to smile and grin. "Then what do you want to take, little lyre?"

"I'd like an audience with Hades," she requested.

He shook his head. "No."

"Then I'd like an audience with you."

He worked his jaw and frowned. "For what?"

She shrugged. "To talk. Doesn't every mortal want to learn what is on the other side of the river while they still have time to ponder it?"

"I do not know what mortals want," he admitted as he stared at the woman. Not only did he not know, but he had never really cared. Most times, he didn't encounter them until they were already dead, their fate set in stone, their wants and dreams left above. "What is your name?"

"Anastacia."

"Is that the truth?" he couldn't help but ask.

She smirked. "I never lie."

He fought to keep his lips from ticking up. "I don't believe that for one moment."

"So, what would it take?" she asked again. "To steal your time?"

His time was not valuable, he wanted to tell her. There was so much of it, unending before this moment and all of eternity left after. His time was the only thing he had that was absolutely worthless. "It would take nothing," he finally answered. "My time is yours."

"And what would it take to return to the world of the living after?"

That was a harder answer. It was his job to ferry the dead across the Acheron. He shouldn't bring a living person across the river, but he had—twice.

Both times, to deliver them to Hades. And here was another mortal that wanted to speak to the god, though the first who would accept Charon's company instead.

"I want to know what you carry behind your back," he said.

Her eyebrows raised in surprise, her mouth dropping open. "I don't carry anything."

He inclined his head. "That is the price of my time, little lyre. Take it or run away before I decide you may not leave."

"You couldn't stop me," she grinned. Her honey eyes were wide, wild. "But I accept your deal."

"You trust me to keep my word?" Charon asked, surprised that she had agreed so quickly. She hopped off the wall, walking towards him teasingly until they were close. Close enough that he could grab her if he wanted, sweep her away like the river would.

She raised a hand and patted his chest. "Oh, yes. If one of us was lying, I know who it would be. You seem like a man who keeps his promises."

"You seem like a woman who doesn't," he commented absently, before he could wonder if it would insult her. She only laughed.

"Yes, I'm afraid you are correct."

She began to walk down the riverbank, her bare feet confident as she stepped through the underworld like she belonged there. Her eyes lacked fear as she walked next to the river of Misery, no hesitation in her steps as it combined with the Styx and crashed together as though going to war.

The waters eventually calmed further downriver, when the two mixed enough that the currents became one. Until that point, it was vicious. Intimidating. Uncrossable.

Charon had never been mortal, had never had to worry about dying. His parents were primordial deities who were there before even the gods and who would exist long after. Therefore, the river did not scare him. Most days, it felt like the blood in his veins. If he cut himself open, he would bleed the mixed water within.

But even the dead were apprehensive of the river.

Anastacia, however, was not. She didn't even glance at it when a particularly large wave crested over the bank, splashing at her feet like it was reaching for her. Trying to drag her into its depths.

"Where are you going?" Charon asked, following behind her.

"I assume you have a home?" she asked.

He thought of his wooden house on the other side of the river, the one that creaked when the water hit the stilts it rested upon, half built over the Acheron itself. Holes decorated the walls to allow the never changing air in, the only noise the roar of the water against the rocks.

Then, he thought of the lock of hair sitting on his carving table, tied carefully with string as though he hadn't wanted to lose even a single strand. It wasn't hidden. Anastacia would see it displayed like a trophy.

"No."

She turned around, hands on her hips. "No, you do not have a home?"

"I have a home. Not one we will visit."

Her lips pursed briefly in annoyance. "Is it because I am not permitted inside of it?"

He gestured around him. "You are really not permitted to be here, either. How *did* you get here?"

"You know how I got here," she answered, her eyes dragging towards her trail on the side of the cavern. "Besides, *anyone* can get here if they try hard enough. If you are going to question me, ask how I got out." Her grin was mischievous.

And Charon realized he wanted to ask her many things. He had promised to give her his time, but wondered how much of her time she would offer him in return. Hers meant much more, after all. How many seconds of her life was she spending here with him? How many did she have left?

"How did you get out?" he asked obediently.

She shrugged. "I walked. Now, tell me what I would have to do to earn a soul from Hades."

He ignored her nonanswer. "To earn one? For what?"

"For freedom. For escape from death. For him to turn his head and deny it a permanent eternity," she answered. Her arms slowly rose from her waist, crossing in front of her.

"For immortality?"

She paused. "I suppose immortality would be acceptable, but simply for the soul to be ignored in death would work too. To be able to escape the confines of the underworld without retribution, to keep their memories. Can you touch souls?"

Her mind was moving a mile a minute, switching too fast for him to comprehend the thoughts behind the statements. "Yes," he answered.

"As for your other question, I do not know what it would take. It has not been done."

"And you will not ask?"

"No. I thought you had been stealing souls. Why not this one?"

She walked towards him again, seeming to understand he wasn't going to take another step towards his boat, was not going to allow her to cross the river today. "Because I've already stolen it once before," she admitted. "And it still does not belong to me."

Her earthy scent tickled his nose. He remembered the taste of her blood on his finger, the way her lips had parted in shock the first time he saw her, the way her skin had felt in his hands.

The way she had tilted her neck, so submissively.

Something stirred within him that he had only heard about, something that he had never understood and never wanted to. He had his purpose; Charon was married to the river, he *was* the river. He had his friends, but they did not distract him. Not like this. None of them were interesting enough, their varying lives and decisions of no impact to him.

Whatever happened above, whatever occurred below, Charon was unchanging. The dead would always be dead. They would always need to cross the river to their resting place.

But Anastacia made him question. Charon was not stupid; he knew what sex was, knew why the gods married, why they broke their fidelity to one another for pretty mortals. He knew why they fucked and drank and consumed. But he had never experienced the need until now. Until the last few days, weeks, months, years, however long it had last been since he had seen her. Since he had imagined what he would do if he had her within his grasp again.

Anastacia. A beautiful name. He liked the way it rolled through his mind and realized he had not yet felt it on his tongue. "Anastacia," he said unbidden. Then he said it again because he liked it so much.

She didn't frown, didn't seem confused at his muttering of her name. She only waited patiently, her face open and accepting. Charon wondered if she could see the heat running through his blood, down to his cock. Did she feel need when she looked at him?

His hands had touched her skin, but his mouth had not. Would it taste like her blood? Would it feel smooth against his lips, would it bruise? How long would his mark stay on her and would men know it as his?

His eyes skimmed her peplos. It was art on her body, mesmerizing. It was still as she stood like marble, as motionless as the woman who wore it. A skill that betrayed her profession. Only a thief or a warrior could stand as quietly as she did and yet look like she was coiled, like at any moment she could burst into movement.

His mind had gone off track. He was so focused on her, the way she stood, the way she watched him, that he could not have spoken anything but her name if he tried.

Charon took a step towards her, wondering if she would run at the look in his eyes. If he appeared as predatory to her as he felt. He did not stop until he had invaded her space, far too close to be acceptable. His hand snaked out to touch her hair again, the same way he had every night in his home.

Suddenly, he was overcome with certainty. He would not allow Anastacia near Hades.

Not now, not ever. She could ask again, she could beg, she could threaten, but no gods would see her face. Hades had always been loyal to Persephone, but if Anastacia could inspire this feeling in Charon, she could do it to anyone.

He did not trust his friend to deny her.

It was not her face itself, necessarily. At first glance, she was not unique. Pretty, but not in a way that made her stand out. No, it was her eyes that did it. The shine, the confidence, the expression.

The way she stood, the way she spoke. Enchanting, intriguing.

Charon would not share her with the gods.

He placed his hand at the base of her skull, wrapping himself in her once more. This time, his grip was so tight to her scalp that she would not be able to cut herself free. He tilted her head up, up, up, until he could feel her breath on his face. She was so tiny in his grasp, a fragile butterfly who had fluttered into a world it was not meant for.

Charon dipped his head, his body folding over her. "Has a man tasted your skin?" he asked.

Her breathing hitched. "No," she admitted.

"And this?"

He brought his other hand up, lewdly touching the fabric of her peplos where it sat between her thighs, not roughly enough to do more than dent it, but she knew where it was. Knew what his fingers were only a twitch away from.

"No," she said again. She was trembling. Charon was too, though his was from restraint. From the exercise of holding himself back.

"Are you scared?" he asked.

He was.

He was scared of her answer. If she told him yes, Charon wasn't sure he could release her, that her fear would dissuade him, that he would be strong enough to watch her run away from him.

They both stood there, her eyes darting between his, her face broken open with an expression he didn't understand, one he had never seen before. Yearning? Understanding? Pity?

He didn't know if she would answer. Charon couldn't keep track of time anymore, each second suspended as they stood in this entangled embrace. He had never been one to pray to the gods, but he did now.

He prayed to whoever would listen that she did not fear him.

And they listened.

"No, I am not scared."

There was a pause where even the river seemed to stall. Then it came rushing back, Charon's mouth crashing down on Anastacia's violently, desperately. He had never kissed anyone before, had never felt the need, but now he couldn't imagine how he had lived without it. His tongue swept into her, his air was hers, she was pressed against his body like they were one.

His hand that had been near her core moved to her hip, his fingertips digging into the skin there. He moved them away, reaching around to grab her backside. It was firm in his hands, strong, soft, a combination he had no words for.

Charon pulled away, his mouth delving to her neck, running his tongue along her jawline and under the sensitive part of her ear. She gasped beneath his ministrations, her hands scrabbling against his bare back. He wanted her nail marks, wanted to see the bright red rakes she left behind.

Wanted the world to see them.

He sucked hard on her neck, his only thought to do the same. To claim. "Charon," she cried.

He shuddered. It was the first time she had said his name. "My little lyre," he responded, his voice rough. Out of all the dreams he had since seeing her, this was the one he dreamt most. His hands roamed up, unsure of what he was doing but focused on the drape of her peplos, of the need for more skin beneath his palms, when he hit it.

He froze in confusion before his hands readjusted, his lips slowing as he wondered what—

Anastacia pulled away from him, skittering backwards. Her face was flushed, her lips bright red. His eyes caught on the purple mark growing on her neck where his mouth had been and satisfaction unfurled in his chest.

"What is it you hide, little lyre?" he asked after a moment, settling his breathing. His cock was still straining toward the woman in front of him.

Her face contorted into a frown, eyes darkening. "Was that—did you only do that to feel my back?"

He stalked towards her again, but she darted away, flipping around until she was walking backwards towards her hole in the wall once more. "No," he smirked. "After all, I had your word anyway, didn't I? No, I did that to feel *you.*"

Still, every step he took forward was another one she took back. It was as if the spell between them was broken. Disappointment lodged itself in his throat. He had never experienced loneliness, but he imagined it felt like this. Like the acute loss of the woman before him. "What of your knife?" he implored. "Will you leave without it?"

"You can keep it," she answered easily. "Another gift to accompany the ring."

Two gifts. Three, if he counted her hair.

No one had given him gifts before. Payment, certainly. Reimbursements, yes. But never a gift. Never for nothing. "And what of your word? Our deal? What is it you carry?"

"I'm afraid it is nothing more than a family heirloom. Sentimental value but nothing else." She paused before her hand went inside the fabric of her peplos, pulling out a staff. He recognized it, though he couldn't put his finger on why. It was just shorter than her forearm, a plain handle with two snakes weaving around it until they kissed at the top, backed by two wings.

It was the wings that held his attention most.

"That is Caduceus," he said after another moment as he examined the staff in her hand. Hermes carried it with him at all times as a symbol of peace. It was the item that enforced his title as messenger, as guide who delivered the dead to Charon's bank. He had never seen the god without it. "How do you have it?"

She rolled her eyes at his serious tone, as though he were wrong. "You've figured it out. I stole it from Hermes years ago."

"I saw him with it just yesterday," he disagreed. He remembered it clutched firmly in Hermes' hand as he guided the souls towards Charon, his eyes lit up with levity and mischief. The two staffs looked exactly the same.

Finally, Anastacia tsked. "You may not know much about the world above, but there *are* replicas." She swung it around to present it to him, unconcerned. As though it meant nothing to her when just moments ago, she had run away from him simply because his fingers brushed against it. "Many people carry them. Besides, it fits me, don't you think?" When he didn't take it, she tucked the head of the staff underneath her, resting her chin on it so the wings cradled her face as she smiled.

He thought about her statement, about the irony that this was the item she treasured. The staff of the thief god who brought him souls, in the hands of the woman who stole them away from him once more. Yes, it fit her.

Jealousy was bitter against the back of his throat though he didn't know why. He didn't want her worshiping other gods. Didn't want her prayers going to the fickle beings, didn't want to share her. "Is Hermes your god, then?"

She hid her smile, though he saw the corner of her lip quirk. "He is the god I'm most like, I suppose. Though for a thief, he is rather unobservant. Conceited."

"They are all that way," he said.

"Are you?"

"I am not a god."

She studied him for another moment, her hand raising to touch her bottom lip. "You certainly kiss like I'd imagine a god does. You look like one, too."

Charon smirked, taking a step closer to see if she'd allow him, but she moved unconsciously, backing toward safety. Another few steps and she would be gone again, forcing him to live eternities in seconds as he waited for her once more.

"I am better than them," he said easily, honestly. "I was here before the gods, and I will be here after. Their fickleness does not live in my skin. Their need for drama and change, their proneness to insult and easy rage, it is the mark of children. I am steady. I am the stone which does not move. I am the son of night and darkness. Chaos flows through me like my birthright. No one worships me because I do not need it. I exist without it. None of your gods can say the same."

Whatever he expected Anastacia to do, however he thought she would respond at his insult of her gods, it was not by laughing. The sound was quiet, joyful, surprised. "Do you speak to them like that?"

"Some of them," he admitted. Those he considered his friends. Hades, Persephone, Hermes, Hecate... the ones who spent ample time in the underworld, those who he had been around for centuries. They existed together peacefully enough, a mutual respect between them.

Anastacia did not ask another question, backing further into her tunnel. He wanted to ask her to stay.

But he stopped himself.

"What will you do now?" he asked instead. "Will you run away again?"

She slipped further into the wall, her face shadowed. "I have errands to run," she said. Then, Anastacia turned around, exposing him to her vulnerable back. Would she hear it if he jumped forward now? Would she dodge in time to escape him?

Charon composed his thoughts, forcing himself not to lunge. Stopping himself from grabbing her to steal her away, as she had stolen his sanity since he had first seen her.

Instead, he followed her steadily. "Why use this exit if you know I'd let you leave as part of our agreement?" he asked as she bent down onto her stomach, crawling through the little tunnel. He could not bend in the narrow space to see Anastacia any longer, and already, his eyes craved the sight of her. He wished he were smaller, if only to have another moment of her time.

"Our deal only promised that *I* could leave," she answered from somewhere in the depths of the tunnel. "But it is not just me in here."

It took a moment for Charon to understand her words, but when he did, he turned around swiftly. He looked aggressively through the souls walking the bank, as if he would be able to find which of them was missing.

He remembered the commotion from earlier, the one he wrote off once he saw the ring. He thought the ring was the reason for the distraction. He had not even stopped to consider she had already stolen from him. He had even *asked* her if she was there to steal from him, and the little thief had said no.

Charon thought he would feel angry, but for the first time in years, perhaps the first time in forever, he bellowed. It was the kind of laugh that echoed, that hollered, that traveled.

He wondered if somewhere deep within the roots of the mountain, Anastacia heard it.

Chapter Seven

Anastacia couldn't hide the bruising on her neck. Every time she noticed it, her skin flushed, heat crawling up to her cheeks. Ophelia offered to heal it, but she declined. Her friend didn't ask where it came from, only gave her a look that warned her to be careful.

Ophelia had her own dalliances, men and women who Anastacia had never met. A far many more than Anastacia, who had only ever been kissed once.

By the Ferryman.

She could feel the tingle on her lips even now, just by closing her eyes. It was easy to imagine his hands on her. They had imprinted themselves into her skin, burning themselves into her memory.

The soul had been returned just fine, following her through the narrow mountain passages. It took longer than normal, but Ophelia had guarded his body well. He was returned to life as if no time at all had passed, only murky memories from his time in the underworld kissing the base of his spine.

Anastacia had been distracted in the hours since he was returned to life, her usual techniques to stay busy doing nothing to keep her mind occupied. Instead, she sat on the side of the Acheron above, her feet dangling in the water. It was such a deep, clear blue that she wondered how it was possible it became such a dark, miserable entity in the underworld.

She shed her peplos, covering her staff with it and placing it carefully with her sandals before she slipped into the cool water. It wasn't deep, her feet touching the sandy bottom with ease. Anastacia dipped her head back and let the water flow around her, trailing through the strands of her hair and dipping into the hollow of her collarbones.

She grinned at the blue sky above her, knowing that somewhere below, Charon was in the same river. They were connected like arteries with the same vein. Did he feel her presence? Was he looking around for her, even now?

She finally washed herself, her hands feeling so much softer with the memory of his still on her mind. He was callused from holding his skiff pole, his grip strong and his forearms large. She couldn't mistake her hands for his, even when she tried.

Anastacia wanted to see him again, as if she hadn't just been down there. Already, her eyes were drawn to the mountain.

But she had things to do first.

***

Anastacia clutched her parchment in her hand tightly enough that it crinkled. She didn't want it tucked into her peplos, worried that it would fall and get lost in the darkness as she descended into the underworld. Already, the flowers within her grasp had begun to wilt, her journey taking its toll. She wondered if the paper would have broken flower petals pressed into it by the time she loosened her grip.

It was rare that she brought something so fragile as an offering.

She had not realized how often she used her hands to balance herself as she walked down the steep inclines, how even when she was not touching the walls or rocks beneath her, she was tightening her fingers reflexively.

Her peplos swayed, a bit heavier than usual with the items she had stashed in the sewn fabric. Even that small difference, she noticed, compensated for.

Her eyes danced across the trail that would deliver her to Charon, but she knew he would have to wait. She didn't have time to see him today, not with the hours it would take to finish her tasks and then return to Ophelia to assist with her spell work. Already, she might be late.

Anastacia turned away from the trail leading to the riverbank, moving further into the mountain as quickly as she dared. The pathway was far more dangerous, less traveled on. Her feet didn't recognize it the same way, hadn't widened the trail enough in some places.

Still, she clutched at her gift and pressed forward. If she were lower in the mountain, it would be a longer journey around the outskirts of the underworld, but traveling high above meant that her descent would lead her to Persephone's grove not much longer than if she were walking to the riverbank.

She ran when she could, her feet slapping against the ground, loud in the hollow tunnels. They were large enough that the strange light within the underworld reached inside, illuminating the walls so that she wasn't blind.

Her breath came in gasps as she reached the grove, chest heaving from her sprint down. It was beautiful as always, thick trees and flowers sprouting through the soil. The first time she had seen it was breathtaking, a sight like nothing else. The grove was thick, the smell of fruit perfuming the air and making her mouth water. It was as beautiful as its goddess was, grown carefully by her hands, crafted like art. She paused to ensure Persephone wasn't sitting within, knowing it wasn't the time to catch her attention fully just yet. She had left gifts in the grove often enough over the years that the goddess would not think it too strange to find something waiting for her, though Anastacia had never left a note before.

When she was certain it was clear, Anastacia forced herself to become silent and invaded the place, not to steal, but to give.

She set the flowers down, their stems cut as nicely as possible without her knife available. Next to them, she placed a dozen fruit seeds she had collected. Last, she took off her ruby ring. It was beautiful and she ached to keep it. She clutched in tightly, trying to remember its weight on her hand, pretending she could still feel the grooves of the gold against her skin. Then she set it down on top of the parchment.

She didn't wait to be discovered, instead fleeing back into the depths of the mountain.

She had sacrificed her ring, something she had cherished.

But it was for something she wanted more. A soul that only Hades could give her. And if Charon would not give her an audience with the god, she knew one other who would.

When Anastacia exited the mouth of the cave, the sun was setting. Her knees weakened at the sight before her, the sunlight dancing across the waves, the billowing clouds stained with pinks and oranges.

This was one of the only times she found the will to pray, to thank the gods. This beauty was a masterpiece, a woven tapestry, something that had no other explanation. She could stare at it for hours without growing tired of the sight. The world changed around her but in this place near the sky, it could not touch her skin.

The ocean sparked as if someone had littered jewels onto the surface. If she didn't fear it so much, she might have run and jumped, throwing herself off the cliffside to see how many of the waves she could steal before she was caught. Might attempt to swim quickly enough that she could catch even the sun and hide it within her home to hoard and peek at.

She gave it one last look, knowing that once she was within the trees, she would not see this sunset again tonight. No, tonight was for the moon. For secrets.

***

By the time she reached Ophelia, she was already standing near a fire, the flames cracking and spitting. Behind her were a group of villagers.

Although they were often wary of the witch, none ever declined her help. They avoided Ophelia because they were in awe of her, not out of fear. Never had she harmed them, nor asked them for something they could not give. No, Ophelia had become a symbol over the many years she had been alive.

She was help. Ageless, undying, kind. She was a story that children grew up listening to. Old men claimed she had been their midwife, walking their mother through childbirth. Then, she was the woman who visited their home during their fever dreams, the one who made them medicine and cast spells to heal their bodies while they were children, the one who eased their parents into death's embrace.

Ophelia was legendary. Beautiful. Revered by the people who knew her.

Anastacia understood why.

As her friend stood in the moonlight, her usually blonde hair appeared silver. Her skin glowed radiantly against the warm firelight.

When her blue eyes landed on Anastacia, she smiled and beckoned her forward.

There, placed beside the fire, was an unconscious female roe deer. Its pelt was a soft strawberry roan, so fine that Anastacia could see the individual strands as the warm light kissed it. Its head was limp, stretched out upon the grass as though it had been killed.

It looked young, smaller than normal. Anastacia bent down, placing her hand on its lightly breathing chest before she ripped her hand backwards and gasped. Her head turned swiftly to look at Ophelia, who only nodded.

It was not a deer at all, the soul inside clearly human. Trapped, then—transformed by magic, an angry god, a vengeful witch, a cruel creature.

Anastacia looked back towards the woman in the doe's body. *Woman*—Anastacia scoffed. Her soul was perhaps seventeen, a girl, really. So innocent, so little time alive, so few experiences with the world.

"Who?" Anastacia asked.

"Zeus."

She bit down on her anger. There was no point in harboring ill will towards the gods. She did not believe in their reasons, but nor did she have the power to defy them more than she and Ophelia already did.

Not if they wanted to continue their work. After all, they could not defy the gods if the gods knew what they were doing. It was their biggest form of payment; they would help, but there would be no stories told about them.

No widespread myths with their names.

No hushed whispers around the fire, no prayers of thanks to the gods. Hecate was perhaps the only goddess who knew of their actions, and even then, she wasn't sure. Ophelia had a special relationship with the goddess, one that Anastacia did not question.

She looked toward the group of villagers, one woman's eyes locked on the doe. The others huddled together, instead looking anywhere *but* at the transformed woman. Perhaps worried that just by being in her presence, they would anger the gods and suffer her same fate.

Anastacia did not comfort them. They should be scared of the gods, who sometimes reminded Anastacia of aggressive dogs; use them for protection, but there was every chance they would bite their masters as quickly as help them.

She heard Charon's voice echo in her head. *I am not a god.*

She had never been more grateful.

She and Ophelia sat around the woman, holding hands. Ophelia directed Anastacia when to chant, when to stay silent, when to cut her hand and where to bleed. It took time, but slowly, the woman began to transform again. It looked painful, bones changing and extending, joints snapping horrifically, teeth falling out to grow in once more. The girl was lucky to be unconscious.

Eventually, though, her eyes opened. They had draped her in an unwrapped peplos, the ground warm and soft enough that she was comfortable on the soil. Her sister—or perhaps her lover—rushed forward, kneeling next to her with quiet, relieved sobs.

They gave them privacy, moving onto the other villagers who had gathered. Some had accrued curses that she and Ophelia discarded, others had come for protection spells to be placed upon them or their family members. Ophelia turned no one away, talking softly and sweetly, like she was calming a skittish horse, until their apprehension at her presence was gone.

It may grow back in the morning, their disbelief at Ophelia's power turning into fear again, but for tonight, the humans who had accrued any curses or needed additional blessings were satisfied. Happy.

Eventually, it was just them once more. They sat in the dirt, exhausted, the stars spanning overhead. "You have been gone again," Ophelia commented.

Anastacia did not look at her, only reached out and grabbed her hand.

"You are trying to leave me?"

"No," Anastacia answered, her eyes darting to each constellation. "Never. It is you and I for eternity. Wherever you work, I will be."

"But I am losing you to the underworld again. Is it not enough, here?" Ophelia was not bitter when she spoke, only curious.

Finally, Anastacia turned towards her friend. "You will always lose me to the underworld. That is my part. We cannot do this if I am not there."

"But *I* cannot do this if you are not *here*."

Anastacia squeezed her hand. "Then you must trust me."

Ophelia searched her face before she sighed and closed her eyes. "I do."

Anastacia's free hand skittered over her peplos, checking to make sure everything was still in its correct spot. She felt the warm press of her staff against her torso, the outline of the items in her sewn folds.

And they did not speak further.

CHAPTER EIGHT

S he didn't bother taking the darker tunnels as she traveled down her trail. She was not trying to hide. Charon's gift was clutched in her hand so tightly she was sure there would be imprints in her palm, that the tracing of it was embedded in her brain. It was not the only gift she had carried when she entered, but she had already rid herself of the others.

Those were the necessary ones, items that were more payment and offerings than presents. But this one... she hadn't needed to bring Charon a gift. She brought it because she thought he might like it.

Anastacia wanted Charon to see her coming. She wanted to know how quickly he would spot her as she descended, to see if he was constantly looking for her the way she was for him.

In the past, he hadn't waited on the bank except for when he was retrieving souls to bring them across the river. He had been easy to avoid. Now, even as she entered the large cavern, she could see his boat resting at the dock.

There were no souls waiting there, either already having been ferried across or serving their one hundred years on the bank of the Cocytus. Her eyes scanned the ground below, waiting to see his familiar build, until—*there*.

Her heart jumped. Charon's eyes were already locked onto her as he rested next to the exit of her tunnel, the one she had used to escape him twice now. He was positioned just beside it, close enough that if she had chosen that route, she would have wandered directly into his grasp. Anastacia would not have been able to see him there.

Like a fly into a web, she would have been trapped before she ever saw the spider.

If there was disappointment on his face that she had dodged his ambush, she couldn't tell. He was stoic, standing gracefully. "Hello, Ferryman," she shouted down to him.

"Hello, liar," he said back. He did not yell, his voice carrying to her easily in the hollow area.

"What will our agreement be today?"

He tilted his head up the closer he got to the steep wall. "Why would I trust your agreements?"

"I honored it last time," she argued.

"After you stole from me," he agreed.

She tipped her head back and laughed. "Then how about I promise you the truth. I have already done what I came here for today."

"And what was that?"

"I won't tell you. You can accept that as my honesty, or you can believe my lies."

He pressed his lips together and crossed his arms. "What is in your hands?"

"My attempt at a new agreement. I will give this to you, and you let me leave."

His gaze was open, curious. She was, as always, struck numb by his face. A seaman through and through. Weathered, but young enough that he wore it well. If Charon could age, she imagined he would be tanned through like leather, skin loose as the years took his muscles but not the way his body had stretched to adjust to them. His hair would be white, his beard grown out.

Instead, he was eternally handsome.

He took a moment to think before inclining his head once. "Will you come down, then?" Charon asked cautiously, as though worried if he pushed her too hard, she would flee the way she came.

"I'm not sure yet," she admitted. His presence was dangerous, an itch under her skin that distracted her constantly. The Ferryman was taking over her every thought, and it was difficult enough to stay away from him without feeling his hands on her skin.

After all, she *did* have other things to do. She couldn't stay below with him at all times, no matter what she craved. Life moved on in the world above, even if it didn't below. How cruel that no matter how she begged time to stop, it obeyed no one.

She tossed him her gift, a pretty shell she had collected from her beach. It wasn't much, but she didn't think he would laugh at it. She had seen the rugged, pretty thing and thought of him. She didn't know why, really. But she thought he would like to know.

He caught it easily in one hand, his palm cradling it like it was fragile as he unfurled his fingers and stared at the shell within. His face was thoughtful, pensive, as he stared at it for far longer than she expected. "Thank you," he finally said.

"Is it enough to earn my escape?"

He tilted his head as he looked up at her, still perched on the trail above him. His hand rose to touch the wall, considering if it could hold his weight. She was certain it couldn't. "I have not decided yet," he said, his words mirroring hers.

She laughed at his honesty. "Then I think I will wait here a little longer." She made herself comfortable, resting her chin on her hands. "So, what does the mighty Charon do while he waits for me?"

"The same thing I have always done, though far more anxiously."
He paused before nodding definitively. "I have changed my mind.
You may leave safely if you come down." His fists opened and closed,
unbidden, as though he didn't even know they were moving. As if they
were clutching her already.

"What makes you say that?"

His feet shuffled, perhaps stopping him from pacing when it was all
his body ached to do. "It is not fair that you can leave at any time and
I cannot stop you."

"That is how it has been all the other times," she teased.

"Yes. I don't find it enjoyable."

She grinned down at him. "I do."

As if he finally understood that her offer to descend fully had
expired, he sighed and looked back towards the river. "Do you enjoy
coming down here, as well? Or is it only a necessity?"

She thought about it. "I enjoy it, though I'm not certain it is enjoyable."

"One does not mean the other?"

She scowled down at him. "No, I don't think so." She dangled her
arm down, judging that the distance was still too great for Charon
to reach her, though she would have loved to have a moment where
they touched one another, something to hang onto when she returned
home. "Do you enjoy living here?"

"It is my home, as much part of me as the power in my veins and
the ancestry in my blood. It is my duty, my purpose for existence.
Enjoyment is too small of a word to encompass what this place means
to me."

Anastacia blew out a breath. "Quite a heavy statement. Very poetic,
too. Tell me, is there anything besides duty running through your
head?"

His head tilted up until their eyes locked, his face serious and hers open. "There is you," he said, and her heart skipped.

"And do you find me... *enjoyable*?"

"I find you curious. Interesting. Puzzling. These things are better than enjoyable." He eyed the steep trail again, the distance to reach her, before he spoke once more. "How old are you?"

"I have lived twenty-four years above," she said after a moment. "How old are *you?*" she joked back, as though his speech had not been replaying in her head for the past few weeks since she had seen him. *Eternal. The beginning of time. A deity.*

She was in over her head, but Anastacia preferred it that way. Life was boring when she wasn't balancing on the edge of ruin. How anyone could stand it, she wasn't sure.

He ignored her question. "So little time in the world, and yet you choose to come below to steal from me, as opposed to enjoying the gifts you were given the right to?"

She shrugged. "I am given the right to anything I can take. If the gods wanted something off limits, they should have ensured it was so."

"Humanity is always reaching farther than its grasp allows," he commented.

"If the gods wanted something completely out of reach, they would not make it so close to our grubby hands. But perhaps they cannot. Perhaps we are to the gods, what the gods were to the titans. One day, they may find they have woken, and the world has left them behind."

"And where would I end up in your godless world?"

"I suppose you would not change. There will always be death, even if there are no gods. Perhaps you will be worshiped instead, as people beg you for mercy to escape your bank."

"Perhaps it is you they should pray to then, thief."

She grinned again. "Perhaps."

Anastacia glanced behind her, towards the entrance to Gaia. She needed to leave soon, had been down here for too long, though she enjoyed Charon's conversation too much for her goodbye to be easy. When she stood, brushing off her peplos and her hands, his body stiffened.

"You are leaving already?"

"I am a busy woman."

"I could make you stay," he threatened. She only laughed and started walking.

"If you could, you would have already." She knew she wasn't wrong, had seen it in the way he stared at the Acheron as though his command of it alone could force it to grasp her from the dizzying heights. Charon was powerful in many ways, but he was not given the gift of flight.

Still, she swore the darkness swirled around her ankles and legs heavily as she left him, begging her to remain. She escaped them nimbly before they could convince her to listen.

***

Months passed, Anastacia sneaking down to the underworld regularly though not always seeing Charon. Sometimes she went down laden with gifts, other times she went to steal a soul while he was away.

Her favorite times were when she watched him from above as he picked up his new trinkets. If she was feeling kind, she would let him see her. If she wasn't, she hid until he gave up his search. Even if she didn't always have time to speak with him, she always let him know she was there.

Though, there were days she still gave him a moment or two. When she called to him from above so she could see the way he assessed the world around them as if it would have changed, as if that would be the day he could convince her to come to him. Every time she visited, she saw his tension grow, his desperation to keep her.

It was equal parts terrifying and exhilarating. *This* was life.

Now that she had his attention, she was worried she would lose it. She couldn't imagine going back to the way things used to be, before his eyes had assessed her knowingly, before she had tasted his skin, before she had seen his lips quirk when he found her amusing.

Time passed, her plans with it. Ophelia's gaze stayed suspicious but she did not interfere, for which Anastacia was grateful.

She had enough lingering doubts; her friend did not need to add more.

CHAPTER NINE

A nastacia stared at the entrance to the underworld. The mouth of her cave was beautiful with the sunset, turning purple as the pastels stained the sky. It didn't matter that it would be dark in the world above; the sun did not reach below, anyway. She had planned it this way, that this view would be the last thing she saw before she walked down to see Charon.

To see the others.

It was pretty, worthy of a spectator who appreciated it. Like a final goodbye to the person she had been.

Because tonight would be different than the other days she had visited. Today, she would feel her Ferryman again. Touch him with her hands instead of her eyes. Find out if he could control himself after her teasing for so long, if she had made him as desperate as she was.

When she began her descent, she did not allow herself to look back.

It was quiet when she made it to her crossroads, one tunnel heading further into the underworld while the other sloped down to the riverbank. She paused and set down the amphora that she had brought with her. There was no need to carry it with her to Persephone, not when her visit would be so brief. No one would discover it here, anyway. No one knew this place existed besides her.

She skittered down to the grove, leaving her gift—a single flower, full of thorns, on the ground. It was in full bloom, beautiful, the color of the sun. She gripped the stem hard in her hand before she released it, blood welling, and then Anastacia ran.

She rushed like she was on borrowed time, the giddiness in her chest encouraging her to hurry, hurry, *hurry*. Her footsteps were silent as her feet pounded back over the returning trail, her hand stretched out to brush the wall. She didn't worry about stubbing her foot. The ground was smooth, worn and flat. Her legs stretched and she laughed, wondering if Charon could hear it from this far above.

She didn't slow until she gathered the amphora again, settling it carefully in her arms. The clay was beautiful, a work of art. It was filled with expensive wine which she had only allowed herself a small taste of. Just enough to make sure it was worth the risk of stealing. She pushed it against her chest as she walked, worried she would stumble and spill it. Even a drop on the ground would be a waste.

Anastacia wasn't sure if Charon always slept on this side of the riverbank or if he had taken to waiting for her in case she arrived, but he was sitting on his skiff when she appeared. His eyes were on her immediately, his hands going still before they lowered. He set something down beside him, though she couldn't see what it was.

He leaned back, crossing his arms as she continued her descent. When she made it to her usual spot, he still hadn't moved. "Do you plan to make us shout the whole night?" she yelled over the sound of river.

"That depends, do you plan on hiding away like a rat in a tree?"

"I don't think rats hide in trees."

"A squirrel, then," he amended.

She tilted her head. "A majestic bird, perhaps."

"Majestic birds do not hide."

Anastacia laughed. "They would if they were smart. But no, Ferryman. There is no need to punish me with distance, I am coming down. Help me."

Charon stood quickly before he could stop himself, though he approached cautiously, as if nervous he would move too quickly and she would change her mind. "What will you offer me to allow you to return?"

She raised the amphora. "A drink."

"And if I am not thirsty?"

"Then I suppose I will simply rely on your good will. What do you say?" she asked as though she didn't know what his answer would be, as though she hadn't been flitting just out of his grasp for months to make sure he wanted her below enough to promise anything.

"Yes," he agreed easily.

Anastacia began the rest of the journey down the steepest part of her trail until she reached the area she would need both hands to climb. She stared at the deity beneath her once more. "Catch," she warned him before she let the amphora go. She waited until it landed easily in Charon's grip before she scaled the wall.

She made sure to rub her hand generously on the rock as she dropped.

Anastacia was so focused on the rocky wall, on making sure her feet dug into the correct spots and she wouldn't slip or make a fool of herself, that she didn't notice Charon had approached until her feet were on solid ground.

She turned around and gasped, his chest so close to hers that she had to tilt her head back to see him. His hands locked her in against the wall, rising to touch either side of her face, creating bars she would have to duck to escape. "You have not come back to me for longer than usual," he said.

"Sure, I have," she offered. "Just because you haven't seen me doesn't mean I haven't seen you." Admittedly, she had peeked at him from afar on the days she did not have time to travel all the way to his shore, or the times when she stole someone without letting him know she had come.

He leaned closer to her until they were breathing the same air. "That is not enough."

"I have other obligations," she said quietly, firmly.

"Perhaps. But none more important than this; than that which you have to the souls you steal away."

She laughed, bringing her hand up to his cheek, wondering if he would let her touch him like that. He did. His skin was smooth underneath her hand, warm, her fingertips tingling.

"I don't just steal away random souls to release into thin air," she explained. "I bring them back to their bodies and give them a second life."

Because her hand was on his cheek, she felt the way he froze at her words. "That should not be possible," he said.

She raised her eyebrow and then looked past him at the cavern beyond. "Not possible, or not advised?" She dropped down to her knees, squeezing quickly underneath his arm and picking up the amphora from where he had set it. "Now, come share this with me."

She squeezed her fist together, letting her blood decorate the ground below as she walked before popping open the clay lid and letting the aroma fill her nose. It was a strong wine, the smell overpowering. Already, her mouth tingled at the thought of tasting more than a sip, her jaw tightening in anticipation.

She didn't check to see if Charon was following even though she couldn't hear his footsteps, light as they were. Anastacia knew he would be trailing behind her like her shadow.

She sat next to his dock, letting her feet dangle off the edge. Her toes barely touched the water. It was frigid, cold against her skin, an unnatural and uncomfortable bite. Still, she swirled her foot around, watching the way it rippled at her intrusion.

Charon settled next to her, his own feet dipping into the Acheron. "You aren't scared to touch the river?"

"Why should I be? It is the same river I bathe in above. The same water that flows there, flows here."

"The water here has experienced far more than it has above."

She tilted her head, looking at it as it eddied beneath her. "Yes. But it is still the same water. And I am safe here, anyway. Just because I would dip my toes in doesn't mean I would brave swimming through it."

He watched the Acheron as if contemplating her words before grabbing the amphora that sat between them, placing it against his lips. He took a long drink and then looked at it critically. She laughed at the expression on his face.

"Is it not as delicious as the nectar of the gods?"

His eyes darted to hers, pupils large. "No, but it is better in other ways."

Her heart skittered at his gaze, the interest there. His attention was a drug, more mind altering than the wine. Anastacia reached for the amphora, taking a drink herself. There was something romantic about knowing his lips and hers were touching through the bottle, that they would taste the same now. She attempted to lower it, but then Charon's hand was on hers, tilting it up once more. "Do not swallow," he instructed her as he filled her mouth carefully. A tiny bit squeezed through the corner of her mouth, dribbling to her chin.

Charon moved the amphora and suddenly, his tongue was there. He swiped up the streak of wine on her face before pressing his lips over hers, coaxing her mouth open. He directed her head over his, drinking the wine from her mouth before he kissed her deeply.

He didn't stop, his body slotting itself over hers. Anastacia's hands rose to his shoulders, her fingers digging into his arms as he devoured her as though *she* were the gift. "Charon," she mumbled breathlessly as he ran a hand through her hair, tilting her head back.

"It tastes far better like this," he said softly, as though it were a secret. Only the river was there to witness them.

She almost put both hands in his hair, but the sting of her palm against his skin reminded her not to. It was lucky he hadn't already noticed her blood staining his arm, the smell of the wine distracting him.

Suddenly, he moved away from her mouth, running down to her neck and sucking hard enough that her body rose off the dock. It was the same place she had touched every night, even after his mark vanished. "You will not allow this to fade next time," he ordered. "You will come back each time it begins to disappear."

"Yes," she answered, her eyes rolling in her head as he laid her down until she was flat against the wood. The water of the river lapped at the stilts, the only sound aside from the blood rushing in her ears. With his hands digging into her torso, skimming their way over her peplos, she would agree to almost anything he asked.

Anything for him to keep going.

Her legs parted around his body as he leaned over her, pressing himself deeply against her core. His hands grabbed onto her legs, spreading them as he moved down her torso and pulled her clothing up.

Anastacia's hands moved of their own accord, grasping at the fabric in a brief moment of panic and uncertainty. She had meant to make him desperate, but she hadn't considered what that would truly mean when she was back in his grasp. That he might devour her before any of her plans were in place.

"I—" she stuttered as his eyes rose to meet hers from between her knees. She knew he claimed not to be a god, but it was difficult to see him as anything different. His eyes were beautiful, holding eternity within them. Wise, young, cruel and kind. The world stared back at her through his gaze.

She was not a child, but for a moment, she felt like one. Inexperienced and unsure. She tried speaking again as he waited patiently, though he did not remove himself. He simply waited for her to adjust, her chest heaving. "I have never done this," she admitted finally.

He laughed, low and deep, grabbing the wine as he inched her peplos higher until her belly was bare to him. She finally understood why animals didn't turn over easily, why they didn't expose themselves like this. She had never felt more vulnerable in her life.

Then, he poured the cool wine gently into her naval before following it with his mouth. "I have never done this either," he finally said after his tongue followed a trail of wine that spilled with her breath. Her heart constricted, and she put a hand on his cheek to stop him.

"Truly?" she asked, shocked.

As if it finally registered that she was serious, that this had meaning to her, he stopped his ministrations. His head tilted to the side. "No." His brows furrowed. "I told you. I have not changed. I do not dally with affairs or meaningless pursuits. I have my purpose and that is enough for me. I have never craved companionship."

She felt the relief settle itself against her skin, her smile lighting up her face. "You're not nervous?"

"What do I have to be nervous about?"

"That you don't know what to do," she added.

Charon laughed, his fingers moving to the linen covering her mound before he dipped them into the waistband. "I said I had never done it before, Anastacia." His eyes darkened as he tore them off of her like they were nothing but thin leaves as opposed to softened animal leather. "Not that I didn't know what to do."

Then, before she could rethink, his mouth dipped down to her entrance, his tongue spreading flat as he licked her languidly. Her hands flew to his hair, her stinging hand forgotten as she wrapped the black strands in her fist while he took her apart. Her body was singing, her eyes flying for anything to look at, to help her hold on, but she couldn't. They squeezed shut suddenly, her body shaking as his hand joined his tongue, strumming against her like she was an instrument he had spent his whole life learning how to play.

When she thought there could be nothing better, his finger entered her, spreading her easily, slowly. Even that felt foreign, his hand so much larger than hers. Her thighs were soaked as he moved, helping her adjust, pleasure zinging through her body.

She tore off the ground as he curled his finger within her.

Anastacia could feel his smile against the inside of her leg as he dramatically dipped his tongue into her once more. "This," he muttered. "*This* is better than the god's nectar."

The sound of his voice in her ears, the feeling of his breath on her mound, the cockiness of his grin—it shredded her apart, his name leaving her lips as she fell to pieces in his hands. Her chest was heaving as she became more aware of the position of her belt against her ribs, the press of her back against her staff.

Charon turned, bending near the edge of the dock, and she worried for an uncomfortable moment that he would leave her. However, before she could do more than clutch at the fabric pushed around her hips, he returned with a cloth in his hand, wet from the river. He cleaned her gently, the water nice against her heated skin. She got on her elbows, staring at his body, the way his cock tented his tunic.

"I can—"

"No, little liar," he said with a soft smile. "I have waited an eternity. I can wait a few moments longer."

She swallowed hard as he set himself down next to her. "I am sorry if I was too forward," he finally stated. "I may look like a man, but I am not one. I have not had to practice restraint or patience often."

"Because you are given everything you want immediately?" she teased, but his face was open, vulnerable.

"Because I have never wanted anything."

Anastacia blinked, his words settling somewhere in her stomach. How would it feel to want nothing? She wouldn't know. Anastacia had never gone a day in her life without *wanting*.

She wanted food in her hand, even when she was not hungry. She wanted art in her home simply to know she had it. She wanted the jewelry she noticed on someone else's skin, even if she knew she would never wear it. She wanted to be the cleverest person in the room, wanted to be ten steps ahead of everyone else, wanted, wanted, wanted.

Her silence was heavy. She could feel it against her skin like a blanket. Finally, he lifted his fingers and rotated his hand before them, the black of his jewel eating the light around them. "This was the first gift I received that was truly for me," he commented. Then he used that same hand to touch the amphora next to them on the ground, picking it up before spinning it to look at the design. "And these. Your shell and your other bobbles."

His eyes traced it carefully, admiring the artwork. She was pleased at his expression—she had thought he would like it. Drawn in black on the clay was an elaborate portrayal of the sun, detailed mountains below it. It had taken her time to find one that didn't depict any of the gods and didn't have any humans painted within.

There had been one of Charon himself, ferrying souls across raging waters, but she had left it untouched.

"Has there been nothing else that has come to you?"

He was still holding the amphora gently, as though if he squeezed it too hard, it would shatter in his hands. "There have been some things. Heracles came and begged my help. Him, I earned a year in chains because of. Orpheus played me a song on his lyre, asking me to take him to Hades to bargain for his wife. For my assistance, I was gifted a beautiful song that still echoes through the riverbank if I listen closely. But those things were still for Hades, ultimately. They were not gifts, only a different sort of coin to gain passage across the river."

She ignored the tiny seed of guilt that lodged in the back of her mind at his words. She pressed her slowly bleeding hand to her peplos, not caring if the fabric stained. Suddenly, she was questioning herself. What she had done. Whose attention she had drawn.

And that was something she could *not* afford to do. Not when she was playing with stakes as high as these, when the reward was large, but the risk was larger.

"Would you have accepted these gifts from anyone, then?" she asked calmly. "Was it only loneliness that endeared me to you?"

Charon set the amphora down, meeting her eyes again. His face was serious. His crooked nose appeared far more severe in the low light, the shadows elongating it. "I have never been lonely in all my days until I saw you."

At her doubtful look, he laughed. "I am a deity. You think I could not find someone to fuck if I wished to fuck? That I could not find someone to please me, could not warm my bed with meaningless partners and pretty faces?" Charon leaned forward, emphasizing his words. "I do not desire you because of your body. You could be mortal, a god, a man, an idea, and it would still only be you that I crave. There has been no other, and there will be no other. So no, I am not lonely. I do not need frivolous company. Do you understand?"

The earth rumbled around them, and Anastacia winced. "This is very inconvenient timing," she commented. His head swayed backwards with confusion. It was clear he had not expected that reaction from his words.

It was not the reaction she wanted to give him either.

She wanted time to explore each of his answers, wished she could sit there and pick apart his brain for as long as he would let her. She didn't want to do anything but drink their wine until it was gone and learn about one another.

Anastacia knew everything there was to know from the surface. The way his body moved as he worked, the expressions he gave the souls on his bank, the way he was polite to the other gods and goddesses she had seen him interact with.

But that told her nothing about his thoughts. Nothing about the real reason *why* she had caught his attention, if he even knew.

"What is inconvenient?" he asked as once again, the underground rumbled.

"Do you trust me?" she asked.

He gave her a look. "No."

She grinned. "I didn't think so. Do you think I have a plan?"

He tilted his head, his eyes searching his face. "I think you must always have a plan."

That would have to be good enough. Anastacia hoped his curiosity overpowered his anger. She swallowed as something appeared in the darkness over the river. "For the record," she added, "those gifts truly were for you, and you alone."

Charon set the amphora down carefully like he didn't quite believe her. "What have you done, little liar?"

She swallowed hard, squaring her shoulders to face her fate. "What I came here to do."

CHAPTER TEN

C haron stared at Anastacia as her lips pursed. Her hands skittered nervously over her peplos—the same peplos he had pushed over her soft belly only moments ago. She patted the fabric as if to reassure herself she was covered and then adjusted it around her back. He idly realized her staff must be there, tucked into the interior of her belt.

He could still taste her on his lips. His hands were tingling with the vibrations of her legs, his ears warm from the imprints of her thighs when she had tightened them against the skin, pulling him closer. Anastacia's arousal still coated his fingers.

It would have been difficult enough for him to comprehend her statements with no context. Add in that his mind was focused only on her, on the way he wanted to explore every part of her body and mind, and he was lost. Nothing she was saying made sense.

Her eyes were locked on the Acheron as he searched for whatever had made her worry, whatever had shaken the earth, until her voice drew his attention back. "You may think me a liar, but I am about to find out if you are, too." Her eyebrow rose as she glanced at him from the side. "If you *are* as fickle and easy to anger as a god."

And then Hades appeared, darkness pulling him through the water as he sat on a boat. The waters of the river calmed where he was, as

Charon had commanded they do for the god when he crossed without Charon's company.

Charon and the god of the underworld had a complicated relationship. Mutual respect, a thing close to friendship, a dedication to their duties. Charon did not consider himself a servant to the god; he was the keeper of the underworld, the primary guard, the first judge. He did not answer to Hades. He answered to the underworld itself.

One day, Hades would be gone. But so long as Thanatos was alive, so long as there were souls to be harvested, Charon would still be the deity of the rivers; the Acheron, the Styx, the Cocytus, the Lethe and the Phlegethon.

Charon stood, his body towering over Anastacia who only crossed her ankles unconcerned, as though she was not in the presence of a god.

A very angry god.

Hades was a handsome man, tall with lean muscle. He had hair darker than Charon's and freezing blue eyes that rivaled the coldest areas of Tartarus. On his own, he was an imposing man.

Next to Charon, however, he was tiny. Only a god.

Hades stepped onto the dock easily, gracefully, stepping forward until he and Charon were almost chest to chest. "Hades," Charon said in greeting.

The god waved his hand towards Anastacia. "What is this?"

"She has not crossed the river," Charon stated.

Hades held something up, his face full of fire. Charon's eyes darted to the handful of desiccated flowers in his grip. Only one was still alive, a thorny rose. It was fresh enough that it had likely just been cut hours before.

Charon's nose flared as he inhaled, noting the familiar scent on the offering. Blood he had tasted before, that he recognized.

His head swung towards the woman who was sitting just beyond them both, a sheepish smile on her face. One hand was still clutching at the fabric of her peplos, and his eyes caught on the way she pinched it together.

If she peeled it away, he knew there would be blood soaking into the fabric. She would not heal here, even the smallest thorn prick bleeding stubbornly until she went back to the world above.

"Where did you find that?" Charon asked Hades as he watched Anastacia. She couldn't have given it to Hades, could she have? Couldn't have reached his palace without Charon's help.

"She has been courting *my wife,*" Hades answered. "Leaving gifts and love notes in her grove."

But the grove—that was—

Charon stared across the river, wondering just how many tunnels and trails Anastacia had discovered within the heart of the mountain. He had not considered that she was going places other than his river-bank, that she had found ways into the underworld that circumvented the Acheron.

Anastacia stood up slowly, brushing her hands off against her peplos. The streak of blood was stark against the light fabric.

"You..." Charon started and then trailed off. Something ached in his chest. "You have come here to steal Persephone?"

Persephone.

The taste of Anastacia, so meaningful before, went bitter on his tongue. He took a moment to dip his hand in the river before swiping it across his face roughly. When he straightened to look at her once more, her eyes lingered on him. On the way his shoulders had caved in just slightly, the downturned angle to his lips. He could not even bring himself to narrow his eyes at her.

His year in chains for Heracles had not hurt. Heracles had not hidden his intentions; Charon made a decision, and though he paid for it, he had known the possible consequences.

Orpheus, too, had found his own way to charm Charon, but he was honest. He had played his lyre, given Charon the gift of music, and Charon had made his choice to bring him to Hades.

But Anastacia had fooled him.

And it wasn't with a heroic story or a mourning song. He had thought *she* was the instrument charming him, but he was wrong.

Charon was the instrument, and Anastacia had been the musician. Picking at his curiosity, pulling at his strings, all while she did the same to Persephone. He could almost laugh if it hadn't curdled the mix of her wine and arousal in his stomach.

Persephone would not leave Hades for anyone, let alone a sneaky, clever mortal woman.

Perhaps not so clever after all, if she had believed such a thing.

Anastacia walked next to Charon, standing with her shoulders back as she tilted her head to stare at Hades. "I have not been trying to court Persephone," she said. "Those gifts are nothing more than sacrifices at an altar."

"I looked at the letters. Do not lie to me," Hades retorted, making the little bit of hope that had lodged in his chest shrivel once more.

"Perhaps you looked at them, but you did not read them," Anastacia argued back as though she wasn't antagonizing one of the most powerful gods in existence. The only god who ruled the ground she stood on.

"I did not need to read every word. You think I do not recognize love? That I did not see your obsession sprinkled between every line? Your gifts from the world above, as though she did not choose me?"

Suddenly, as if reality had come back to her quickly, her eyes darted behind Hades and she took a step back. "That is not what they were."

Charon frowned. "What were they?"

She glanced at him. "I didn't lie when I asked for an audience with Hades. You wouldn't grant me one. There is something I need that I cannot steal, and if I could not ask it of Hades, I knew I could ask it from Persephone. I did go to the grove, yes. Those gifts are from me. But I needed time to explain things to her, a way to allow her to listen and consider before she made her decision."

Both men scowled, Hades' face looking more intrigued as Anastacia spoke. Even that interest, Charon did not like. *That* was Anastacia's skill. To look so average, to so easily blend into the world around her, that when she opened her mouth it was mesmerizing.

If she had cowered to Hades, made bumbling apologies with timid mannerisms, Hades would not have even given her a moment to explain. His wrath and protection of his wife was unmatched. Their loyalty to one another had never wavered, though Hades still did not appreciate those who tried to steal his wife away. If Anastacia had not stood toe to toe with the god like she was not a mere mortal but a goddess herself, Charon was not sure she would be there now.

But she had caught Hades' attention the same way she had captured Charon's. Once more, Charon found himself posturing, wanting to tell Hades to leave. He was not sure what *he* would do to Anastacia, but whatever punishment was chosen, whatever she had earned with her disregard for the underworld, the grove, the river, Charon wanted to be the one responsible for it.

Before anyone else could speak, another noise echoed on the water, Persephone appearing as she cut through the waves. Her gaze was locked unhappily on the group of them, and while a small smile grew on Hades' face, Anastacia began to pale.

This was what she wanted, though he understood why she might feel a moment of regret. She was about to be in the presence of two powerful gods. Charon was used to the way they moved, the way life and death emanated from their very pores, but Anastacia was not.

She may have seen them from a distance, might have imagined what it would be like to meet the rulers of the underworld, but he remembered the way she had trembled when she was in Charon's presence the first time he got his hands on her. The fear, the exhilaration, how her body had twisted because instinct told it to *run*. Watching from afar might have given her the confidence to attempt contacting them, but it could not have prepared her for what their meeting would be like.

For the first time, Charon wondered how much of him she had seen before he noticed her. How long had she studied him before they met?

"This dock is beginning to feel a little small," she made an excuse as she began to back herself off slowly, her feet leaving the wood until they were bare on the soil of the bank. He didn't know why he was so certain she was going to slip away, but suddenly, he was positive.

Perhaps because she had pulled the trick on him before.

Charon moved before he thought about it, the feeling in his chest screaming *hurry*. Before Anastacia could take another step toward her little rat tunnels, Charon was behind her. He towered over her, her back bumping into his torso, her head barely brushing his chin. He molded himself so tightly to her body that he could feel her staff squeeze between them.

He leaned down, hands gripping her biceps. They were strong as she flexed in his grip, though still so fragile compared to his hands that he felt if he pressed too hard, they would snap. He let his fingers dig in enough that they left indentations in her skin.

He wondered if they bruised—and why part of him wanted them to. Charon wanted his marks to litter her entire body, even with the anger and betrayal simmering in his chest. Charon had months of staring at Anastacia while she teased him from above, out of reach. That time had only given him leave to think about everything he craved to do with her, things he had never imagined before that now haunted his every waking moment.

They had spent hours talking together, though it felt like she hid more from him than she offered. Even in that way, he learned about her. But with her in his arms, his mind fled and his rushing blood replaced it.

He wanted to suck on the skin of her thighs until they were purple and angry, wondered how she would look with her face flushed with need.

Wanted to see how pink her body could become after he worshipped it for hours.

Whatever happened today, she had ruined herself. She had burrowed under his skin, and though she had teased him, baited him, perhaps visited him only out of a want for Persephone, Charon had not lied.

He had made his decision. The little lyre was his, whether she was a thief, a sneak, or a fraud. Charon was not a god. He would not cast her away for her mistakes, would not turn her into an animal, punish her in the river, drown her in tears.

Charon was worse than a god.

He would keep her, whatever she was, until she was only his. If she strayed to another, he would drag the soul to the depths of Tartarus himself. He would make sure Anastacia knew he was the only choice she wanted, the only one she had.

Once his mouth was at her ear, he spoke. "Where are you trying to go, little lyre? Did you think I'd let you escape me this time?"

"We had a deal," she said back as she kept her eyes on Hades, and now Persephone as she joined her husband.

He laughed. The sound was dark, even to him. He was angry. His tongue slid up the side of her neck. "You lied. So can I."

Perhaps he would have let her go if the gods had not visited. Either way, he hadn't hesitated when he made the promise, knowing no matter what she had offered him, wine, no wine, deal or no deal, he would have agreed to anything to lure her to him.

Her absence had almost convinced him to journey to Gaia. He knew he would find her eventually. He had all the time in the world, and she was only mortal. But he had known she would come back underground eventually. Charon had even taken to sleeping near the tunnel entrance, listening for light footsteps and a lithe body slinking through the narrow walls.

What he would have done before didn't matter, though. Now that he knew how easy his little thief was to make promises, to put herself in the paths of angry gods, he would not make the mistake of allowing her out of his sight without assurance she would return. More assurance than her word, which clearly meant nothing to her.

"Hades wants to harm me," she hissed as she struggled in his grip.

"Worry about me. The one who has you within his grasp *now*. Hades might get to you later, but I have you first." He didn't bother comforting her. If Hades was going to harm her, he would have done it already. The god would hear Anastacia and his wife out before he made any decisions.

Knowing Persephone, that meant Anastacia would be just fine. By the look on her face, she was fond of his little thief already. The goddess's smile was soft, half of her gold-brown hair swept up to frame her face. She tucked herself beside Hades, pulling his arm around her shoulders before patting his hand.

"You must be Anastacia," she said.

Anastacia was trembling in his grip, her body pressing deeper into him. Suddenly, the arms that had been fighting against him began to hold him tightly. She had realized she could not escape and was instead using him as protection.

He did his best to hide his grin, though Hades gave him a knowing look.

"Yes, goddess," she answered.

Hades huffed at her polite tone. "Your reverence only extends to my wife?"

Persephone stepped forward before Anastacia could answer him. "Do you understand what you have asked me for? Your letters speak of your desire for to earn a soul back from my husband, but I worry you have not thought through the consequences."

Anastacia nodded her head, staring at the goddess's feet. "Yes, goddess," she said again. "I wouldn't have asked if I wasn't sure."

The goddess stared at the woman in his arms for a long moment. "It has been you bringing me gifts all these years?" she asked as she tilted her head. Anastacia nodded again. "You are brave to have come down here so many times. No others have done such a thing."

"Where stupidity leads, bravery must follow."

Persephone let out a small laugh before looking up at her husband. "She has asked me for a soul. I would give it to her."

"She has insulted me," Hades answered. "And just how many years has she been leaving you gifts that you have not told me of?" He looked at Charon. "How long has she been sneaking beneath my nose, in my home, unattended?"

Charon frowned and glanced down, but Anastacia only shrugged. "I have not kept track."

Charon was certain that was a lie. Hades met his eyes and Charon dipped his head. He could admit when he had made a mistake. "The first time I saw her was only a few months ago. I did not know she had access to areas other than the riverbank."

He did not mention that she had already been stealing souls. *That* was something he did not think Hades would forgive. Those were his domain, his responsibility. Charon could argue that they were not Hades' until they crossed the Acheron, but it was a weak statement.

"Then let her earn it," Persephone proposed. "We will give her labors to complete. One for each stage of delivering a soul. The guide, the ferryman, and the final resting place. It will be fair."

Anastacia began to shake her head. "The guide? I would prefer not to—"

"You do not get a say in this, little lyre," Charon whispered to her as his hand slid up to cover her mouth. "You are lucky they are considering it at all. *I* would not."

She intelligently stayed silent, letting the two deliberate. Finally, Hades' blue eyes landed on Anastacia. "Three labors. Hermes will choose the first. You will not leave the underworld unless it is to complete the trial you are given. If I am pleased with your completion, I *may* consider letting you leave my home with the soul. Is that understood?"

"Yes," she responded quietly, perhaps worried if she said even one more word, it would change the god's mind. "Thank you."

Charon didn't release her as Hades' gaze found his once more. "You and I will discuss this."

Charon inclined his head in agreement.

The king and queen of the underworld departed, stepping onto Hades' boat and disappearing into the gloom. Charon didn't give Anastacia the chance to wiggle away from him, lifting her over his shoulder until she dangled there. Her elbows landed against his back.

"Charon," she said in a hard voice. "Put me down."

"I do not trust your feet to obey," he explained.

"I promise I will follow."

"I do not trust your mouth to speak truth."

She began to struggle in his arms as his feet hit the wood of the dock. He brought up his free hand, swatting her behind with it once, his hand stinging. He hoped his handprint would appear underneath her clothing.

Her gasp made him smile. He walked confidently to his skiff, grabbing his pole. "You had better stop moving, lest we fall into the Acheron," he commented happily. She froze.

"Please, Charon. I do not like deep or fast water. I would rather stay on the bank or find a better place to cross."

"Then you should have chosen another deity to play your games with. I am the Ferryman. The river is my home."

He pushed off the shore, finally setting her down softly when the skiff had floated far enough away that she could not reach the bank even if she threw herself into the water.

Although he had questioned her fear when she told him of it, he didn't now. It was obvious she hadn't lied about her discomfort on the deep water as he watched the way she crouched low, her fingers white as they grabbed onto the wood. Her eyes frantically ran across his skiff as though she could fall off, as if he would even let her get close.

His river would not touch her.

No, only he would do that.

Chapter Eleven

Every time the boat rocked beneath her, Anastacia grew one second closer to throwing up. The wine she had consumed was roiling within her stomach, threatening to come out all over Charon's feet. Her hands tried to grab onto something solid, anything, but there was nothing but smooth wood.

Charon's deep laugh rang out above her as a wave crested over the side of the boat. He maneuvered them skillfully, but though she had never seen him fall, that didn't mean it was impossible.

He only ferried the *dead*. She was very much alive. This river could absolutely kill her if he wasn't careful. The Acheron provided so much life, but she had never forgotten what it was. What it was capable of.

She squeezed her eyes shut until they made it to calmer waters, though her muscles refused to loosen. Just because the surface was calm didn't mean there wasn't a current raging underneath or that the water was shallow. It was simply deep enough that the rocks weren't there to disturb their pathway.

Charon shifted, the boat moving beneath him and sending her heart into her throat.

"I will not return this way," she demanded.

"You will," he responded smugly.

She didn't answer because she knew he was right. Instead, she focused only on breathing, promising herself that they would be across the river soon. She knew she should look around, do her best to memorize where they were, but she couldn't bring herself to lift her head high enough.

When Anastacia finally felt the boat nudge against the opposite riverbank, she wasn't sure she could move. Her legs were heavy, stuck in place. Instead of requesting she stand, Charon bent down and scooped her easily into his arms. She tucked her head into his chest, keeping her eyes closed as he stepped away from the Acheron and onto the dock.

The world still felt like it was rocking long after she knew they were back on solid land.

"Gods and deities do not scare you, but the river does?"

She shook her head. "It is impossible to explain to a being that cannot experience death."

"Then pick your head up, Anastacia," he said, amused. "There is no death for you here."

She finally opened her eyes, curiosity getting the better of her.

The riverbank near the entrance of the underworld was no longer visible, swallowed by gloom, and she turned to discover what the other side of the Acheron looked like. After all, she had always wondered what type of home Charon would have.

It was a simple place, wooden walls and with an unblocked window. Half of the home rested on stilts, hanging over the river. It wasn't large, wasn't decorated or pretty. Moss grew up the sides, the wood stained darker where the river kissed it often. A warm glow emanated from within.

The air was cooler on this side of the river, perhaps because it was deeper in the underworld.

Her skin pebbled, her light summer peplos doing nothing to keep the chill misting from the river out of her clothing. As if he felt the shiver in his arms, Charon's lip tilted up. "You are cold?"

"We are deep within the underworld, and I am wet. Yes, I am cold."

He nodded, his hands adjusting until his fingers were positioned just barely outside of the junction of her thighs. Just lower than where his mouth had been earlier. Their encounter had been pushed from her mind in the chaos of the minutes after, but it rushed back with a vengeance now.

She had seen the anger in his face at the god's arrival. Anastacia didn't know what that meant, what would come of the dark betrayal in his gaze. She wished she could explain, almost convinced herself to talk to him, but she wasn't stupid. He wouldn't trust her, even if she were honest.

Charon was interested in her. She had captured his attention, convinced him to think of something other than his duty, but she was not delusional. There was no love or trust between them. He may not be a god, but he was certainly not human either.

Already, she was at a disadvantage. He had captured her in his web, ripped her apart in ways she hadn't imagined. It wasn't meant to go like this. She couldn't give him more of herself yet. Not when she wasn't sure what he would do with it.

Anastacia had heard the stories. She should have known he would have no control, no patience, that whatever limits society placed on her and other mortals would not apply to him. He did not feel shame in what they had done. There had been no regret on his face.

Anger, yes. Hurt, she thought so.

But as Charon carried her to his home, nudging the door open and shut before even setting her down, she had the distinct feeling that she was in over her head.

The air was more bearable inside. He walked her to the corner of the room where a bed was situated. It wasn't huge, but it was large enough to fit Charon's body and then some. There was a tiny area for cooking, though the only table in the room sat scattered with wood carving utensils and parchment. He set her down softly on the bed before grabbing a blanket and placing it on her.

"You will not be able to escape from me here, little liar."

She didn't argue with him, though she was certain she could. She knew Persephone's grove sat to the north, and that Tartarus was to her east. There were other ways out of the mountain besides the one closest to her home. Shallow places she could cross the rivers at.

But Anastacia stayed silent, instead looking up at the deity who stood above her.

His chest glowed in the warm firelight, the flames making him appear more ethereal than usual. When her eyes rose back to his face, he was smirking, enjoying the way she devoured his body. The longer she perused him, the more she noticed the way his cock tented the fabric of his tunic. Her eyes locked onto it, and though she knew it was inappropriate, that she should look away, she didn't.

The ferryman didn't know what was improper and what wasn't. He didn't acknowledge the expectations of the world above, had likely never even visited it. She had no doubt that he would listen to her if she said no, but without the chains of propriety, why should she?

Anastacia would never be married. She would never find love with a normal man, would not grow old with him. All she had was Ophelia, and her friend had a new lover every week. No, if Charon wanted to ruin her, she would let him.

"Have you touched a cock before, Anastacia?" he asked.

She nodded. "Yes. My friend is a healer. Naked bodies and maneuverings come with the territory." It had never been of a sexual nature, but of course she had the accidental or necessary brushing. Injuries high on thighs, to the pelvis, the changing of soiled clothes and bathroom accidents.

"That is not what I mean," he clarified.

She swallowed hard. "Then no."

His hand dipped into her hair, pulling her head backwards and forcing her neck to arch.

"You are not angry?" she asked slowly.

"Oh, yes. I am angry. You used me to get to Persephone."

She shook her head. "I did not. I could have gotten to her without you. I didn't need to visit you, didn't need your favor."

"And to steal the souls? Did you not need my favor for that?"

"I have been stealing souls for years without your approval. If I wanted to continue to do so, I could have."

He leaned down towards her. "Who is this soul you are trying so hard to save?"

"It doesn't matter until I save it."

"Will you try to disappear from me then? After you have gotten what you want?" His gaze was intense on her face, unsmiling.

She was honest, though she was certain he wouldn't believe her. "I have been trying to run away from you since the first time I saw you. I haven't been able to do it yet."

He hummed but released her, walking to the seat at his table. "Do you need to eat?"

"I don't know," she answered. Would her hunger return on this side of the river? "Do you?"

"I can, but I don't need to. It is more for enjoyment than for sustenance." He stood back up once more, pacing the little room twice before leaving, the door shutting quietly behind him.

Anastacia wasn't sure what to do, if she was meant to stay here or follow. She stepped off the bed when he didn't return, moving on silent feet to the table.

She picked up the carving utensils. They were well used, the handles worn and imprinted with Charon's palm, the blades sharp. Anastacia looked around the room but couldn't find any carvings, nothing on the walls to indicate that he had worked on the home.

She walked to the window, looking out as though he would appear at any moment. He was silent enough that Anastacia knew she would not hear him approach. She wasn't certain how long he would leave her here alone, but she would have to make the best of it.

She was lucky the home was small. It wouldn't take long to explore.

The door didn't have a lock, and the window was large enough she could crawl through if needed. A dresser sat near the bed. She opened it, finding a few different tunics. All were soft against her hands, the fabric delicate, though sturdy. She grabbed the only black item within, unfolding it until a cloak was before her. It was thick, warm.

She had never noticed the weather change on the riverbank and had never seen him wear it. She folded it back up before moving to the next drawer.

Within it was a box, small and light in her hands. She tried to open it, but a lock stopped it from budging. She had just moved her hands toward her lockpicks when she heard a thud outside the door.

Anastacia scrambled to put it back, shutting it and flying back to the bed. She did her best to arrange herself naturally.

Charon didn't look at her as he entered, carrying a tray laden with fruits and nuts, bread and fish. He shut the door with his foot and set everything down on the table. "Did you find anything interesting?"

She frowned, crossing her arms. "What?"

He gave her a knowing look. "You think I am foolish enough to allow a thief into my home without making sure everything was put away carefully?"

Her mouth dropped open. "I wouldn't steal from you."

"You would, and you have."

She pursed her lips. "Well, I wouldn't steal anything right now." He didn't answer, instead pulling out the only chair at the table. "And how did you know to put things away? You didn't know I was coming."

He gestured for her to wait, then walked out once more but left the door open behind him. He was hardly gone from sight when he came back, a heavy wooden chair in his grip. It was well made, sturdy. A pretty color, each leg intricately carved with leaves and branches.

He set it by the table before sitting. Anastacia stood slowly and sat next to him, crossing her legs. She wasn't used to sitting on chairs. She and Ophelia used mats to sit on, their table low to the ground when they ate.

He picked up an olive, holding it out to her with his head tilted. She leaned forward, wrapping her lips around his fingers as she took it from him. He seemed pleased at her action.

"I did know you were coming," he finally admitted. "Perhaps not today or tomorrow. But I knew there would be a day that you came to the underworld and I could not bear to let you go." He picked up a piece of bread, ripping it so that it was bite sized before holding it towards her mouth.

"And when you get tired of me?" she asked.

His thumb lingered in her mouth this time after she took the food from him. "I have done the same thing every day, for all of my days. I gather my coins, I ferry the dead, I navigate the river. Never have I felt bored, never have I wanted something different. So no, Anastacia. I will not get tired of you. Is there any food you do not like?" He changed the subject.

"No," she said. "Is this how I will always eat, then?"

"Perhaps. I like this." She watched him carefully. For a man who claimed to be furious, he didn't act like it.

"You are still angry?" she asked after swallowing.

"Yes."

"Even though I told you the truth?"

"I do not believe it is the whole truth. And even if I did, I would be angry. I do not appreciate that you have put yourself in the ways of the gods, that you have agreed to their labors. I hate that you need something I cannot give you. I do not like that the gods even know you exist."

She was silent for a moment, mulling over his words. For all that he seemed to work with the gods, their familiarity with one another, he didn't seem to trust them any more than he trusted her.

"You don't act like an angry man," she finally said.

"How would an angry man act?" he asked.

"Loudly, physically, emotionally. He would yell or perhaps throw something. Grow distant or say cruel things."

He held out another piece of food, his eyes locked on her mouth. "I have nothing to yell that I could not say. If I need to be physical, I have an entire river to take out my frustrations. I do not want to be distant from you or hurt your feelings. I am angry, but doing those things will not make me feel less so."

"What will?"

He shrugged. "This is a start, but I have plans, little liar. However, as you don't share yours with me, I don't need to share mine with you. Don't worry. You will earn my forgiveness."

She swallowed nervously, finishing her food in silence. He never ate, not one bite, instead only focusing on feeding her. When she could eat no more, she turned her head away and picked up his chisel.

"What do you carve?"

"Boats, mainly, though I made both of these chairs. I built this home, the bed, the table. I make my oars and my skiff poles. There are many ways to pass the time. Did you carve the bone of your staff yourself?"

Anastacia grabbed the staff at her back, pulling it out and rolling it in her hands. "No, I got it like this."

He held out his hand to see it, and she gently gave it to him. Her eyes watched him cautiously as his hands cradled it. "Got it, or stole it?"

Anastacia rolled her eyes. "What's the difference? It's mine."

"It's beautiful," he commented as his fingers danced across the bone. "I am sure even Hermes would have a hard time telling his apart from this one, they are so similar."

"I am sure he would," she agreed. She doubted the god had studied his staff in years. "What is he like?"

Charon blew out a breath, setting the staff down on the table. "He is like all gods. Better than some, worse than others. He is a noble guide, kind to the souls he brings me. To others, he is a troublemaker, a trickster. Hermes is granted access to the underworld because he is more neutral than the others, no strong loyalty to any one god or goddess. He is a good messenger. I think you will get along well enough."

"When will he come retrieve me?"

His eyes turned flinty. "Eager to start your labors, or ready to run away from me again?"

"I have never truly wanted to run away from you," she said, her fingers trailing down to her waist absently. The item in her pocket.

"You should have," he commented. "You should have sprinted the first time you caught my attention and never returned."

"And yet I still would have come back eventually. You said so yourself."

He laughed. "Yes, but perhaps I would not have known you so well then. I might have let you cross the Acheron with only a lingering glance, perhaps a question or two."

She narrowed her eyes. "Do you really think so?"

He didn't respond to her question, pushing his chair back and standing. He held out his hand and she slid hers into it lightly.

He led her back to the bed before his hands went to her belt, removing it from her waist. If he noticed how heavy it was, how ladened with tools and items it had become, he didn't comment. He left only the band around her chest and her underwear.

"You will need rest before we accompany Hermes," he said.

"Is it possible to sleep here?" she asked.

He nodded. "On this side of the river, yes. Your finger has stopped bleeding. You will feel hunger and thirst. You will need to sleep. The riverbank is different, a place of waiting. It is a kindness to take away the perception of time for the souls there."

The thought back on her own time there and agreed. The souls would go insane if their minds were present and they could not leave, stuck in the place between life and death.

She tilted her head up to look at him. "I'm not sure I can sleep," she admitted. Anastacia was still too curious. She wanted to go outside and explore.

More importantly, she needed to find a way out that didn't involve crossing the Acheron again. She wanted to find her way back to the grove. Even though she knew she couldn't leave yet, that she was exactly where she had hoped to be, it felt wrong to be stuck.

Suffocating.

"You are not tired?" Charon asked.

"No."

His grin was slow, languid. He sat down across from her, his eyes running down the length of her body. "That is lucky for me," he said as they snagged on her breasts. They paused and then darted up to meet her gaze once more. "Did you mean it?" he asked.

"Mean what?"

"That you came here for me," he answered. The words were quiet, small. Vulnerable.

"Yes," she breathed, honest.

She meant it more than he could possibly understand. More than she could explain without revealing too much, too soon.

"And you are not lying?"

She looked at the Ferryman. He was somehow the same as he always was, and yet not. Whatever was between them was fragile, new. "Sometimes I don't even know if the words I speak are a lie or not. Sometimes I mean a promise when I make it, and I break it without second thought later. This is one truth that has always been certain. I didn't have to come back to you."

He searched her face as though trying to gauge for himself if she was genuine. Finally, he nodded. "Okay, little liar. Crawl to me."

Her mouth dropped open. "What?"

"Crawl. To. Me."

It was an order, undeniable. Her mouth went dry. She remembered the way he had moved so confidently between her thighs even as he claimed he had never touched a woman in that way. The way he had looked when he asked her if she had ever touched a cock.

Charon had not been ashamed of his inexperience. In fact, she hadn't noticed any hesitation at all. He had not faltered, had not questioned himself.

Anastacia wouldn't either.

She knelt to the floor slowly, her knees touching first as she kneeled. "Take off your band," he ordered.

She raised her hand to her breasts, undoing it and watching it fall to the side. "Beautiful," he said. She inhaled sharply, her breasts rising and falling with the movement. Her nipples pebbled and she was certain he noticed, his tongue darting out to lick his bottom lip.

"Now crawl." She placed her hands on the ground, her shorter hair falling into place around her chin as she moved. Anastacia kept her eyes up, locked on Charon's. He couldn't quite hide his satisfied grin. When she reached him, she placed her hands on his thighs.

They were strong, warm. His muscles flexed beneath her fingers, his legs shifting wider so that she could settle in between them. He dug his hand into her hair before gripping it slowly, tightly enough that she could feel it but without it hurting. "You look so pretty sitting there," he commented as he moved her head further up, forcing her shoulders back and her breasts forward. "I have never understood the allure of a woman's body until I saw yours."

He reached forward, taking one of her nipples in between his finger and thumb before tweaking it. "I always thought, we all have these. This flesh. It is nothing. It ages, it dies, it decays. But then I saw the soul in your eyes and the way your body houses it so beautifully. I understand now."

His hand cupped her breast, the weight sitting in his palm as he caressed it. The action was gentle, though his calluses were rough on her skin. She sat there before him, trembling at his words. Anastacia had never minded that she wasn't beautiful. She had never needed the compliments or the stares. Had never hoped to change it or prayed that age would give her something special.

But the way Charon was watching her, the way his eyes had locked onto her with rapture and intensity, she finally felt it—why a woman would crave this feeling. The power that came with entrancing a strong man. She was on her knees, but she felt like she was the one in control.

She could ask Charon for anything right now, and he would say yes.

He leaned back, giving her a dark grin. "I still have your taste on my tongue. Now I want mine on yours."

A shiver wracked her body, her eyes darting down his torso until they landed at the junction of his thighs. There were divots in the skin of his abdomen, dipping into his clothing.

Her hand reached out, trembling slightly. Anastacia didn't know whether it was with nerves or anticipation. Still, as she undid the fabric and let it fall away, she felt her legs begin to grow slick. She shifted, hoping to relieve some of the tension, but it did nothing.

His cock stood proudly, larger than any she had ever seen. It curved just slightly, a vein running up the side that she wanted to run her tongue along. A bead of liquid grew at the slit, and Anastacia reached out with her finger, swiping it away before placing it in her mouth.

She didn't think it was possible for Charon's eyes to get any more intense or possessive, but as he watched her taste him, they did. He pulled her head gently towards him. "Lick," he ordered.

She stuck out her tongue, flattening it the best she could before she placed it against his skin and stroked upwards. His cock was harder than she had expected. Anastacia had never touched one that was aroused, and didn't realize how much like a bone it would feel. Like a jewel wrapped in silk.

"Again," he said quietly, obsessively. A thrill ran through her at the need in his tone. She licked him again until he was as slippery as the apex of her thighs.

"Good girl," he praised her and she melted. Was that it? Did that make him feel as good as she had earlier? But then, he positioned her differently, bringing her higher so that her mouth was at the tip of his cock. "Now, I have work to do," his free hand went to the table, grabbing a small piece of wood and a chisel. "You said you are not tired. You will kneel here, with my cock filling your mouth, for as long as it takes you to get sleepy. When you are ready, you will begin to suck and stroke until I spill myself. You will swallow every drop. If even one bit escapes your lips, I will put you to bed aching. You will have to dream of getting filled for even a bit of relief. But if you listen, if you earn it, I will make sure you go to bed satisfied. Is that understood?"

Her breathing was ragged at his words. Saliva had gathered in her mouth but she refused to swallow it, knowing now why he had her lick him so thoroughly.

Because her jaw was about to be stretched around his girth. And she was anything but tired.

He pushed on her head with encouragement, and she spread her lips wide as she took him within her mouth. He let her go at her own pace until he reached the back of her throat, and then just once, he pressed down on the back of her head. His cock pushed deeply into her throat before she could react, and he held her there for a moment. She willed herself not to pull away, but her eyes began watering immediately.

His groan was worth it, loud and low.

When he released her, it was only to bring her far enough off the base of him that she could breathe through her nose once more. Her tongue had molded to the underside of his cock. She moved it experimentally but found that aside from flexing it, his girth was too much to allow it to roll over him the way she wanted it to.

As if he could read her mind, her intentions at trying to adjust and take more of him, he tsked. "Look at me, Anastacia."

Her eyes rose, mouth still full of him. "I could keep you here for hours. Days. I would deny myself pleasure to stare at this view forever." His thumb touched her bottom lip, pulling it down before tracing his own cock where it met her skin. "Every piece of you will be mine, Anastacia. Every lying, thieving, clever, and good thing within you will belong to me. I will touch and explore every inch of your body. I will fuck every hole, taste every bit of skin you possess. Just so you know my intentions."

And then he released her head, leaving her there with her mouth covering his cock while he gathered his tools.

She could hear the knife against the wood, it was so silent. Slowly, she became more and more confident in herself, though she wasn't doing anything different. The nerves disappeared the longer she stayed perched over him, doing her best to swallow occasionally. Most of the time, the mixture of saliva and his release was too much, and she had to adjust to let it slip down the area of his length that was exposed to the air.

She wondered how it would feel within her body. If he truly meant it when he said he would fuck every hole, touch every inch. She didn't think he had been lying.

Anastacia wasn't sure how she would ever grow tired with the arousal rushing through her body like a raging river, but eventually she did. Her jaw began to ache as did her knees, and though she shifted, it didn't ease. She wasn't sure how long it had been, but at her noticeable discomfort, she heard Charon put down his tools.

They thunked against the wood of his table. She hadn't noticed the way her eyes had grown heavy, her lids beginning to fall, until she had to force to raise them towards Charon's face. It was kind as he glanced at her.

He pulled himself out of her mouth softly, liquid dribbling over both his skin and her chin. "Spit," he said. It was the first thing she had heard since his statement earlier, the one that had been replaying itself over and over in her mind. She did so, positioning her lips over the head of his cock before forcing whatever was left over the head. She thought he might fuck her mouth as he had promised, spill himself between her lips, but he didn't.

Instead, he took his hand and swiped it over her chin before bringing it to the apex of her thighs, pushing aside her underwear and rubbing it over her entrance. His chuckle was dark. "You may be sleepy, but your entrance still weeps," he commented.

Charon gathered her into his arms and stood before walking her back to his bed. She splayed out on the comfortable mattress, her thighs parting easily. He slipped her underwear down her legs before discarding it somewhere on the floor. Then, he positioned himself between her legs, his cock slotting easily against her.

She thought he might enter her. They both stared at the place where their skin kissed, the way his cock had turned an angry red. He pushed forward just slightly, letting the crown just barely disappear within her.

They both groaned, her hips rising involuntarily and taking him just slightly deeper. It was not enough. He had pulled his hips back to stop himself from entering her further, and her head thrashed. "Please," she begged. She needed him, needed to feel him inside of her.

If her mouth could fit him, so could the rest of her body. She wanted his promises, his threats. She would take it all tonight if he let her.

This was better than any mark. Better than stealing expensive jewels or art, better than sneaking souls out from the underworld and watching them come back to life. She would trade it all, her life, her friends, her very self, to feel him within her.

"So greedy, my little liar," he whispered. "I should have known you have no impulse control from the way your little hands grab at anything pretty that your eyes lay upon."

She should have been insulted, though he wasn't wrong. She couldn't help herself when she stole. If she wanted something, her skin would itch until it was in her grasp. She had the same feeling right now, the need, the frantic energy.

Instead, Charon pulled himself out fully and ran his cock along her slit, allowing it to press against her clit. He did it again and again, each time letting his skin rub hard along the little bud. It was driving her mad, slowly allowing her to circle higher and higher. His hand gripped his cock tightly, angrily, his thrusts growing more and more uncontrolled.

Then, he straightened just a tad, his other hand pushing inside of her easily. Two fingers disappeared within her, and she felt them curl just as he groaned.

They fell apart at the same time, his orgasm pulsing over her pelvic mound and belly as she came on his hand. He was staring at the spots where his spend painted her body as though it was a work of art, eyes wide with something akin to wonder.

She sometimes forgot that all of this was as new to him as it was to her.

Charon pressed a kiss to her forehead before rising, unashamed. He walked to the other side of the room, grabbing a cloth and wetting it in a bucket before bringing it back to her and cleaning them both up quietly.

She was warm, her skin finally content. She moved to the corner of the bed easily. Deep in the recess of her brain, she wondered if she should offer to sleep elsewhere. But then, Charon got in beside her, wrapping her in his embrace as she snuggled against his torso.

They were both still naked, their skin pressed against one another easily. His hand found her hair once more, this time running his fingers through it softly, sweetly.

She fell asleep against him, firelight dancing on the ceiling and the usual buzz under in skin settled. There was no reason for her to run, to leave, to take.

She had everything.

CHAPTER TWELVE

When she woke, there was a blanket covering her. Charon was speaking to someone outside, his voice just barely filtering into his home.

Her peplos lay on the bed next to her, her underwear too. She grabbed it, noting it was slightly damp as though it had been washed. She got dressed quickly, staring at her staff for a moment.

Anastacia didn't want to acknowledge it, but she had to. The other voice outside—the one that did not belong to Charon—she recognized as Hermes. And if he was present, the staff should be left behind.

Her staff was something that she did not like to be without, that she had grown so used to carrying, it was like another limb. However, she didn't want Hermes seeing it, lest he believed she prayed to him or emulated him. Worse, she didn't want him touching it or watching her closely because of it. It was bad enough that Anastacia was being watched by two gods already.

She tucked the staff between Charon's bed and the wall, putting her belt on without it. Then, she steeled herself and left the house. It was strange, the light different than it was on the other side of the riverbank. There, she had never noticed a difference between day and night, though here, the sky above Charon's home had lightened.

Was it was a mere mimicry of the world above or was there a way for the light to filter in? No matter how hard she stared at the cavernous sky above her, she couldn't tell. The sand was different here too, softer against her skin than the hard ground of the other side. There were a few rocks and boulders that the water lapped at, but it was otherwise clear of any debris.

Charon's boat was pulled onto the bank, and she walked towards it. Her eyes ran down the design, the finished carvings. They were beautiful, warriors with spears and swords, horses pulling chariots, flora, leaves and landscaping all interwoven around it. It was an artist's boat.

She was still standing there tracing the wood with her hands when Charon slid up beside her. His arm brushed her shoulder and she looked up. "Where are the other boats you craft?"

He put his hand on the solid wood. "Scattered throughout the underworld at strategic crossing points."

"You have never made too many?"

He shrugged. "They have many uses. I always need firewood."

"You can't burn these," she gasped.

"What else would I do with them?"

Her mouth gaped like a fish. *Sell them, give them away, drop them in a fishing town. Gods, anything but burn them.* "Someone would want them," she said. "You should have someone bring them to my village. They will always use boats, if not for the water, then for history."

He hummed but did not respond. "Are you ready?"

She took his hand as he walked her toward the god leaning languidly against the side of Charon's home. He had an easy smile and friendly eyes, though they had locked onto her, far too intrigued. The last time she had seen Hermes, he hadn't cared for her—hadn't noticed her. She could have been anyone.

Even now, he didn't recognize her. He only looked at her strangely because she had caught the attention of others.

Hermes' hair was dark, his skin color the same olive as hers. His eyes were a pretty hazel, greens and browns so closely intertwined that they blended into each other. He held his staff loosely in his hand. It *did* look just like hers, the artistry so similar they easily passed for one another. Even the bone seemed to have been carved from the same beast.

He wore a cream colored tunic that covered his chest, fastened at each of his shoulders with golden laurels. His sandals were made from leather, two wings near his heels.

The thief god, the messenger, the guide.

They were so alike it was intimidating. She was just as worried he would not like her, as concerned that he would. Anastacia didn't want his approval, yet she craved it just the same.

Even now, the way he looked at her like she was a curious thing, made her chest warm. She shoved the feeling away, reminding herself of all the other times his eyes had skipped over her, marked her as unimportant. He didn't feel a bond toward her. There was no connection.

There was no responsibility between them.

She bowed her head slightly, not bothering to talk kindly with him. "What is my task?"

Hermes tilted his head at her short tone, twirling his staff easily with amusement, but otherwise answered. "I have a soul to retrieve, a crafty little thing. He has run from me while on the brink of death and found himself on an island he has no business being on. One that Thanatos will not touch out of respect for the gods. He thinks he has found a way to immortality. I am here to remind him there is no such thing for mortals," he said lightly. Then his eyes narrowed on her and his hand waved. "No offense, of course."

She raised an eyebrow. "Where has he gone, then, that Death is scared to follow?"

Charon gave her a look at her insinuation of his brother fearing anything, but he did not speak.

"The island of Delos," Hermes answered. "Birthplace to the twins Apollo and Artemis. No one else is permitted to be born, nor die, there. The gods are not allowed to interfere until he is off the island. The fates shall not cut his string while he hides there, Thanatos shall not sever his soul from his body, and I shall not retrieve him. So... *you* will go get him, my little protégé."

"Do not call me that," she answered sternly.

His eyebrows raised, full of mirth as he looked at Charon like she had said something funny. "Testy, that one. You have your hands full. Are we all ready, then?"

"We?" she asked.

Charon answered instead of Hermes. "I told you, little thief. I don't trust you to stay where you are told. If you think I will let you out of my sight, you are mistaken."

Perhaps she should have felt insulted that last night had changed nothing between them, but she didn't. There was only relief that she would not be alone with Hermes.

"I cannot fly into Delos," Hermes admitted. "But I will take us to Mykonos and we can sail from there. After all, we have the underworld's best ferryman, don't we?"

Before panic could set in at his words, they disappeared from the underworld.

It was a jolt to her system, the riverbank vanishing even as Mykonos appeared before her, blurry at first and then there all at once.

She gasped, her stomach roiling as she fell to her knees. A hand touched her back lightly as she barely stopped herself from heaving. "What was that?" she sputtered.

"Hermes' flight," Charon responded. "His winged sandals can be... disorienting, when used too quickly."

For all his comforting, *he* didn't seem to be affected. Anastacia took a deep breath as she did her best to distract herself.

There was sand beneath her hands, but it felt different, the grains larger and rougher than on Charon's riverbank. The sound of the ocean was loud too, angrier than it was at her village. She and Ophelia had built their home on the innermost part of the ocean, where the waves had time to calm and quiet before they reached the shore. This portion of the beach was far more violent.

Her head rose and snagged on a medium sized vessel bobbing in the water. Hermes was already standing upon it, fiddling with the sails, careless of what his flight had done to her.

She glanced up at Charon, ready to make her excuses and beg for another task, when she noticed his face.

Anastacia had never seen him in sunlight. Hadn't even known he could leave his spot in the underworld.

Didn't know if he ever actually had.

His skin soaked up the sun as she stared, browning in seconds. His eyes were wide with wonder as they gazed out towards the sea. He had not blinked once, his mouth parted slightly in amazement. He was leaning forward as though a string was dragging him to the water, his body looking like it might topple if he didn't take a step soon to support the change in weight.

Still, he did not stop touching her back, his thumb moving in soothing circles as though he could feel her anxiety at the thought of sailing.

She swallowed her protests, following the way that Charon's eyes danced over the sailboat, his free hand flexing. Whatever he had said about not wanting, she knew now that he had lied. Or if he had not lied, then he had simply not experienced it until now.

She had compared him to a seaman so many times, to the men in her village who spent their lives fishing on the water, but never had she connected the thoughts to the realization that he had never left the Acheron. That his hands had not touched the sea, his eyes had not seen the sky at the horizon when it melted into the water.

His eyes devoured the view, and she finally stood to allow him to walk forward. His feet were bare as they slid lightly through the sand. His toes curled into the rocks when he walked, little footprints left behind. She slid her own foot into the imprint as though it would be warm from his body.

He was silent as his skin finally met the sea, his eyes closing. She wondered if he could see spots behind his eyelids from the sun, if he had ever felt this warm before. Charon knelt to dip his hand in the waves, the spray skipping up and landing on his cheek. She placed her feet in the water next to him, content to touch the sea so long as she could run away from it.

Charon seemed to have no timeline, happy to simply soak in the summer sun. Hermes felt differently, his voice carried to shore by the wind. "Let's get on the water, I have a soul to guide!" He smiled as he hung playfully on the wooden mast in the center of the boat.

From this far away, she could not believe he was an adult, let alone a god.

Charon glanced at her and his smile was breathtaking. She had seen him smirk, watched the corners of his lips turn up, but never had she seen him like this; and she had been staring at the nuances of his face for years.

Far longer than he knew.

He reached his hand out to her and she grasped it tightly as he led her into the waves. She waited for the moment her feet wouldn't be able to touch, memories swirling around her like the water did.

Anastacia knew how to swim. She was born in a fishing village, after all. When she was young, she learned within the calm waters of the Acheron, and when she grew older, she braved the waves of the sea just as often when they were rough as she did when they were kind.

But the memories that flooded her now were not of her childhood. They were violent and fearful, images of hands gripping her neck and biceps, of bubbles blowing out of her nose and mouth while she screamed out the last of her air. Feelings of struggling and thrashing until she was limp.

Charon's hand squeezed hers and she dragged her eyes away from the deep. The waves were up to her hips, warm enough that it didn't bite her skin yet there was a chill in her bones. "I will not let you drown," he said as though he could see her turmoil.

They would need to swim to get to the boat. Then, they would have to sail. The entire time, she would be over open ocean, waves threatening them with every lap against the wood. Reaching for the interior of the boat, threatening to capsize them until it swallowed the three of them whole. Poseidon did not care for mortals. He would not save her.

But Charon didn't promise her they wouldn't tip over, that they wouldn't fall into the sea. That was something no one could swear.

But he said she would not drown. And she didn't need a god to save her when she had Charon.

So, she would do her best to believe him.

Anastacia nodded once, bolstering herself before she flung her body into an oncoming wave. If she waited even another moment, she worried that her courage would flee.

As she dove, water surrounded her, bubbles popping against her skin. There was a moment when she was suspended, the sea licking at her face, pressing into her lips, playing in her hair. Then, she burst through the other side, taking in a large breath of air.

It wasn't long before she felt the warmth of Charon as he swam next to her, his head breaching the surface. His hair was dark, slicked back with water. Droplets beaded on his thick lashes, and the smile still had not left his face. She knew this was Poseidon's domain, and yet Charon belonged here. The ocean suited him, lightening his features and the responsibility his shoulders carried.

She pushed herself through the water, toward Hermes' boat. Charon could no doubt outswim her, but instead stayed firmly by her side until she was pulling herself up and over the edge, her foot hooking on the wood until her back was against the hull and her face was turned up towards the sky.

Charon climbed over gracefully as she took a moment to orient herself, his body sleek, his chest on display. There was a light dusting of hair that shone in the sunlight. She stood to watch him easier, her legs shaky against her will. Anastacia was so focused on him that when Hermes approached her, she didn't have the wherewithal to stop herself from reacting. She moved backwards instinctively, almost flinging herself back into the sea in her haste.

Hermes wasn't much taller than she was, their eyes looking at one another easily. He didn't seem insulted at her reaction, perhaps attributing it to his godhood. Hermes picked at a strand of her hair, staring at it strangely before flicking it out of his hand. "For someone who doesn't like the sea, it loves you. You're a plain thing otherwise, but when your hair is wet it's rather... unique." His eyes were assessing. His words didn't sound like a compliment.

She looked at him the same way, searching for something that made him so special. Something that would draw a woman's eye, to see if he was as loveable as it was claimed. Was it a mortal's curse to always fall in love with a god when one appeared?

Did they even have a chance? Was it choice, or was it some natural draw to those who controlled the world? Did he truly have redeeming qualities?

She didn't know. But whatever they were, she didn't see them. He seemed like any other man, though certainly more intense. Perhaps she was searching too hard. After all, there were plenty of times that gods had disguised themselves, hidden their traits to fool mortals into loving them.

Maybe that was the truth.

"The water doesn't love me," she finally said as she turned away from him. "What about you? What do you love?"

Hermes raised his brows as Charon busied himself with the sails, preparing the boat. "Many things, little girl. I love flight, pretty trinkets and jewels, a good trick or a funny joke. I love clever plans, nice clothing, I love the mortal need for exploration and invention. I love to fuck, I love to eat, I love to see Gaia change and prove that even gods can be surprised." He began ticking off his fingers as he listed one thing after another, his voice filled with levity.

"What about a woman?" she asked as she looked to the horizon, the boat rocking beneath her.

She could hear the smirk in his voice. "I have loved many women, many times."

"Never one any more than another?"

He laughed. "Why waste my love on only one, when I can give it to any number? There is too much time in the world to only spend it on one woman."

It was the answer she had expected, if not the one she wanted. "And to the women you leave behind, heartbroken?"

Hermes scoffed. "They are blessed, fucked by a god. No great sacrifice for them, is it? I make sure my lovers are all satisfied and happy." He paused, and she could tell from her peripheral that he was looking at Charon. "Though, I don't think *your* lover would appreciate your questions. Is he not doing well enough for you? I could certainly offer my advice to—"

"No," she interrupted him swiftly. "He doesn't need your advice. In fact, you shouldn't give him any tips or tricks at all. Please."

Perhaps thinking her embarrassed, he only laughed. "Okay," he acquiesced. "But it is to your detriment."

Anastacia didn't answer, instead turning around as the boat caught the wind and began to cut through the waves. She watched Charon move like he belonged there, grateful to witness such a thing even if it meant sailing over the deep ocean. His hands were strong and sure as he maneuvered the sailboat, his muscles flexing, golden and sprayed with a dusting of water.

She wished his tunic were gone, not because she wanted to stare lustfully, but because it felt wrong for him to wear clothing when he was such a work of art. If she could chisel him into marble, she would. If she knew how to paint, she would beg him to stand still in order to capture this moment perfectly.

It was criminal to have this memory only in her mind.

His hair ruffled with the wind, his eyes focused ahead. He was carefree, wild, the most beautiful thing she had ever seen.

When the boat began traveling through calmer waters and in the correct direction, Charon walked to where she and Hermes waited. He was not the least bit out of breath, though a sheen of sweat glistened on the side of his temple.

Hermes grinned, his hair rustling with the wind. "I'd argue the sea suits you more than it suits the girl."

Charon's eyes rose to the expansive water around him. "It is like nothing I have ever seen."

Hermes clapped, turning just enough for Anastacia to note he stored his staff in the same place she did. "Well, for the son of darkness, you were made for the world above, my friend. How will you ever return to your river, now?"

Charon grinned, his arms spreading. "To have been here once is to have been here one hundred times. If I come back, it will be no hardship, but my home will always be the rivers below." He took a deep breath and nodded his head at Hermes. "Now, tell us about this soul."

Hermes pursed his lips before grabbing the very thing her eyes had been drawn to, rolling it between his palms as Anastacia had done to her own so often. "He is a demigod," Hermes finally answered. "Not one of any importance, he has not done anything to earn godhood. He has lived a mortal life and will have a mortal death. He is still rather young, but sick. When his time approached, however, he fled. It was interesting at first. He was clever, but not as clever as I. Wherever he went, I followed, even beating him there sometimes. I enjoyed our little game. But then he went to Delos, the one place he could not die, and the other gods got involved. Now he has given me no choice."

Charon glanced at Hermes' staff. "You could not convince him to follow you?"

"My staff has never convinced souls, only been a symbol of peace. That I am a safe god, trustworthy in my messages and in my guidance. Though I admit, it used to be a beautiful sight to behold—it would glow, lighting our way to the underworld. It was easy for mortals to follow the light, simple. But whatever magic it was imbued with is gone now, damaged through time. Just a symbol, once more."

"Apollo couldn't fix it?" Charon asked, and Anastacia held back her laugh. Apollo had gifted the staff to Hermes long ago, and though she had never met the god, she couldn't imagine he was any kinder than the others.

Hermes rolled his eyes. "I didn't even tell Apollo it had broken. My arrogant brother would only believe I did something to it. His attitude and wrath are not worth my peace when I can do my job just fine either way."

"What would you have Anastacia do with this man, then?" Charon asked when it was clear she wasn't going to speak.

Hermes shrugged. "Convince him to leave Delos so that he may face his fate."

"You want me to kill a man," she finally said.

"No, he cannot die on Delos. And once he is on our boat, the fates and Thanatos will do their jobs perfectly well. You won't need to touch him."

"Yes, but I will be convincing him to leave. To walk towards Death."

Hermes rolled his eyes. "If you want to be dramatic and morose, then yes. But he was facing death long before he was facing you, girl. He has postponed it for years, earned more time than he ever would have otherwise."

"How should I get him off the island, then?"

"I will not complete your trial for you. You'll figure it out yourself. I believe in you, underworld walker. After all, it sounds like you have experience in being places you are not supposed to, charming men who cannot be charmed." His eyes darted teasingly to Charon, who didn't take the bait.

They were silent for the rest of the trip. Anastacia kept her arms crossed to hide her trembling and distaste. Her only saving grace was that in these waters, she could swim. She would be able to keep herself afloat if she fell within them.

It was not like the Acheron and the Styx, with raging currents that would drag her beneath and away quicker than Charon could retrieve her. Not like the Lethe, where if even a drop entered her mouth, she would forget who she was. She would not burn here like she would in the Phlegethon.

No, this was simply the sea.

She didn't allow herself to think on the lives it had claimed.

Far more than the Acheron had.

No, if she thought about that, she would fall apart. Instead, she focused on the god and her Ferryman. She watched them interact as though they were friends, like they knew one another as well as they knew themselves. When one shifted, the other compensated.

Anastacia supposed they had worked together for as long as there had been souls to ferry, as long as they had been assigned their jobs. Forever.

She wondered if she and Ophelia moved like that. If one day, they would know each other as well as these two eternal beings did.

Her friend would not be worried about Anastacia's absence yet. It had only been a day, and she had been gone for far longer than that without sending word before. Still, she wished she could see Ophelia. That she were here with Anastacia for this.

Even though it was a journey she needed to take alone.

When the island of Delos appeared over the horizon, she readied herself. She wished that she could have planned something, but she didn't know this man. There was no way to know what would help convince him, whether she could trick him or if he was frail enough that she would be able to drag him away from land herself. Anastacia would have to think quickly on her feet, adapt as she went.

For an island that didn't have anyone living on it, the wood of the dock was well maintained. It had not rotted, legs free of algae, and it didn't creak or move as they secured the boat and she stepped on it.

Charon and Hermes both settled themselves back comfortably, not budging even as she took a step away. "You're not coming?" she asked.

It was Charon who answered. "This is your labor, little liar. Your agreement with the gods. We have helped you by getting you here, but we cannot complete it for you."

"What happened to not letting me out of your sight?"

He grinned. "Where can you go that I cannot find you? You cannot swim back to Mykonos, and Delos is not that big. I may not go get this soul for you, but I have no problem retrieving *you*." He glanced up at the sky before putting his hands behind his head. She had never seen him so free from burden. "Take your time, my thief. I find I'm enjoying myself."

Anastacia scoffed but strutted away, her feet eating up the ground angrily now that she was back on land, guilt growing at the base of her spine for agreeing to this task. She and Ophelia had spent their lives saving men, women, and children from the underworld, giving them longer lives. They had been spitting in the face of Thanatos and the Fates for so many years that if Charon or Hades knew the truth, she was certain they would not have heeded her request no matter what Persephone thought.

It felt wrong to deliver someone to their fate when they had escaped it so cleverly. If he had found Anastacia and Ophelia before he captured the god's attention, perhaps they could have helped him. But it was too late.

Once one caught the attention of the gods, it was not easy to lose it.

Unless it was for fucking, of course, Hermes statements earlier ringing in her ears. Perhaps if the man had fucked Hermes instead of running, the god would have forgotten him the moment he spent himself.

Anastacia didn't look back as she wandered the island. It was easy to see why he had chosen this place. Immortality sat against her skin like fog. She could feel it, the way there were no aches, no kiss of death in the air, no change. It was Gaia's version of the riverbank.

She wondered if the flowers here ever died, or if they were the same ones that had been here since the island had formed.

The silence reminded her of the underworld. There were no birds or bees, no chatter of wildlife. It was as if even they could tell this place was sacred, and they didn't like it.

Finally, she located prints on the ground. They were bare, so faint that she could hardly see them. Anastacia followed them anyway, pondering what kind of man was so scared of death that he would sequester himself on Delos alone.

She had spent years by herself, but that was different. She hadn't had a choice. She didn't think she would do it again, not even in such a place as this. The boredom alone would drive her crazy. No animals to watch, no things to peruse, no people to interact with. How anyone could choose this over a swift death, she wasn't sure. This wasn't living.

Though, this man wasn't trying to live at all. He was only trying to hide.

Anastacia heard the singing first. It wasn't particularly good, nor was it bad. It was a joyful tune, one she didn't recognize. She followed it, her eyes roaming over the pillars soaring overhead. They appeared ancient, the stone sun-kissed. Standing at the top of each pillar, peering down at her, were statues of Apollo and Artemis in different poses.

In each one, they were beautiful.

The man who sat below with his back against the towering stone was not.

He was frail. It was no wonder his footprints hadn't been deep within the soil. A strong wind could blow him over, his muscles so atrophied that there was only bone. His skin was pale and worn, drooping far too much for how young he was. She couldn't tell if he was naturally handsome, his eyes carrying bags beneath them and his cheeks hollow.

His eyes were closed as his voice swirled into the air. She walked towards him silently, watching the way he shifted gingerly like he was in pain. It wasn't until she had placed her back against the side of his same pillar that she cleared her throat.

His eyes popped open with a gasp, his head turning towards her. He didn't scramble away, though she wasn't sure if it was because he adjusted to the shock quickly or if he was simply too tired.

"I'm Anastacia," she introduced herself as she looked out at the island around her.

He was silent, though his gaze felt heavy against her skin. Anastacia was almost worried he had forgotten how to communicate by the time he responded. "I wondered if the gods had forgotten me here. I see now they have not." He sighed and leaned his head back so it was against the pillar once more. "They have sent you to collect me?"

"Yes."

She said nothing else, content to sit with him for a few moments. It was companionable, polite. She set her hand down in between them with her palm up. He slid his own fingers into it softly. "How long have you been alone?"

"I don't know. I haven't counted the days, and they all pass the same. Wonderful sunrises and sunsets, pretty flowers and tasty fruit. Sleep comes easy and restful while the waking hours are peaceful. The sun sets and rises, and I live."

"It doesn't seem like much of a life," she commented.

"No. But it is still a life."

She thought about all the years she had lived and how she had spent them, and didn't think that was true. "You stay here because you fear the underworld, then?"

"Doesn't everyone?"

"It is not so bad," she answered. "Dying is unpleasant, but death is not. And you look like you have been dying for a very long time."

"I cannot die here," he argued. His body moved to look at her and she moved with him so their faces were close.

"Maybe not your body. But your soul is. Where are the people you love? The things that get your blood moving, the fun, the excitement, the happiness and laughter?"

He was breathing hard just at supporting himself on his own. He leaned back once more. "You don't need those things to enjoy the world. Contentment is within me."

"If you were content with your life and how you lived it, then you wouldn't be so scared to leave it behind. You would feel fulfilled. You wouldn't still be here trying to prove something to yourself."

He laughed lightly at her reprimand, inclining his head. "Maybe. I didn't live like I meant to. I had potential and I did nothing with it; I didn't love, didn't marry, didn't have children. And now I never will. There is no one to mourn me, no one to give me a burial. At least here, I can speak my own name. I can remember that I lived at all, even if I did not live how I wanted. Once I am gone, so too will my impact." He sighed. "I look at my footprints, at the stones I have worn down, and I see that I am here. I see that I have changed the world, even if only a little bit."

She sighed too, squeezing his hand. "I have seen your footprints," she finally said. "And I have heard you sing. I will remember you. What is your name?"

"Epiphanios," he answered. Then, "You speak of death like you know it."

"I do know it," she admitted. "It was scary, though mine was different than yours will be. Violent, cruel. But I earned it," she said sadly. "When Hermes came to collect me, it was all very polite. Sweet. Cordial. His eyes looked at me but he did not see me. I suppose he can't have empathy for all the souls he collects, though. After all, there are so many of us mortals. Always dying. And I have never been particularly memorable."

"Yet you are here," he said. It sounded more like a question.

Anastacia inclined her head. "Yes. I didn't give my coin to Charon when it was my time. I don't know why, only that in my moment of clarity, I kept it for myself. I wandered the bank next to him for years, only fleeting memories of my life returning when he was near. Charon became my memories, my tether to myself. The underworld will try to pull you away, try to give you peace. But it won't if you don't let it."

It had taken her years to build herself back to the person she once was, snatching little pieces from Charon each time he visited the bank. It took her even longer to create her pathways out of the underworld, to sneak through the tunnels until she discovered a way that led home, back to Ophelia.

Her friend had preserved her body as if she knew Anastacia would find a way to cheat death. She was lucky the witch was so long lived and had not forgotten her.

"I do not think I will have the luxury of Hermes or Charon allowing me to wander the bank for long enough to find myself again." He chuckled derisively, gesturing to himself. "And what is there to find? I have nothing to hold on to, anyway. I am a failed demigod. Hermes' blood runs through my veins and all it ever gave me was more time to run." Her head whipped towards him at his words, her eyes searching his face as her hand tightened on his.

"You are a son of Hermes?"

"For all the good it ever did me," he scoffed. "Yes. He made me clever enough to find Delos, but not clever enough to find a fate worth living before I was already dying."

Her hand roamed her peplos, feeling the item within it. One that she did not leave without, one that meant more to her than even the staff. She pushed her hand into the fabric and pulled it out.

It was an obol. Old, from her life before. Likely long before Epiphanios was even born. She squeezed it hard in her free hand, brought it up to her lips and kissed it. Then, she leaned over and set it on his thigh.

"You will die, Epiphanios," she said softly. "But if you trust me, I have a plan."

"And why would I trust you, woman who has come to me at the behest of the gods?"

Anastacia looked around once, glancing up at the statues who stared upon them. But they weren't listening. The gods didn't care for lives like theirs.

So, she opened her mouth, and she spoke.

CHAPTER THIRTEEN

C haron didn't know what to expect from his little thief.

He thought Anastacia might appear dragging the man by his foot, or perhaps with his arms trussed up and his face broken with defeat. What he had not expected was for the sickly man to be walking with her, hand in hand, as they chatted quietly.

His face didn't hold the fear of someone running from death, the disappointment of one who had escaped it for years only to give in at last. He also didn't seem peaceful, like he had accepted that it was his time.

No, his smile was too large and hopeful to be peaceful. His steps were light on the ground even though sickness ravaged his body. Charon didn't think he would have long at all once he stepped off the island.

Still, the man didn't pause as he walked onto the wooden dock and off the island of Delos. He only looked at Anastacia once. "We must stick together, yes?"

The words were quiet, his voice already fading.

"Yes," Anastacia promised him.

Together, they stepped into the boat. Every second that passed seemed an eternity to the little demigod, his life leaking out of him. Hermes watched the two with assessing eyes, but Anastacia did not look away from the man as she helped him lay down before lifting his head to settle it in her lap.

They stared at one another, his hand gripping something tightly, her own covering it. Finally, she leaned down and pressed a kiss to his forehead. Charon thought he might feel jealous, but there was nothing romantic about the gesture.

It was as a mother would kiss a child, a sister her brother. There was only kindness in the movement. When Anastacia pulled away, the demigod had passed.

Hermes grinned at them both. "Clever boy, but never cleverer than me. I knew a pretty face would get him out." To Charon, he inclined his head. "I trust you know the way back."

He disappeared, likely to take the soul to Charon's shore. Anastacia closed the man's eyes before laying his head lightly on the ground as though he were only sleeping. "We will take his body to my home," she demanded. "My friend will take care of the rest of his burial."

"Okay," Charon said easily as he stepped forward to move the body to a more convenient location, away from the side of the boat. When he shifted it, the man's hand fell to the side and an obol rolled from his grip.

Charon grabbed it before Anastacia could. He moved it around between his fingers, examining it. "This is old. I didn't expect him to have a coin."

Her eyes had locked onto the item. "He didn't. That one is mine. Or, it was, at least."

She reached forward and snagged it from him quickly, opening the man's mouth and slipping it under his tongue. "It is his, now. You can wait to touch it until he gives it to you at the riverbank." Her tone was short, though not unkind, and he forced himself to swallow his questions as he moved the man to a more secure spot.

He gave her time with her thoughts as he readied the boat before he caught the wind and they moved back towards Mykonos. "Where should I go?" he asked.

"To the mouth of the Acheron," she instructed. His eyebrows rose with surprise.

All this time, and she had been right there. So close without him even aware that he should have been searching.

"How did you convince him to come so easily?" he finally asked.

Her eyes dropped to the wood at her feet. "I promised him I would steal his soul away before he could give you his coin," she admitted.

Charon frowned. "You cannot. Your task won't be completed until he has been judged and is safe in the underworld."

"I know." Her voice was hard. "I lied."

She wiped at her face, though whether it was a tear or spray from the sea, he wasn't sure. "Are you okay?"

She waved him off. "He will forget my betrayal when he drinks from the Lethe, anyway." But she looked sick, ashamed. She wasn't happy with what she had done here.

"Whose soul do you want so badly that you are willing to go against your values?"

"You should stop asking."

"You said you have had no lovers. A family member, then? A mother or father?"

Anastacia stood, walking over to the side of the boat and tapping her fingers against it. "My mother wouldn't want to return to life and my father still lives."

Charon paused for a moment before speaking slowly, timidly. He didn't know if it was a thread of hope he heard in his voice or if it was worry that she would do so much for him. After all, what would she want his soul for? But still, the words left his mouth. "Mine?"

"No," she laughed, and a piece of him shriveled at having asked. Of course it was not his. He was a deity who belonged to the underworld, a being of darkness, the great Ferryman. There was not one person who had ever *wanted* to be upon the river that he loved so dearly. But then she turned, and her fingers brushed his chest. "Why would I ask for something I can steal?"

He stared into her honey brown eyes and considered ripping his heart out if only to offer it to her. They could stare at it together, see what color it was and how quickly it beat when she touched him. She could hide it within her peplos or carve open her own chest and tuck it in with hers.

He didn't care what she did with it.

But he didn't say any of that. He knew mortals had reservations about love and time. She did not understand the way Charon had been alive for eons and found nothing that made him curious or happy. He had never once felt the need to have something apart from his duty, from his home.

So of course, it was easy for him to look at her with no intention of ever stopping. Gods and deities bordered on obsession with the things that captured their eyes during their best days, and Charon was worse than all of them because he only had one focus.

Only the river and his job bringing souls across it.

But now, he also felt the constant pull to Anastacia, the need to take her apart and learn every nook and cranny.

"Tell me about your mother," he said as he adjusted the sails towards her home.

"There isn't much to say. She was a pretty woman, she caught the eye of a man, she birthed me."

"You were not close, then?"

"Her mind was broken by my father's leaving. She believed his promises when she shouldn't have. He stayed with her for a time, but left while I was still young. I have very few memories with him."

"Do you still speak with him?"

She laughed, a short chuckle, a barely there huff of breath. "No. He wouldn't know me, even if I did."

Charon pursed his lips. "I am sorry."

She shrugged. "I am better off. My mother knew who he was—she should have expected it. Luckily, he taught me early enough that he only broke my heart once. My mother's, he broke every day that he didn't return. Perhaps I get my lying from him."

"On the day he comes to my bank, I could let you speak with him," he offered.

Anastacia only shook her head. "I have nothing to say. Even if he could feel regret, it would be fleeting. I need nothing from him. Not his approval, not his pride, not his attention."

Charon did not comment on the longing in her voice. Instead, he switched between watching her and navigating the sea. She stayed near the man's body, keeping it positioned comfortably even in death.

"How did you come by a coin so old?" he asked.

She glanced up at him. "I didn't realize it *was* that old. Just chance, I suppose."

Charon had a hard time believing chance had anything to do with Anastacia. Whatever she had helping her, it was something she had crafted herself.

Still, he let it go. It was hard to ask her questions when he could not tell if her answers were truth anyway. Especially when he had a niggling suspicion in the back of his mind that they weren't. No, whatever pieces of her he gathered, she would force him to put them together himself.

Charon sailed until he felt the Acheron call to him like a light in a dark tunnel, directing him home. He adjusted the boat towards shore, allowing it to jump along the waves until the beach appeared. She inclined her head, her hair flowing around her in the wind.

The longer he stared, the more he knew of her, the less average she appeared.

She was beautiful in her simplicity. There was something honest about her face, even if her words didn't match. Something familiar, too, in the way she moved.

Her grace, her ease, her balance. Her penchant for thievery and the way it was so natural for her to lie.

Charon looked away from her, focusing instead on her directions until he reached a small home on the beach. It was pretty, peaceful. A bit secluded from the village, though not so far that they didn't have easy access.

As if the woman inside could sense their presence, she walked out slowly, her steps cautious until her eyes locked on the woman beside him. "Ana!" she shouted, as though they had been separated for months instead of only a day and a half.

He couldn't blame her.

The months he had been apart from Anastacia had felt longer to him, too.

Despite Anastacia's bravery on the boat, she didn't enter the water until they were near shore. He threw a small anchor overboard, waiting for it to catch while Anastacia reached her friend. He wished he could hear what they were speaking about.

Instead, he did his best to tactfully throw the demigod over his shoulder, jumping into the water and moving to shore. The waves were calmer here than they had been deeper in the ocean, lapping against the beach like a lover's fingertips.

The two women stopped speaking once he approached, Anastacia glancing at him appreciatively whereas her friend stared at him like he was Hades himself, come to steal Anastacia away for good.

Only part of that was true.

"Where would you like his body?" he asked.

"Behind the house is good," the woman said. She was beautiful, long blonde hair and fair features rarely seen. Her eyes were a radiant blue. Next to her, he understood why Anastacia was able to steal, how she could slip under the detection of men and women alike.

He wouldn't have noticed Anastacia's classic beauty next to this woman's unnatural one, not if he hadn't noticed her cunning eyes first. The way she studied the world around her like it was a game she intended on winning. She used her body to her advantage, a tool, one that could blend in anywhere and gain her anything.

Charon wondered, not for the first time, how many souls she had taken from him. How, if he had not seen that flash of red from her ring, he would have missed her entirely. Might have continued on his life like normal, with her existing under his nose, their eyes never catching one another.

He walked as quickly as possible to put the body down, worried that if Anastacia had too much time with her friend, she would find the nerve to leave him. Perhaps she would decide the soul she cherished so much wasn't worth it after all, and she would rescind her deal with Hades and Persephone to come home.

He couldn't allow that to happen.

CHAPTER FOURTEEN

Ophelia was not happy with Anastacia, her arms crossed firmly over her chest and a worried frown on her face. "I cannot believe you brought him here. This is delusional, Ana. Absolutely insane. Not only your idea, but the fact that you trust him enough to show him even a sliver of our plans, of the things we have done—"

"It wasn't on purpose!" Anastacia interrupted her, shaking her head as she fidgeted with her hands. "He saw me when I went to retrieve the boy's coin."

Ophelia gave her a knowing look, and Anastacia shut her mouth. "You and I both know that if you hadn't wanted him to see you, he wouldn't have. You can lie to yourself, lie to the world, but you cannot lie to me. What did you do?"

She swallowed hard, shifting back and forth on her toes like she'd be able to escape this conversation if she bolted fast enough. "Flashed the ruby ring at a convenient time," she admitted after a moment, hardly loud enough to hear over the sound of the ocean waves breaking on the shore. Ophelia continued to stare at her, eyes narrowed and disappointed, until Anastacia added, "Twice."

Ophelia shut her eyes slowly, her hand rubbing over her forehead. "Why? Why would you ruin everything we have done? It was working. We were saving people just fine before you got your silly idea."

"It was just a matter of time before one of the gods caught us, Ophelia. They may not always be watching, but *someone* is. We would have healed the wrong person, or word would have spread too far. I have seen the gods' wrath, their anger and their pettiness. The plan I have will make it safer for us. You have to trust me."

Ophelia rolled her eyes. "Then tell me your plan, Ana. Because right now it looks like you did all of this to have an excuse to capture your Ferryman."

Anastacia let the corner of her lip slip up. "I mean, that was a benefit."

Ophelia huffed. "You have so many things going on in your head that I don't think you could even separate your motives."

"Do my motives really matter if they have a desirable outcome?" Anastacia reached out and took Ophelia's hand, squeezing it hard. "Just do what I have asked, please?"

Ophelia's eyes softened. "Of course, I will. You already know it."

She sighed with relief. "Thank you. I am sorry I didn't tell you I was going to be gone for a little while."

Before Ophelia could respond, Charon appeared from behind their home. It was strange seeing him on Gaia, near their cozy little house. She was so used to thinking of him as a deity, as some strong and powerful being, that to watch him in such an ordinary place made her question how much of his intimidation came from where he resided.

The Ferryman.

Ophelia was right. Anastacia might have more than one reason for her actions, but he was the main one. He had stolen more from Anastacia than she had ever taken from him, and he didn't even know it.

He had done it all on accident, enticing her for years as she handed him little slivers of herself, as if she had been slipping things into his tunic or his boat instead of stealing them. It was the opposite of who she was, of what she did, and it was too late for her.

She had caught his attention now, though, and it was far scarier than she had imagined. His intensity, his obsession. It rivaled hers, though she had been adjusting to it and dealing with it for far longer. Anastacia wasn't sure how he would feel if he knew that none of their meeting had been left to chance.

That she didn't believe in such things.

Charon stepped next to her, his head tilted down to glance between herself and Ophelia. Ophelia was taller than Anastacia was, far more beautiful. When she stood next to Charon, it was like seeing the sun next to the night sky.

What would strangers think when they saw Anastacia next to Charon? Would there even be anything to compare her to? She didn't think so. Simply a mortal next to a deity.

If they noticed her at all.

Likely, Charon would do the same thing Ophelia did, all eyes gravitating towards them. Anastacia tried not to smile at the thought.

She had always done her best work when no one was paying attention to her.

"Are you ready to return home?" Charon asked, and Ophelia cleared her throat.

"She is home."

Charon turned to frown at her. "She is staying with me."

"But she will return here once she is done. *You* are temporary."

His responding grin looked more like a wolf baring its teeth. "Nothing about me is temporary, witch."

Both women flinched in surprise and he laughed darkly. "You think I cannot feel the power in your soul? The way the earth warps towards you? I have spent years with Hecate. I know her influence, her worshipers. I see the way sacrificial blood stains the wood of your home. You may have her mercy, her blessing, but you do not know eternity the way I know it. Your very bones will be dust long before I have even noticed the time passing. I am one of the only things in the world that is *not* temporary."

Ophelia did not back down. "Then Anastacia is temporary too, Ferryman."

Charon slid his arm over Anastacia's shoulder, pulling her into his side possessively. "Anastacia is mine. There will be no death for her for as long as I live."

Ophelia waved him off. "A half-life, to be stuck on your riverbed forever. She would hate it. One day, she would sneak out and your brother would find her, just as Hermes would."

"And even then, I would have to ferry her soul over before she could enter the underworld. In life, in death, in purgatory, she cannot escape me. I am inevitable."

His words were branding, bordering between setting her heart aflame with happiness and screaming at her mind to run before he trapped her. Ophelia was right.

She couldn't be stuck in one place forever. Her feet yearned to travel, her eyes required changes of scenery, her body needed to feel the rush of life. Anastacia wouldn't be able to stay in the underworld forever.

But that was why she needed this deal.

She stepped towards Ophelia, pulling her into a hug. "Trust me," she whispered.

Ophelia's hands gripped her hard, but when Anastacia pulled away, she let go. "I will do as you've asked," she ground out. "So, I will see you soon."

Anastacia smiled, ignoring the way her friend's eyes were worried as she glanced between her and the Ferryman.

Anastacia took Charon's hand and began leading him towards the mountain. He glanced behind his shoulder, his voice rough. "Keep the boat," he told Ophelia.

She kept walking, Charon vibrating with anger beside her as they traversed over the land. "Where are we going?"

"Trust me," she said.

He looked at the small trail they followed critically. "We should return to the underworld."

"We will. It is only a small detour."

They walked briskly, his impatience forcing her to stretch her legs to match his pace as they covered the ground. He moved as if he knew where he was going, rather than Anastacia leading him. She wondered if he even noticed, if he could feel the way his body was directing him towards the Acheron.

Still, she didn't comment on it. If they spoke now, she was worried he would ask her for things she wasn't ready to give. His tongue had been loose, barbed, his anger barely restrained, a fear at losing her strong in his words.

They reached the river, the sound of the water slipping across the ground finding her ears first. As usual, it was empty this far from the village. Closer to the sea, there would be children and boats, families enjoying it and bathing, but it wasn't often that they traveled far inland.

Charon's footsteps slowed as he stared at the Acheron.

The blue waters, so different than the raging creature it became in the underworld. The way animal tracks were scattered around and through it, the bubbles of a fish swimming up to catch a bug on the surface, the way the sunlight shone like jewels as it danced on the water.

This Acheron was not misery. It was not cold from residing within darkness.

She undid her belt and peplos before Charon said anything, his eyes still locked onto the river. It wasn't until she stood before him, bare, that his gaze turned towards her. "This is the Acheron," he breathed.

"Yes."

"This is my river," he said as he glanced toward it again.

"Yours, whether above or below," she confirmed, hoping he heard the meaning in her words. She reached up to him, her hands touching his broad shoulders before she slipped the sleeve of his tunic off, deft fingers undressing him easily.

He wore nothing underneath it, the fabric revealing his chiseled body. She couldn't decide how she liked him better. Naked, shadowed in the underworld where each divot was even further defined in the darkness, the way they ate at his skin like lovers in the dark, or the way he shone in the sunlight, nothing hidden. She looked for imperfections and found none.

It was the first time she felt like she was reaching too far, as if her hands were about to steal something that would burn them.

Her body was not like his. She had scarring on her cheek, her hands, her torso, arms and legs. Her nose was slightly too large for her face, her breasts rather small. She was thin—too thin to be womanly, too callused to be soft.

But she didn't say those things. Didn't allow them to take root in her mind, pushing them away and into the river until they were swept downstream. Doubt didn't have a place here.

She had chosen to love herself long before Charon did, and his appreciative gaze wouldn't give her any confidence, nor remove it. She knew what she was.

He gathered her naked body into his arms, his hands sliding against her skin. Already, his cock was hard against her stomach. He didn't pay it any mind, didn't acknowledge it or make their embrace sexual.

"Will you swim with me?" she asked.

He nodded quickly, his throat bobbing as he swallowed, the anger from earlier disappearing from his face. "Whatever you want."

She grinned, pulling away and rushing into the water. It was warm enough that it didn't sting her skin with ice, but still provided relief from the hot day. She laughed as she dove in.

This was where the water loved her. Hermes had been wrong when he claimed it was the sea. The sea didn't care for her one way or the other, didn't caress her the way the Acheron did. Didn't allow her to float without threatening to drown her with waves, didn't allow her to drink from it or stand without trying to drag her in or push her out.

When she stood, Charon was stepping in gingerly, only up to his shins. He was still glancing around at his surroundings, his eyes eating the world like it was dessert. She couldn't help but stare unabashedly at the way his cock bobbed with every step, how the muscles in his thighs flexed, how his torso rippled when he turned at a bird call.

It was impossible for even the gods to look as good as her deity did.

Finally, he paused and took a deep breath before plunging into the water. The sunlight didn't allow him to hide beneath it, his body shining, distorted through the surface. Anastacia watched him take long strokes toward her, waiting with anticipation as he got closer and closer.

She felt hands against her ankles and suddenly, she was disappearing beneath the water.

Anastacia thought she might try to fight, feel the need to scramble away, but there was no fear in her chest as her head was engulfed. This was not the past.

This was Charon.

His lips touched hers, their tongues meeting as his hands grasped her closely to him. When she needed air, he breathed into her. She didn't need the surface when she had him. She didn't need anything other than her Ferryman.

The water wasn't deep, but she felt the silt of the riverbed against her back, the way she was pressed against it, bobbing slightly with the current. How he kept them so steadily beneath the surface, she didn't know or care. If she could stay here forever, like this, she might. His hands trailed down her belly and to the apex of her thighs, his fingers dipping into her easily.

He used his hand to thrust inside of her, his palm moving over her clit while his fingers strummed against a spot that made her toes curl. She almost forgot that she couldn't breathe without his mouth, attempting to turn her head away until Charon's hand tightened on her neck in warning.

It was difficult not to gasp, not to cry out as he quickened the pace of his hand, her body bucking beneath his. There was heat growing in her pelvis, need that she couldn't sate.

Anastacia reached down, grasping his hard length in her hand and placing it against her entrance. She thought there might be doubt or fear, but she felt nothing except anticipation. He pulled back for a moment, their eyes open in the water as they stared at one another. Whatever he saw in her expression, he grinned in response.

His hand covered hers confidently, rolling her fist over him once before he pressed carefully into her, watching her face.

She thought it might hurt, but it didn't. She was so soaked between her own arousal and the water around them that he slid into her easily, his eyes fluttering as if in a mixture of pleasure and pain. She arched against him, moving her hips to adjust, tiny thrusts that took him deeper and deeper each time until he was seated fully. He leaned down to kiss her once more, giving her air. She gasped into his mouth as he pulled out and thrust himself back in, his finger circling her clit as he began his long, languid movements.

Anastacia was so focused on the pleasure working its way up her spine that she had to shut her mouth closed quickly when he pulled away, his eyes looking down between them where he met. As if the sight was too much, his body bucked uncontrollably.

His pace picked up, hard even in the water. Her eyes had started to swim by the time he placed his mouth back on hers, allowing her to breathe once more. He did it over and over again, Anastacia getting farther and farther lost in herself as time wore on.

Only Charon mattered.

It was *him* that gave her life, that gave her air, that gave her pleasure. She was so close to shattering but it was as if he knew, slowing down whenever she began teetering on that knife's edge.

She became uncontrolled, frantic, her body undulating beneath him. His hands were everywhere, and where they weren't, the water was. Brushing against her sensitive nipples, cold against her clit in the moments that he moved away from it.

Sensation was everywhere but it all felt like an extension of him.

She heard his voice in her ear, clear as though he was speaking through air.

"This time, you don't breathe until we both orgasm. You'd better come over my cock quickly if you don't want me taking your coin on the other side."

Then, his lips pressed against hers once. She desperately took a long breath before he was gone.

His words sent a thrill through her, her body reacting even if her mind knew it was a bluff.

Either way, she wasn't worried. She was so close that it was only another moment before she was coming apart on his cock, her own hips reaching up to swallow more of him even as he pulled away. His face watched her with rapture until he, too, was spending himself inside of her.

Before she could even begin to strain for air, he was pulling them to the surface.

She was still clutched in his arms. They rose calmly, his lips moving to gently caress her own.

Anastacia felt like a different woman than the one who had gone under the water. They were still connected, her legs wrapped around his waist, her arms draped loosely around his shoulders. She was closer to him than even his clothing had been, her body his armor.

"My little liar," he whispered before he buried himself in her neck. "I cannot go back to an existence without you."

"You won't have to," she said into his hair as she ran her fingers through it, scratching lightly at his scalp.

"You are not temporary to me," he said, referencing Ophelia's words. "There is no half-life below. Whatever you need, I will give it to you, if you will only stay."

She pressed a kiss to the top of his head. That was a promise she wouldn't make yet.

He pulled his head away from her, eyes dark. "I don't know how I have lived so long without seeing you every day."

Anastacia finally laughed. "You have seen me many times over many different days, long before you knew it," she admitted.

Charon's face went slack with surprise, and he shook his head. "No, I never saw you until that day with the boy. Until then, I didn't even know that you were coming below, that you were stealing souls."

She grinned sheepishly. "That might have been the first time you *noticed* me, but no. It was not the first time you saw me, or met my eyes. I have been skirting around you for years."

"Years," he said, his voice weak. "How?"

"You won't like the answer," she said.

"Tell me anyway."

She sighed but nodded her head, finally pulling away from him to clean herself in the river while she spoke. She didn't want to look at his face, couldn't bear to see his reaction. Anastacia didn't think he would be angry with her, but she knew he might be upset with himself—with their circumstances and the time they had missed.

She didn't regret her choices. Knew that if she had done things differently, they wouldn't have happened at all. She hadn't been ready for this when she first met Charon.

Hadn't loved him yet.

And despite what he thought, he wouldn't have loved her, either. She had still been only a child, unsure of herself and cockier than she should have been.

"When I was twenty-one, I stole from someone I shouldn't have. Someone traveling on horseback with a group of slaves. I should have known he was rich." She paused, amending her statement. "I *did* know he was rich. And so, I didn't think he would have much of an attachment to his items. See, it is dangerous to steal from poor people. They *care* about their things. They want them back, they are desperate, they are needy. But people with wealth, with plenty, sometimes they don't even notice. They will think they merely misplaced an item, that it fell while they were traveling or was accidentally left behind."

She smiled bitterly. "This man had a keener eye than most. I stole from one of his slaves carrying a bag. Grabbed a pretty dagger. Gods, it was well made. So sharp it could cut a butterfly's wing. Beautifully designed, the hilt like nothing I had ever seen before."

Even now, she remembered how solid and heavy it was in her hands. The way it caught on the light and how she had trouble looking away from it.

Anastacia didn't know what she was going to do with it, hadn't really even meant to take it. She had just stolen from the bag because of the potential of what it held within.

"Anyway, the slave noticed it was missing very quickly, and I hadn't been careful. I was still close by, looking at my loot instead of running away. It was stupid, arrogant. By the time I noticed that I had made someone very angry, it was too late. I am not a fighter. Even with the dagger in my hands, I was no match for the men who chased me."

Charon watched her intently, and she swirled the water around with her fingertips. "He asked what to do with me, and I told him to let me go. He asked what I had in value to repay him, but I had nothing. So, he took the only thing I could give him. My life."

She didn't look at Charon for this part, her embarrassment still following her. Anastacia's failure to pick a safe mark, her inability to escape once she had been caught.

"We were near the sea. They dragged me there and pushed my head under the waves to let it wash away my mistakes, they said. I couldn't escape them, so I drowned. It was a very unenjoyable death," she added. And it was. It had been painful, conscious for long enough she had to accept she wasn't going to escape. Her throat had burned, nails biting into her arms and hair.

She had held her breath for as long as she could, but the ocean waves had shoved themselves into her mouth until she was choking on them. Anastacia would never forget the way she felt when her body gave up and swallowed the salty water, when it truly knew that she was dying.

"I was lucky they pulled me out of the water instead of leaving me to the sea. Ophelia knew where I had been traveling, and when I didn't come home that night, she went looking for me. This was back when we still ate together every day, when neither of us were comfortable apart for long."

Anastacia shook her head, a bitter smile on her face. "They might have killed me, but they still gave me an obol. A small mercy. I suppose I did take something from them in the end, even if it was only a coin. Ophelia and I had not been stealing souls yet, or at least not like now. We were going to sick people on the brink of death and healing them the best we could. Ophelia wasn't strong enough that it healed them forever, but it prolonged their lives.

In the meantime, I was working to find my way into the underworld. We had the idea to try saving souls once they had passed, because her gift had always worked better on the dead. She thought she could fix whatever was ailing them permanently if they died from it first. It just hadn't been working because I couldn't find a way in.

Ophelia was smart, because she trusted me. She knew that I had a way into the underworld now, and that maybe I could find a way out. She took my body and preserved it instead of finishing my burial rites. She was able to get my body into a stasis, although my soul wasn't within it anymore."

"How long ago was this?" Charon interrupted to ask, his eyes angry.

She waved him off. "Far past a man's lifespan. Those men are long dead."

If Charon was surprised by her admitting her long life, certainly somewhere over a century though she had not quite kept track, he didn't look it. Maybe it was because she had still lived only a drop in a bucket compared to him, or maybe because it didn't matter.

She was who she was, whatever her age.

"That doesn't mean they are out of my reach." His face was full of rage on her behalf.

She laughed him off, leaning her head back so her hair floated in the water around her. "They were within their right, although it was a harsh punishment. It *was* a very nice dagger. I made a mistake, and I paid for it. And anyway, that is not the point of this story." There was a large cloud in the sky, white against the blue backdrop and so perfectly fluffy that it looked fake.

"I met Hermes," she finally said. "And I was... very disappointed in what I saw. I had heard many things about him, I had made excuses for the god that I shouldn't have, imagined promises and reactions that were not realistic. I had crafted myself in his image, a clever trickster, a thief, and he didn't notice. So, when he collected my soul, I was angry. I looked at him and I saw his kind smile, I saw those wings on his feet that allowed him to travel the world, be so many places in just as many seconds. And I realized that this thief god I had looked up to for so long was nothing but a powerful man who I had put on a pedestal. His god blood meant nothing. He hadn't cared for me, hadn't protected me from being caught all those few years I had lived, the times I narrowly escaped that I attributed to him."

It had been a devastating realization—that the god she had called her own cared nothing for her.

"I wanted to take from him, make him feel what I felt. But what mattered to a god that a mortal could take?" she added quietly before huffing. "It didn't matter, because then he left me at your bank, and I forgot it all. There was no time, no life, no anger or passion or wanting. It is a strange place there, for a soul. A fever dream, a befuddled mind, a world that has no meaning. No change, no learning, no growth."

She grew quiet, recalling the journey. Following Hermes and his staff to the underworld, losing herself to the bank. Charon watched her quietly, his hands clenched at his sides, his jaw muscle fluttering.

"But then, I saw you." She reached out to take his hand, loosening his fingers. "I was waiting in line for you to take my coin. It wasn't a busy day, perhaps only two or three other souls waiting with me. My first thought was that it was strange, the way the first soul flinched away from you.

You were standing on your skiff, pole in hand, looking like a sailor. Your hair was windswept, your muscles strong from navigating your way to us, and you looked so kind. Whatever I saw was not what the soul in front saw, because he shook with fear. Yet, you held out your hand, took his coin, and allowed him to board.

I felt fear, then. I remembered that I wanted to find my way back to Ophelia. That if I could find a way out, it would change everything. Me, our lives, the lives of the people who had come to depend on us. I remembered my anger at Hermes, the feeling that I got when he let me go towards your river with not even a glance goodbye. And then I simply looked at you. How handsome I thought you were. I knew if I crossed that river and drank from the Lethe, I would never see you again. I would not recall your face, your kind eyes."

She shook her head and laughed, shrugging. "I have never been good at accepting things. So, I didn't. You asked for my coin and I hid it. A trick of my hands, a slip of my fingers, and you guided me to wait. You touched my shoulder so lightly." She smiled at the memory. "When you let me go, I started to forget again, as all souls do. But I never quite let myself. You were my anchor, my tether to the world. Whenever I gained my memory from you, I gave you pieces of me in return.

Whenever I heard your skiff come across the water, my feet would find their way toward you. Close enough that I captured remnants of myself, held onto them like the stolen treasure I had always coveted.

We spent years like that, you and I. Me, watching you from afar, and you, not knowing I was there. Once I had enough pieces of myself back, I began wandering father and farther from the bank. I would watch Hermes come down with souls, Caduceus glowing in his hand like a beacon. I began to form my own trails while you were gone, carving pathways in the side of the cavern walls until my feet didn't stumble upon them. Until they were smooth and solid enough to carry others with me.

I diverted water into little tunnels, letting them carve for me until I had multiple ways to travel through the underworld. Time did not pass for me, as a soul. I didn't have to sleep or eat. Most of the time I didn't even know why I was doing what I was doing. I had purpose but no real thoughts unless you were there."

She glanced over at the Ferryman. His face had gone pale, his eyes tortured. He looked like he was in pain.

"On my last day there, Hermes came below. He was oblivious toward me, though for good reason. None of the other souls had ever accomplished what I had.

I had studied his staff, Caduceus. Every day he came below, I stared at it. I learned its grooves and divots, the places it was worn, the areas Hermes touched most. I found bone after bone in those mountains, spent time practicing my carving over and over until I could only make that one thing. My fingers traced its outline even in my empty moments where I lost myself, my empty, waking dreams were filled with it. I am sure it wasn't exact, but it didn't need to be. Whatever didn't add up, Hermes would dismiss. No one would steal from him."

She grinned. "But I did."

"You stole Caduceus," Charon repeated, his voice void of emotion.

"Yes. Replaced it with my replica before he even felt it leave his belt."

"That staff you carry, the one you keep hidden within your tunic—"

She tried to control her smile, but she couldn't. Caduceus was one of the finest things she had ever stolen. "Yes, the fabric hides the glow when I lead souls. It's why I didn't bring it today. I didn't want Hermes seeing it, recognizing it." He stood quickly, his steps sloshing through the surface violently as he left the water. Anastacia stood too, watching him go. "You're angry I stole the staff?"

"No," he said gruffly. Water sluiced off his body, his chest heaving as though he had finished a run. "No, I don't care about Hermes or his silly little staff. Though, I wouldn't tell him you have it. He can be kind, but he would not be happy to know he was tricked."

She followed him slowly as he began donning his clothing. "Then what's wrong?"

He scoffed before hooking his sleeve over his shoulder and turning toward her so quickly that her eyes hardly tracked the movement. "I didn't see you. I was with you for years and I didn't even know?"

She threw her hands up in the air. "Why would you have known?"

"I don't know!" he shouted. He paced the riverbank, back and forth, while she stood there quietly. "Because I should have known. I should have seen the look in your eyes and known you were different, known that you were *mine.*"

She smiled softly, exiting the water and grabbing his hand to pull him to a stop. "But I wasn't yours," she said. "The version of me that met you then was not *me* yet. Perhaps I have always been arrogant, but I am wiser now, too. Smarter, better at planning things out. There is more to love than simply finding the right person. You must find them at the right time, too."

His brow furrowed, his head shaking. "You're not angry at me? For ignoring you all those years, for missing you?"

She brought his knuckles up to her mouth. "No. I wasn't ready for something like you, then."

Charon's eyes locked onto where her skin touched his. "But you are now?"

Anastacia grinned. "Yes," she confirmed.

He brushed a wet strand of hair behind her ear. "How do you know?"

"How do I know the sky is blue? That water is wet? That summers are hot and I need to eat every day?" Anastacia shrugged. "I just know. There wasn't one particular moment I could name. It happened slowly. But I still know."

He breathed in deeply as he processed her words, looking back towards the river. "How many secrets are you still hiding from me?"

She smiled at him as he turned toward her again, a wide grin. "Who knows. I hardly remember my own until they come to haunt me. Eventually, you'll either get used to it or get rid of me. My tongue will always find a way to lie, whether I mean to or not."

He placed a hand on her throat, nudging her head up so that she was baring it to him. "I won't get rid of you, but I think I can find better things for your tongue to do." Charon leaned down and kissed her gently, his mouth roaming over hers languidly. "I hope you understand what you have done by claiming me in this way, Anastacia."

She swallowed hard.

She hoped she did too. If she had made even one mistake, timed something wrong, underestimated how his affection would protect her and how far this deal would let her stretch the rules, then she would cause herself quite a bit of trouble.

Trouble she might not be able to weasel her way out from.

CHAPTER FIFTEEN

The underworld was unchanged when they came back, though it was her first time traveling down the famed steps to Charon's bank. They were narrow and steep, winding through the cavernous mountain, but it was surreal to know this was the same path she had taken after her death. The same trail Orpheus and Heracles had braved.

It was still difficult to travel over the Archeron, but Charon was kind enough to take her alone so she didn't have to share the minimal space with others. Then, Charon left her at the bank near his home while he returned to his skiff to go ferry the souls across. She watched him disappear, staring into the waters where the Archeron and the Styx melded.

When Charon was gone, the water became even more violent. If she even risked stepping up to her calves, her feet would get swept out from under her with the current. Anastacia would be pummeled with waves instead of hands, but the outcome would be the same. Her, swallowing mouthful after mouthful of water, her body struggling for air, her lungs pounding and swimming until blackness surrounded her.

If she fell in, she wondered if she would be able to convince herself to simply exhale early, breathe in water quickly enough that death wouldn't last as long. Perhaps her body wouldn't allow her to do such a thing, though. Would force her to fight even if she knew she wouldn't make it out.

She was still staring into the dark water when Persephone walked up beside her. Anastacia didn't flinch, having felt the air shift when the goddess arrived. She could tell by the soft presence who it was. After all, Anastacia had spent years watching Persephone in her grove, seeing the way the world moved around her, the way she walked a line between peace and power so delicately.

"Hello," she said calmly as she followed Anastacia's gaze to the river.

Anastacia glanced over at her, inclining her head.

They stood in silence for a bit, only the sound of the river echoing around them. "It's good to finally put a face to the woman who has been leaving me gifts for so many years. I have enjoyed them."

"I am sorry they weren't fancier," Anastacia admitted. The years she had been down here as a soul, in fact, her gifts had been sad little things. Pretty but worthless rocks, mainly. But even then, she knew she needed to curry favor where she could get it.

And though one rock might not mean anything, thousands of them did. Thousands of visits showed dedication, commitment, a willingness to follow and listen. Once she was back on Gaia, she was able to tailor them more carefully to Persephone—fruits, flower seeds, plants, *life*. It was only occasionally that she would leave something expensive.

A gorgeous necklace. A crown. An elaborate dagger.

A red ruby ring she had loved.

She didn't know what the goddess did with these things, whether she kept them in a room somewhere or threw them out. Anastacia couldn't picture her wearing them. Even if they were nice for mortals, expensive, they weren't fit for a goddess.

Persephone smiled, turning to glance at Anastacia, her hair cascading over her shoulder as she shifted. "Have you finished your first task?"

Anastacia nodded towards the river. "Once Charon brings the demigod over the river, yes."

"Was it what you expected it to be?"

Her stomach twisted, nerves and pressure swirling within it. The trial had forced her to make promises she wasn't sure she could keep.

Not particularly new to her, but she had made them to someone who mattered. Who she wanted to keep her word to.

"No," she finally admitted.

"But will it be worth it?" Persephone asked, a tilt to her voice.

Anastacia blinked. "Yes. I need my soul."

"What will you do with it?"

Anastacia shrugged. "There are plenty of things."

A great many things. Most of those, she couldn't tell Persephone about.

Persephone's skin was so smooth in the low light that Anastacia thought it might feel like the petals of a flower, though her question distracted her from staring. "Will one of those things be to keep the Ferryman by your side?"

Anastacia raised her eyebrows, a small smile appearing on her face. Persephone pursed her lips, her body otherwise still.

"I have known Charon for many years. He is a private being. Kind to some, not as much to others. Black and white in his understandings of the world. He is a friend of mine, though I am not sure I am one to him. He will not be an easy deity to love."

She didn't plan on sharing her love life with the goddess, no matter how much she liked her. "Thank you, but I know who he is."

"You know who he is on the bank," Persephone corrected. "But he is more than that, though not even he realizes it. He is the first judge, the gatekeeper, he is one of the most trusted and eternal beings in the universe. To love Charon is to love the underworld. To love him, you must love the river."

"I have always loved the river," Anastacia said.

Persephone shook her head, sadness rimming her eyes. "Not only the Acheron above, but the one below. You must love the misery and hatred, the wailing and the forgetting. The pain and torture of the Phlegethon and all that it punishes in Tartarus. There is joy here, Anastacia. So much beauty and joy. But there is no middle ground. For every piece of absolute happiness, there is an equal amount of damnation."

"And yet you chose it," she argued.

Persephone sighed, so softly that Anastacia almost missed it over the raging river.

"But I didn't. Perhaps I would have come to, in time. Naturally, without force. I don't know."

Anastacia's mouth dropped open slightly before she could contain the reaction. "You would go back to who you were before you ate the pomegranate?"

"No," she laughed. "But I am different now than I was. I was bent into who I am today, made stronger for it surely, and I don't regret the events that led me here. I love Hades. I love my home. But the maiden of the world above? Demeter's daughter? The girl of life and flowers and all things sweet? She didn't survive the underworld. I was created instead."

Anastacia straightened her shoulders. "I have never been those things. A girl of flowers, of sweetness."

Persephone's face was sad. "Of course you were. Perhaps life took them from you early, but you were. All women are."

And she spoke true, for although Anastacia didn't want to, although it made her ache, she remembered.

She recalled the days of wearing her father's cap. The one she hid once the weeks between visits got farther and farther apart, hoping he would stay because he didn't want to leave without it.

The days she would slip her tiny feet into his sandals, wondering if they would take her where they had taken him. If she could make her own sandals just like his to follow. The times she began to steal little items, her small and nimble fingers quick, her innocent face and young age hiding her from suspicion.

She left them on his altars. Placed them outside her door like he might come by and see them.

When he was home, she would take his staff and sleep with it cradled closely to her body like it was her child. She remembered the way her fingers tangled in the snakes, the way the wings felt pressed against her cheek.

And she remembered how it felt when Hermes took it sweetly from her grasp, promising her he would return as he gently pried her fingers off of the bone. She had believed him. And he had lied.

Until one day, he kept his promise. But it was the day she died.

He hadn't even recognized her.

She hated him as much as she loved him. Knew it was his blood that had made her who she was, even as she cursed it for making him who *he* was.

Seeing him had pushed those memories to the front of her brain, Persephone's words only forcing them forward harder. Anastacia rubbed at her temple.

"Yes, maybe you're right."

Persephone allowed her to stop talking, as if realizing she didn't want to continue the conversation. Instead, she changed the subject. "Charon will give you your next task tomorrow."

"So soon?" Anastacia asked.

Persephone smiled. "We thought it would take you longer today. I am excited to see how you handle tomorrow. That is when you will know if you are meant for your ferryman or not."

"Then I know I will have no issues," she said.

"I see your confidence hasn't faltered," Persephone commented, raising a brow.

"Why would it have? I have been proving myself my entire life. This will be no different."

Persephone went still again as she stared into the Acheron, unnaturally so. As still as Anastacia had only ever seen stone go. Perhaps it was a trait of all the gods. "Mortals always think they are proving themselves worthy. Many times, they are only doing the opposite. Greedy, ungrateful things. Beautiful in their flaws, but flawed all the same."

"We are made in your image," Anastacia shrugged. "Whatever problems you have with us are the ones you gave. Look in a mirror if you want someone to blame for our shortcomings."

She felt Persephone look at her more than she saw it. "You are quite mouthy. Did your parents teach you manners?"

Anastacia met her eyes. "They taught me many things. Manners were not one of them."

"I would watch which gods you use that tone with." Persephone was still smiling softly, her good nature overriding Anastacia's irreverence.

Anastacia pressed her lips together. Her mouth had gotten her into more trouble than it was worth. "That is why I need the soul," Anastacia admitted.

"Because it will help with your tone?" Persephone questioned smoothly.

"Because it will make the consequences less severe."

They stopped talking as her Ferryman started to come through the gloom of the river, his body surrounded by shadow behind him. His arms navigated the waters easily, the areas where it was calm just as simple as those that raged.

She thought Persephone may ask something more, but she only stepped back. "Enjoy your night, Anastacia. I hope to see you after your trial."

Anastacia didn't say anything as the goddess left. Charon docked, and she watched as Epiphanios followed the ferryman. He had a look of sad acceptance on his face as he glanced around before he met her eyes.

He would be led to the Lethe now, to drink.

She walked towards the two men, her steps slow. "May I take him?" she asked.

Charon looked at her with pity in his eyes. He knew it was too late, that she had missed her window to take his coin like she had so many others. He nodded in response to her question, as though the least he could do was give her time to mourn what she had done. The man she had betrayed. Epiphanios.

"Follow me."

Epiphanios didn't speak with her as she stepped beside him. He didn't even look at her.

The walk wasn't long over the empty ground, nothing for a wary soul to stumble over. Once they arrived at the Lethe, the river of emptiness, of forgetting, she knelt with him at the shallow bank. "This will make you forget. There will be no longing, no wishing you had been better in life. It will bring you peace."

He finally looked at her, and she waited to see what he would do. His eyes were hard, convinced. "I made my choice."

She nodded and put her hand on his back, acting as if she could protect him from what she had already imposed. "Then dip your hands in the water," she ordered as she guided him down. The water was mist more than it was liquid, but it still gathered in the palm of his hand as he ducked to drink.

When he rose, his eyes were unfocused, his dislike of her gone. Water dripped from his chin.

She looked at Charon, tears in her eyes even as she tried to fight them. "It is done," she said as she retreated.

Charon glanced at the soul of her half-brother and nodded. "I will take him for judgement."

"I would like to go back to your home. How long will you be?" She did not want to see Epiphanios's judgement. Charon could tell her where the man was led to—Elysium, she hoped.

She rubbed her eyes, scrubbing her face as Charon accepted her request.

"I will see you there in a few hours."

He walked away with Epiphanios following him blindly, off to Hades' palace to meet the judges.

Anastacia took a moment to watch him leave.

Then she took off running like extra speed would absolve her guilt, her feet eating the ground quickly as she tried to fit in as much work into that little time as she could.

The underworld would not map itself, after all. And she had promises to keep.

Chapter Sixteen

By the time Charon returned to his home, Anastacia was already fast asleep. Her short hair was splayed on his pillow, her body bundled beneath his covers. In the past, he hadn't cared for sleep. It was simply a thing to do, a way to pass time in between ferrying the dead.

Tonight, he had found himself itching in his skin to get back to her. He wanted to wrap himself around his lyre, feel her body in his arms, berate himself in the quiet for missing out on her beautiful mind for so many years. She could tell herself whatever she liked, but Charon knew the truth.

He would have been just as enamored with her when she first entered the underworld as he was now. Or was it only her cleverness that had caught his attention, her fearlessness of him? He didn't know. It bothered him greatly.

Charon took his tunic off, the fabric falling away easily as he climbed into bed. She, too, was sleeping naked. He ran his hands down her arms, her back, reminding himself that she was alive and well. The story she had told him about had passed long ago, so long ago that he hadn't a clue how to find the man who ordered her death.

Despite what Anastacia had said, Charon knew he would do terrible things to the soul if he found him. Throw him into the depths of

Tartarus, give him an impossible, eternal task. He was tempted to take Anastacia throughout the underworld simply to have her point him out.

In the months since he had seen her, he had changed in ways he had not thought possible. The feeling in his chest was possessive, worried, a dangerous thing. There were reasons that he had not been given leave to go elsewhere in Gaia, that he did not often go away from the river.

Charon didn't use his gifts often, but that didn't mean they were not underneath his skin, writhing. His control of souls was unmatched, his ability to force them to his will something he didn't use often. His control of the rivers of the underworld, his ability to kill gods, his inability to be killed in return.

There was a reason Hades appreciated Charon guarding his gates, and it wasn't because Charon didn't have any other choice.

This was the job Charon was created for. It was still in his blood and bones, but now, he had a heart too. And the little thief was stealing it from him.

Charon pressed a kiss to her forehead, closing his eyes as he settled beside her. He would make sure the other gods and deities knew she was his.

That she was untouchable.

***

Anastacia woke slowly. There was light outside, more natural than usual. She wondered if the underworld reflected Hades' mood, or if there was another aspect of this place that she didn't understand yet.

Charon was wrapped around her like a snake, his limbs entwined with hers, his hands grasping her body like he thought she would sneak away in the night if he was not careful. She smirked to herself.

Her fingers rose to his back and shoulder, rubbing over them lightly. She explored his body softly, confidently. There were so many days where picturing her hands on his skin was all that brought her back to herself. She wasn't sure how much of her love toward Charon had developed from her soul's need to be around him versus a natural attraction, but it didn't matter now. He was so ingrained within her being that she couldn't see a way to separate herself.

Like Persephone, she found she didn't want to anyway. Whatever had brought them together, she would thank it.

Charon's eyes fluttered open, darkness gazing back at her.

"Good morning," she said lightly.

He leaned forward and kissed her once on the lips before they wandered to the spot on her neck that he seemed to love so much. He sucked on it hard, possessively more than romantically. She gasped, her hand automatically going to his hair in surprise, but he only shook her off and pressed his teeth against her skin.

When he finally released her, his eyes were looking at the spot with satisfaction. Her hand rose to feel it, picking out each little indent he had left behind. At her questioning look, he did the same, his hand slotting itself against her neck, his thumb rubbing against what she was sure was a forming bruise.

"You are mine, Anastacia." His voice was rough from sleep. "I will have the whole world know it. The gods and goddesses, the deities and titans, from the depths of Tartarus to the tip of Mount Olympus. They will remember your name and know you are untouchable."

Her face blanched. *That* was something she certainly didn't want.

"Charon, I don't think that's necessary. The gods have left me alone just fine without me drawing attention to myself. If anything, bringing their awareness to me will only cause issues."

His gaze grew stormy. "You don't want them knowing you are mine?"

"No," she reached forward and touched his face. "I don't want them knowing me at all. Hades and Persephone, I had no choice but to tell because I needed their help. Hermes, too, because of the trials. But I would rather the rest of the world never know of me or who I am to you. You are powerful, Ferryman. You have never had a weakness before, never had something to be used against you. But now, I am that thing."

It was the truth, although there was more to it than he would understand.

Charon wasn't pleased with her statement, rising from bed swiftly and grabbing his clothes.

"Then I will tell no one, as you wish. Get dressed. We will start your trial soon."

Anastacia watched him go and sighed, following his lead. She wished she could comfort him, but there was nothing to be done for it except hope that whatever she could give him was enough. The gods' attention had never helped anyone, and it certainly wouldn't help her.

Charon was waiting for her at his skiff, standing on the wood already as the water swirled beneath him. It was choppier than usual, short and shallow as opposed to the usually large, foamy waves.

She stepped onto the boat, swallowing her fear the best she could. Still, her hands shook. The Acheron above was kind. This one would drown her.

This one would grab her with unforgiving hands and steal the breath from her lungs without ever offering it back.

She glanced at Charon who moved so easily, so trusting. She remembered the way she had loved the water when she was with him yesterday, the way there was no fear even as he held her against the silty river floor and kissed her senseless. The way he was her air when she had nothing else.

Anastacia pried her fingers from the edge of the boat. It wasn't much, but it was enough for today. Perhaps in the future, with little steps taken each time, she could grow to feel as comfortable here as he did.

Her breath trembled as she exhaled, focusing on her breathing. Charon glanced at her every few seconds to make sure she was doing well. He didn't coddle her, but nor did he berate her for her fear. His face held a sliver of worry and uncertainty.

It looked wrong on him. She was used to only seeing his calm and confident expressions.

The journey to the other side of the riverbank felt short. It was only because she was paying attention that she noticed the moment they passed far enough over the river for time to pause. It felt distinctly different from the rest of the underworld now that she had spent substantial time there.

It must have only been ten minutes or so to cross, but the danger made it seem longer. Every time the boat tilted too much, every time that Charon had to sway his weight to compensate, her heart jumped into her throat.

She knew it was ridiculous. She had spent her childhood on boats, both in the ocean and on the river. She knew how to move her body with the water, remembered how to adjust her feet when necessary and how to balance.

She was a thief. Of course she had nimble feet.

But her drowning had left invisible scars, and they were difficult to ignore in a river this violent. One that, although she told Persephone differently, she was not sure she loved or trusted. *Her* Acheron would not kill her.

But this one didn't care one way or another.

When they arrived at the riverbank, there were a few souls waiting there. Their eyes were vacant as they stood patiently, puppets discarded until someone picked them up and told them to move.

She expected Charon to let them board, to accept them onto the boat and ferry them across, but he didn't. Instead, he kept going, only slightly further down from where the new souls were.

"You seemed unsure this morning," Charon commented. Her head whipped up towards him. "When I told you that I wanted the world to know you were mine, and only mine. That you wouldn't leave me. And I wondered, is it because you think you will be happier somewhere else? With someone else?"

Her heart constricted. She hadn't meant to make him feel that way. "No, my Ferryman. That's not it at all."

He leaned forward. His eyes were dark, burning, glowing like embers. "I don't believe you." He pulled away from her quickly. "Your task today will be to guide the souls across the river. You will learn how to navigate it, how to move with it, how to stop fearing it. You will dip your hands and feet within it, you will swim in its calm waters and submit to its rapids. You will become a master of it."

He brought them to the riverbank of the Cocytus. There was only one man waiting there for them, his coin clutched tightly in his hand. He was handsome and tall, though not as tall as Charon. Even with the blankness of death on his face, she could tell he had been a lady's man while he lived. "I will show you how it is done, first. I will show you the difference between the control we have and that which we do not."

Charon stepped of the bank and walked towards the man, speaking to him softly. Anastacia couldn't hear them, but the conversation took longer than she expected. Usually, Charon took the coin and then allowed the soul to fall back into that strange place between life and death. This one though, he spoke with.

The man peered at her over Charon's shoulder, a roguish grin taking over his face as he nodded. Charon shook his hand and then led him back to the boat. It shifted a bit with their weight, her eyes darting back to the waters below them. She couldn't help the nerves that engulfed her. Anastacia wasn't sure Charon would be able to rid her of this fear as easily as he thought.

She expected them to leave right away, but Charon didn't grab his skiff pole or untether them from the dock. "Lay back, Anastacia."

She frowned. "What?"

"Lay. Back," He said again, the command in his tone and eyes clear. She sat down on the bottom of the boat and leaned back on her elbows.

"What are you—"

He interrupted her. "This man's name doesn't matter because he will drink from the Lethe once we arrive on the other side. This will all be forgotten, though he has agreed to my offer. I admit, it was a kind one. Now, my little lyre, do you trust me?"

"I—"

"Yes or no," he cut her off again.

"Yes," she said, surprising even herself.

"Then I will show you why there is no other man for you. Why it would be best for you to stay with me."

He maneuvered until he was behind her, settling her against his chest. His legs intertwined with hers as he pulled her peplos up, over her knees and to her belt. Anastacia's eyes widened as she tried to close her legs, but he stopped her. Instead, he undid her belt and set it to the side before he unwrapped the peplos entirely. "He is an attractive soul," Charon finally said. The man stood before her, and while yes, she could admit it... he had nothing on the deity behind her. "Come," he told the man.

The man crouched before her, his shoulders rippling as he lowered himself, but Anastacia glanced away and turned toward Charon. "No, no, my little lyre. If you are to choose me, then you should know what you will be missing out on. The love of *mortals*," he scoffed. "You will see that it is nothing compared to what I give you," he whispered into her ear. And then, there was a mouth against her core, fingers sliding into her underwear, stroking her.

Anastacia gasped at the suddenness, the unexpectedness. She attempted to move her hands but Charon grabbed them. Although he nudged her chin forward once more so she could see the man in front of her, she couldn't stop her gaze from going back to Charon's face instead, possessive with dark hair, thick, beautiful. Godlike.

The man's tongue was skilled, but while her body reacted to his ministrations, she wasn't fooled. She knew that she only felt this way because of Charon. Because of his heat against her back, the feeling of his arousal between them.

"Don't go so fast," Charon said, and for a moment Anastacia thought he was speaking to her until the tongue on her body slowed down. "Point your tongue now, circle the little bud before you flatten it on her slit."

The man groaned as he obeyed and Charon did too, as if he were the one between her legs. "Is she not delicious? I hope you enjoy this now, because you will not remember it. Perhaps there will be some days in the underworld when you taste something just as good and wonder what it reminds you of, but it will escape you. *I* will not have that problem. Now, use a finger and place it within her. Crook it up toward her—yes, just like that."

Charon instructed the man, making it clear that she might be touched by the mortal, but he was nothing more than a toy.

Her Ferryman was in control here.

Just as she was worked higher and higher, Charon stopped him. Anastacia was writhing in his arms, ready to plead.

"For being so gracious, I will let you have another part of her. Bend down lower and lick her. Let your tongue play, get her body nice and wet, because I am going to fuck it once you are through." To her, he licked the side of her neck. "There will be no part of you that is not mine. Do you understand now?"

"Yes," she cried. And he was right, even if it was for the wrong reasons.

She had doubted if she was ready to stay here with him, even though that was all she ever wanted. She was questioning if it was truly the right time, if Ophelia would be alright without her, if she had really thought this all through.

But he was wrong in thinking her doubts were for another man. Even now, she knew that if she ever left, she would still only ever return to the Ferryman. There was no one else.

A finger entered her most private hole and she squirmed, her arousal rising with the confusing feeling. Still, she had promised Charon her trust, and she had meant it. If this was what he needed, then she would give it to him. He wouldn't believe her words alone. *She* may not even believe her word alone.

Already, Anastacia had lied so many times, was still lying. He needed this reassurance, and she understood why.

She was floating away, her body in a strange place, caught between discomfort, vulnerability and want. Charon continued to instruct the man, fleeting commands Anastacia lost track of. It took her body another moment to adjust, but soon she was distracted in the feeling again, not caring what it took if she could just find release.

She felt empty, like she needed more. Hollow, as though Charon was the missing piece of her.

"Charon, please," Anastacia pleaded.

"Do you see how it is me you beg, even with the mortal pleasuring you? You are mine, Anastacia. My liar. My thief. My soul."

Then he pushed his tunic aside, his cock hot against her back. He lifted her further up, slotting the head against her. "There is no part of you that will be untouched by me," he stated just as he tilted his hips up, replacing the man's tongue.

Anastacia's eyes closed as he stretched her, her legs still wide, the cool river air running across her thighs as the man moved back. The emptiness at her core still begged, though this new feeling was so foreign that she could focus on nothing else. She didn't look at the soul, her eyes only on the deity behind her, currently working his way into her body.

The man moved back to her clit, but she no longer felt like he was separate from Charon. They were both under his control, all tools of his, and he wielded himself like a master. He carved himself into whatever parts of her he hadn't reached yet, tearing her apart and putting her back together again until she was sure she must look different.

She wasn't the same woman she had been before Charon, and now she would never get her back. Persephone was right. She wouldn't have wanted to if she could.

Charon thrust into her gently, even that little friction feeling amazing. At her begging gasps, her echoing moans, he placed his hands under her knees, standing slowly until she was hanging in the air, only his body holding her up as his hips bucked his cock deeper into her, his pelvis hitting her each time.

Her weight pulled her down just as his strength pushed her up, her body suspended. The man's tongue swept against her entrance, fingers slipping inside of her once more, curling and undulating until she was shattering around Charon. His breath skated along her cheek, his groans and grunts loud as his fingers dug into her skin.

"This is the last time anyone besides me will ever touch you in such a way. Do you understand?"

"Yes," she said as she fell limp against him. As if her acceptance was enough to send him over the edge, he stilled and spilled himself inside of her.

A blush began to steal over her cheeks, embarrassment sweeping through her now that her sense was returning. Her eyes rose to the man, wondering if there would be judgement in his eyes, but already he had retreated from them as if Charon had forced him away, consciousness leaving with his distance.

Charon adjusted her in his arms kindly as he slipped out of her, walking them both back onto the dock until they were at the bank of the river. He placed his hand within it and it calmed enough that she no longer needed to worry about being swept away if she entered.

He walked into the water with her, not flinching although it was frigid as he dipped them both beneath it, his hands gentle and sweet as he swiped them over her body.

"Why are you so quiet?" he asked, frowning as his warm hands took away some of the cold.

She mulled over her answer. "I'm embarrassed."

"About what?"

Anastacia finally looked into his face, finding it open and content.

"I feel like what we just did was forbidden, wrong," she said and almost laughed. She had been a criminal her entire life, and never had she felt uncertain or ashamed of it. But *this* made her insecure.

"He will not remember," Charon said as he caressed her face. "He agreed to my terms when I offered them."

She shook her head. "It's not just about that."

His head tilted back with understanding. "Ah. I apologize, I did not realize I made a mistake, that it was something... wrong. Is that something you would like to do to me? I do not know human sexual customs, I'm afraid."

"No, no, I..." she trailed off and simply allowed herself to look at him. At his lack of shame, his contentedness in what they had just done.

And she let that same feeling wash over her too. Let the river take away whatever had plagued her mind, and simply let Charon clean her.

"Do you still feel that you need others beside me?" he asked, curious, and Anastacia laughed, exasperated.

"I never felt like that. I don't want any other, now or before."

He frowned. "You seemed like you didn't want others to know about us. I assumed... Well, I assumed it was because you wanted another; god, mortal, or soul."

She turned and looked at him, scrubbing herself better, determined to be clean before her task, though frustration bubbled up into her throat. "You didn't listen to what I was saying. I don't, but it's not because of you. It is because the gods always meddle, but they only involve themselves when something grabs their attention. I do not want their interest; I would rather they know nothing of me."

Charon sighed but nodded his head. He pushed a strand of her brown hair behind her ear, his eyes gazing into her.

"I have never had something I was afraid to lose before, little liar. The only thing that has mattered to me is the river, and that is something that cannot be taken. I am sorry if I am overbearing at times. If I do not understand your words or feel you are being untruthful."

She smiled up at him. "I am not always the most trustworthy woman, but I wouldn't lie about this."

He leaned down and kissed her softly, running his hands through her hair. When he spoke, he didn't move back, his lips staying close to her own. "Okay," he accepted.

She hoped he believed her.

Chapter Seventeen

"You will not like your task today, but it is important," Charon stated as he separated himself from her, picking her up to set her on the dry bank before stepping out himself.

She nodded, her smile fleeing at his words. She had told Persephone that she planned to complete her trials easily, but this was something she would struggle with. Anastacia was not particularly strong. She had seen the muscles Charon developed from ferrying across the Acheron, his ability to navigate the river making it look easy. She knew it would not be.

Charon guided her back to the boat where the man waited. "Stand with me," he offered.

"I would truly rather sit," she said as she stepped onto the wood.

"You won't be able to navigate most of the river by sitting when it is your turn. You must feel it now, Anastacia."

She swallowed her complaint, slotting herself in front of him. His chest was sturdy against her back and she leaned into him, using him as a crutch. She might not trust the Acheron or her skills, but she trusted Charon not to let her fall.

"Put your hands on the skiff pole."

She grabbed onto it, wondering if he could see the way her fingers trembled. His oar was down by their feet, ready to be used when the waters got too deep to maneuver.

"Are you ready?" His voice was soft above her, patient. Her hair felt warmer where his breath skittered against it. She tilted her head back to see him, the way he towered over her, how he watched her so intently.

She wouldn't fail his task.

"Yes."

She held onto the pole with him as he pushed them off the shore. Charon moved slower than usual, allowing her clumsy and unsure hands to work with his, to feel the way he moved like the water itself. Her body was pressed so tightly against his that she had no choice but to adjust whenever he did, to bend her legs and move her feet.

Anastacia paid attention to how he used the skiff pole, how he pushed off the river bottom in some areas and used it to avoid large rocks that she wouldn't have noticed without his guidance. Many didn't break the surface of the water, big enough that to hit them hard would capsize the boat yet small enough that she could not see them.

The water roared beneath her, trying to trick her on purpose. It *wanted* her to fall into it, wanted to claim souls that weren't supposed to be here. And Anastacia wasn't meant to be here, many times over.

When the water got deep enough, Charon donned his oar. Already, the waves were much larger though calmer, bigger swells but less spray. Her hands grasped the wooden oar below his hands, her reach smaller.

They steered with one another until they made it to the opposite bank, where the water once again grew choppier, easier to navigate than in the beginning. She sighed in relief when the man walked off the boat, glad it was over.

Anastacia was about to step off to lead him to the Lethe when Charon grabbed her arm. "We must go gather the rest."

Her eyes widened and she shook her head. There were too many for her to ferry, and the boat needed would be much larger. She could hardly handle this one.

"I will only have you take a few," he comforted her. "I will bring the others behind you."

She felt like yelling. Simply after this exercise with Charon, her arms felt a bit limp. She didn't think she would be able to handle another trip there and back.

Charon pushed them off the back together again, and she did her best to focus on the way he moved with the river. Still, she was aware of how much work he was taking from her, how much he was doing.

Another larger boat appeared next to them, and she looked up to find Charon focusing on it.

"Are you moving that through the water without touching it?" Anastacia asked incredulously.

"Yes."

She took her hands off the pat and turned to look at him. "Then why are we ferrying souls this way if you can control the boat and the river without any work?"

She crossed her arms to give them a break, allowing her forearms to rest on one another.

"Because this is a soul's journey to their final resting place. It is an honor to escort them there and should be treated as such."

A particularly intense wave struck their boat, making it rock wildly. Anastacia had no choice but to turn back and grab the oar, hoping to stay balanced.

"And if I overturn those souls into the Acheron with my ignorance? That doesn't sound honorable or dignified."

Charon's torso shook against her back as he laughed. "Then don't let them fall in. Though if you do, they won't remember. We will just have to fish them out together. I will pin them, you will jump in and save them."

She huffed but quieted as they neared the opposite bank. Still, the souls waited for the Ferryman as they always did.

Both boats docked together on opposite sides of the wood. Charon took her hand as she stepped out, leading her to the group. He separated three souls, inclining his head towards Anastacia. "Take their coin."

She stared at them, remembering this day. Did they feel like she had? Were memories itching in the corners of their minds or was it her god blood that made her different?

Either way, she was careful to avoid touching their skin as she took an obol from each of them. Anastacia had awoken many souls, but always with the intentions of bringing them back to life. The idea of sending these ones to eternity instead didn't sit well with her.

Perhaps some of them would enjoy it, but she could not see how. An eternity of peace sounded terribly boring.

She retrieved each coin, hoping the souls didn't feel the way her nerves wracked her. She didn't want them worried that they would not make it to the other side. It was bad enough that Charon would witness her struggle; she didn't need the pressure of strangers watching as well.

Anastacia forced herself to step away from them, guiding the three souls until they boarded the boat. She wished she could run her hand along her staff, but it was safe in Charon's home. Even the coin she used to keep tucked away was gone, given to Epiphanios. She had no crutch, no piece of luck other than herself.

Each of the souls sat down carefully around the boat, balancing it naturally. She swallowed hard and glanced over at Charon. His own boat was waiting, just as hers was. He inclined his head with encouragement.

Anastacia sighed and checked to see if the gods were watching, but she didn't see them. Wherever they were, it was beyond her mortal sight. She was glad; the three who were aware of her tasks were the gods she was most anxious to impress. Hades and Persephone, because she needed their favor, and Hermes...

Well, she wouldn't examine why she wanted to impress him.

She steeled herself and remembered what she was doing this for. The river would not stop her.

Anastacia picked up the skiff pole and pushed off the bank without looking back. *The water is the same,* she promised herself. *This is the water I learned to swim in, the water I bathe in, the water I have kissed Charon within.*

As if to contradict her thoughts, a particularly hard current caught the boat and jerked it downstream. She used the pole to counter the movement, her arms mimicking Charon's actions and failing. The boat turned slightly, but she was unable to correct it fully. The river sent them careening into a rock, the souls shifting as the boat slammed against it.

Anastacia cursed as she did her best to keep her balance, shoving the pole in the water to fight against the current. Instead, her body flinched forward when it found no ground. They had passed into the area of the river where it was too deep to touch.

She brought it up quickly, shifting to the oar, and plunged it into the water. As if it could feel her anxiety, her uncertainty, the river got rougher. Water up began licking the side of the boat, spraying her legs and the souls within.

Her arms trembled as she rowed, trying to get them out of the current. When she finally muscled her way free, she thought it might get easier, but instead they were pushed into a tumultuous area of angry waves.

Anastacia let out a hard breath as she fixed her eyes to the opposite shore—she couldn't see it yet, but every time she pressed forward, she reminded herself that she was closer.

She rowed harder, fighting the waves, the boat rocking precariously as it crested one and slammed down hard on the other side. She cursed louder, angrily, her voice echoing. She wondered if Charon could hear it, wherever he was.

As if to retaliate, her face was splashed with frigid water. Her peplos clung to her skin which was shaking in the cold. In contrast to her misery, the souls sat, passive. They did not fight her, nor did they help. She was left to struggle on her own, her arms doing their best to counteract the river even as her hands went numb.

Anastacia fingers began blistering, wood cutting her skin when the oar was ripped out of her grasp. She scrambled for it with stinging hands, pain in her bones as she gripped it again. When her legs began trembling as well, her back aching, she finally had to stop fighting.

She gave in, allowing the river to move them as it wished, only adjusting to keep them afloat. The Acheron was too stubborn, too impossible to win against in a battle of strength. It would beat her every time.

But as Anastacia did her best to work with the water, to take what it gave her and move with it, she realized strength had never been her best trait.

Her adaptability was.

She found herself moving across, albeit downstream. She swallowed her worry. It didn't matter if they needed to walk, if she fell slightly off course. So long as she reached the shore before the river morphed into the Phlegethon and took them to Tartarus, she'd be successful.

Anastacia was tired to her bones by the time she made it to calmer waters. She tried to grab the skiff pole but her hands refused to wrap around the wood. Charon had told her she would be a master by the end of this trial, but he was wrong.

The river had mastered her instead.

When the boat scraped up against the shore, it was difficult to convince herself to step out and pull it further up. It was only knowing that these souls would not move, would not help her, that forced her to rise.

She stepped past them, yanking and dragging the skiff until it was secure. Then, Anastacia finally directed the souls off the boat and began their trek to the Lethe. All she wanted to do was to find a place to lie down, to rest her muscles until she felt like herself again, but there was no time.

Charon was already there, waiting stoically. His souls were all sitting along the bank of the absent river, their faces peaceful as they stared around in wonder. She had a violent reaction upon seeing them, a fierce disgust at their blank, happy stares. They had given away their memories, their sense of self, and had transformed into nothing. Mirrors of one another. No way to tell them apart, there would be no moments of recognition for family members, no love or hatred. Hollow beings. Empty souls.

She hated it. Anastacia was tempted to touch each of her souls before they drank so they could recall their lives one last time, but decided it was too cruel to give them those precious memories only to yank them away moments later.

Instead, she guided them to the Lethe and watched as they drank, like sheep led to water.

Charon touched her shoulder lightly. "Someone else will assist me with guiding them to Hades' palace today. You and I still have more to do."

He pulled her along, and she protested. "I completed my trial."

"Not to my satisfaction," he said.

"It isn't about your satisfaction. It's about my deal with the gods, which I completed."

"I am not a god," he reminded her. He pulled her onto the skiff. Her exhaustion and time spent fighting and fearing the river earlier had lessened her trepidation. Anastacia was simply glad that he grabbed the pole instead of her.

When they made it to the middle of the river, he stopped moving. He let the river take them where it wished. "Is it drowning you fear, or is it man?" he asked.

She stared at the water. "It's both. Man may be what forced me under, but it was still the water that flooded my mouth."

"You were not scared of it yesterday," Charon commented.

"I had you."

He paused for a moment, his hand moving to her shoulder. "And you still do."

Then, he pushed her. She flailed, her arms doing their best to help her keep her balance, but she could do nothing but stare at his face with betrayal as she fell into the frigid, angry Acheron. Anastacia took a deep breath just before she submerged, though at the all-consuming cold, it threatened to abandon her.

She opened her eyes, but saw only blackness. She didn't know which way was up, couldn't feel the bottom beneath her feet or the air at her fingertips. Her lungs began burning immediately, panic making air feel more necessary. There had been a time when Anastacia could swim under the water for many minutes, but it was long gone.

She strained to find the surface but couldn't orient herself. Anastacia blew out a few bubbles, hoping to find the way up, but it was too dark to see them. Her hands cupped her mouth, but the river was too frothy as it pummeled her for her to feel any difference.

Her muscles screamed at her as she picked a direction and began swimming, begging herself not to yell in frustration. If she thought she could force herself to breathe in the water sooner, she had lied. There was no part of her that wanted death, that wanted to feel the pain of drowning a second time. Fear overwhelmed her at the thought that she was only swimming deeper, farther away from the boat that would save her life.

But no matter how she fought, she didn't win. Her mind began to slow, time condensing as she realized that she was going to drown again. And it would be Charon who did it to her.

It might not be his hands, but it was certainly his river. His actions. The thought made her pause.

She remembered the way she had submitted when on the boat, the way she had given herself to Charon piece by piece for years. The way Persephone told her that to love Charon was to love the river, both above and below. How the ocean suited him, all water that her deity touched finding a way to make him somehow even more gorgeous.

And so Anastacia did the only thing her body begged her not to, and stopped. She felt the water around her, felt the way it dragged against her skin like Charon's interest, the way it wanted to devour her the same way he did. It wanted to claim her. Even on the boat, it had tried touching her skin, begged her for its full attention.

Charon and the Acheron were the same.

Her lungs were ready to burst when the water swept her up, allowing her to resurface and take a breath. She thought it might plunge her beneath again, but she had traveled while beneath the waves, back towards the shore and into calmer waves.

She hadn't expected Charon to be next to her, the water too dark for him to monitor her above the surface, but her foot kicked the side of his boat and she turned to see him floating there. Anastacia scowled even as she grabbed the side and hauled herself up, her arms shaking with fatigue. "What was that?" she tried to shout, but there wasn't enough air in her lungs to do so.

"That was you beginning to master the river," he commented easily, as if she hadn't almost just drowned. "That was you learning what it wants, and how to get what you want in return."

She wrapped her arms around herself, bumps overtaking her skin as she huddled into herself, looking away from the deity.

"You are cold," he said.

She whipped her head towards him. "Yes, Charon. I am cold. I was just dunked in the frigid waters of the Acheron."

"You will get used to it."

"I don't want to!" she yelled. "I do not want to get used to it. I don't want to fight to row across it, or get dragged beneath it."

"Then stop fighting it," he said easily. "You ferried your souls as you were meant to, you navigated the river adequately. You experienced its roughest waters and survived. What is there left to fear?"

She rolled her eyes as she huffed, forcing herself to ignore him before she said something cruel. His face was set in stone, stubborn. He wouldn't understand that the river was different for her than it was for him, that while he was in tune with it, she was not.

Charon said he was not a god, but in so many ways, he was.

And it would do her well to remember it.

Chapter Eighteen

Anastacia slept beside Charon again that night despite her lingering irritation with him. He could tell that she was cross, though he still kept his arms wrapped around her.

If anything, her anger made him hold her tighter as though she might run. And he was right to be concerned. Despite her exhaustion, her eyes stayed open while she listened to him breathe, and she began to understand further.

The way that her anger and reluctance made Charon cling to her was the same way the river treated her when she fought it. It wasn't until Anastacia relaxed into him that his grip loosened enough for her to rest comfortably.

As if he could feel the moment she shifted, his breathing hitched. "Where are you going?" His voice was rough with sleep, gravel filled and tired.

She shifted to look at him, face neutral as she ran her gaze down his face. The dark eyes, the broken nose, the smooth skin.

"Nowhere," she finally said.

And they both closed their eyes and slept.

***

Anastacia woke slowly, warm and heavy. Charon was naked beneath her, their bodies pressed together like stocks of wheat. He was already looking at her, unashamed in a way that warned her he had been awake for minutes, or perhaps hours, prior.

"How do you feel?" he asked.

She didn't need to move to answer. "Sore."

"I will see if Persephone can postpone your last trial."

She sat up despite the way her body protested. "No, it is better to do it now." She could not risk them changing their minds, going back on their word. She might be untrustworthy, but they were more so.

Charon frowned but didn't say anything as she stood and dressed herself, preparing for whatever trial Persephone had created. Anastacia knew that she had a hand in all three of the labors, whether Charon had gone above and beyond with his or not.

Her labors hadn't been so hard that they were impossible, but she knew that was not Persephone's intention. No, the goddess was trying to get her to change her mind. Trying to convince her that she didn't want her soul, that to live forever would be unfair, that she should want to die as opposed to spend the rest of her existence here.

The first trial, forcing her to convince someone to die—the very fate Anastacia was fighting against.

The second, facing the reality of her future with Charon and the river; what it contained, and where she would be expected to stay if she chose this path.

She could only assume the last would do the same. Already, she had learned things she did not want to about herself.

She had had a moment where she hoped Epiphanios would accept his fate when he drank from the Lethe, that he would want the peace they both seemed to hope to avoid. Like brother, like sister, she supposed. Maybe discontent ran within both of their veins.

Then, yesterday, the knowledge that she couldn't control the river and would never be able to. That she would have to learn to submit to it to get what she wanted, that she could not only take. She knew that the Acheron reflected Charon and vice versa. The two of them were connected in ways she hadn't ever imagined, down to the marrow of their bones.

But she was learning.

She had loved the Acheron above even longer than she had loved the Ferryman. These were only different facets of those things.

But this third trial, Persephone's trial, she didn't know what to expect. Could once again, not prepare herself

As though he understood, Charon didn't speak with her as she finished getting ready and walked outside to sit on the riverbank. She gazed across the dark water, looked up to the strange cavern sky, touched the soil beneath her. This was a beautiful place. Desolate, yes, but not everywhere. And even in its simplicity, it was breathtaking.

When Persephone arrived, she walked to Charon first. Anastacia didn't turn to look at them, but she could hear the cadence of their voices as they spoke. Toward the end of their conversation, Charon's voice rose, his temper aggravating the river. Waves that had been lightly kissing the shore began digging their claws into the sand, creeping closer towards her toes with every moment.

She considered pulling her feet up, remembering the frigid cold within. How it would bite her and make her numb. How it wanted to take her away, keep her trapped within its depths.

But she stopped herself, letting it cling to her toes instead. Anastacia didn't think she imagined when it paused there, content to touch her without growing further up the shore. She wondered, not for the first time that day, if the river was truly tied to Charon in the way that the underworld was tied to Hades.

Her toes had just begun to numb when Charon touched her shoulder, his face like a storm. "Did she tell you what the trial was?" she asked.

He nodded his head once, but his jaw was so tense that the movement was forced.

"You don't seem happy about it. What is it?"

"I was not permitted to speak with you about it. I will take you to her, if you're ready."

She searched his expression to see if there was any hint of what she was to face that had him so frustrated, but there was nothing. His eyes stayed locked on her but didn't shift to her muscles as though he was nervous she hadn't stretched. He didn't glance backwards towards Tartarus or to the palace.

And yet she had spent years learning the nuances of Charon's expressions. This was one she had never seen, and certainly not since they had begun their courting of one another.

Fear.

"I'll complete it just fine, Charon. Like I have the others."

His eyes bored into her like he was memorizing her face. "I will believe you, little liar." She reached out and grabbed his callused hand, squeezing tight. His responding grip was light. He might call her the liar, but she thought he was, too. Whatever Persephone had told him had made him worry she would not return to him at the end.

Would it truly be that difficult of a trial? After all, even if she died, she would still come back to him. Perhaps there was a caveat in their deal that she hadn't explored. Maybe Anastacia should have asked what failure would entail—if it meant she would simply have to return home empty handed, or if there were larger consequences.

But the truth of it was, failure wasn't an option.

If Anastacia failed, there was no consequence larger. No bigger incentive she could offer herself. If she failed, then it didn't matter what became of her because she wouldn't remember anyway. She would drink from the Lethe one day and fall into some empty, eternal rest. A hollow toy that worked only when told to, that had no thoughts or growth. She wouldn't remember her Ferryman, the way he looked when shadowed on his river, the way he felt when he moved inside of her, the places on her body his skin had touched.

Yes, her eventual death was consequence enough.

She left Charon staring at the empty Acheron behind her, walking until she stood beside Persephone. The goddess was radiant as usual, life pouring off of her in waves. It was peaceful, sweet, tempting.

She much preferred her Ferryman. Anastacia turned toward him one last time.

He stood still as stone, his tunic hanging on one shoulder, simple. No golden clasp like Hermes, no fair, glowing skin like Persephone. From a distance, Charon looked like a dedicated seaman, and that was all. At least, to her.

Perhaps one day she would get the courage to ask if she saw him as he truly was, or only how she wanted him to be. If there was something else beneath his skin, the deity different in his own eyes. What did he see when he looked upon his reflection?

Persephone began walking away and Anastacia took one last moment to burn him into her memory. He turned to watch her go as if doing the same.

"Where are we going?" Anastacia asked as they followed the same trail she had brought the souls yesterday.

"To your last trial," Persephone answered. Anastacia tried not to roll her eyes at the intentional vagueness.

"And this is the one you designed?"

Persephone turned to smile at Anastacia cordially. "Hades and I, yes. You have proven that you can convince souls to follow you, that you know the value of death as opposed to an immortal life. You have showed that you understand the river, that you understand how violent both it—and its Ferryman—can be, the way it threatened to kill you yesterday, drag you beneath and never release you from its clutches. Today, you will learn the peace of the underworld."

And Anastacia could have laughed. The goddess had been watching Anastacia, but clearly not close enough. She was only seeing what she wanted to impart, not the message that was being received.

Because Persephone was wrong.

When she had convinced Epiphanios to come with her, it wasn't because either of them valued death. It was because together, they had a chance to escape their father and his guidance.

When she had seen the river's violence, she had also seen its needs. The way it reacted to her. How the water might have been through different things, but it was still the same water she had been in while on Gaia.

If Persephone's goal was to dissuade her, she was doing the opposite. But Anastacia only nodded, unwilling to tell the goddess any different.

Until she was led to the Lethe.

Persephone crouched and let her fingers run through the nothingness until she rose, a drop of the smoky water hanging from her fingertip.

"Open your mouth," Persephone commanded.

Anastacia flinched back automatically, her jaw clenching. She was certain her shock was plain on her face.

Persephone only waited patiently, that drop dangling like a death sentence. "Will I forget forever?"

The goddess shook her head. "No, Anastacia. Only for a time."

"And what then?"

Persephone shrugged. "For my trial, you will experience Elysium. Eternal happiness, no pain, no worries. You must understand what you are sacrificing. That you are giving up a gift, Anastacia. Death is a kindness, immortality a curse. If you still do not want Elysium after you experience it, then I will consider your trial completed."

Anastacia eyed her finger warily as Persephone held it out towards her face.

"Now, Anastacia. Before it falls and I consider your trial failed."

She didn't question it another time, darting forward and letting the drop hit her tongue before the goddess could change her mind. It was refreshing, sweet, what she imagined peace might taste like. Anastacia had just enough time to wonder what it would be like to lose herself, if she would even know that she had lost something, when suddenly it didn't matter any longer.

***

Charon didn't move from his spot on the riverbank. The souls could wait. For the first time in his long life, his day felt unnecessary. There were things to be done, but he couldn't focus.

The Acheron was more agitated than usual as if it felt his discomfort, mourning Anastacia's loss the same way he did.

The underworld felt empty without her consciousness within it. He didn't know how long it had been that he had spent searching for simply a glimpse of her, but even when she didn't appear, there had been something interesting in his day. Something to look forward to, a chance that he would see her face, smell her skin, feel her touch.

And then, the past few days, he had thought things would be different. That he was past separating himself from her, that when he had captured her, he would never have to let her go again. Even if she escaped from him that first time, she would come back.

Of course she would.

Because Anastacia knew him. She had watched him, had given her time to a deity who never had a reason to spend it. A creature who had no need for love, for joy, for permanence. Nothing was more eternal than he was. There was no point in sharing himself.

And she had still found him. A liminal being who had nothing but himself and the river, and now... Anastacia.

Anastacia, Anastacia, Anastacia.

He had missed her for years. And not only a few years, one or two that would have passed like minutes, but almost a *century*.

She thought he wouldn't have loved her or wanted her. Perhaps it was true. Maybe it was the clever gleam in her eye that he recognized, the way she responded to him and his souls that resonated deep within him. It didn't matter.

She was his now. And she would always be his.

Charon did not know how long he stared after the little lyre and the goddess, but it was long enough that he knew her memory was gone, taken by the Lethe.

But Anastacia had grown to love him once, had fought for her memories long before now. She would do it again.

He wouldn't lose her. It was too late for either of them.

CHAPTER NINETEEN

Anastacia sat with her back against a tree, smiling into the cavernous sky. There was a piece of fruit in her hand, a small bite taken out. It had tasted sweet, the juice dripping down the palm of her hand when her teeth broke the flesh.

She didn't know how long she had been holding it. It didn't matter, because she wasn't hungry. Every now and then, she touched her tongue to the exposed flesh simply to let the flavor tingle her cheeks, to feel the way her jaw ached at the tartness. To feel something at all.

There were people playing happily in the distance, their laughter easy and carefree. She could see them in the light, the landscape around them bright with color. The nights were just as beautiful, the weather always perfect. Even when there was thunder in the distance, it didn't reach her.

Her tunic felt like silk against her skin as she shifted, her hand squeezing the fruit too hard for only a moment. A bit of the juice spilled out, landing on the cream fabric covering her chest. For one distinct moment, she thought it looked like blood.

But then the thought was gone.

The stain didn't matter. She would wake tomorrow with it clean, having disappeared.

People spoke around her, but she didn't join them. She wasn't one for empty conversation, and in a place where nothing mattered, there was no reason to use her voice. She didn't know them and she didn't want to.

There was only one woman who she spoke to, and that woman hadn't visited recently.

Their conversations used to be cordial. Anastacia knew that. When she had first arrived, the peace of Elysium had enveloped her and she was glad. Happy. Full. The woman had been pleased, and Anastacia felt good to have caused her smile. She felt powerful, like she had done something rare. She wanted to make the woman smile more.

But then the woman had left, and Anastacia fell into an unchanging routine. And she found that although she was supposed to be happy, there was something *wrong. Bad. Empty.*

The woman came back and Anastacia lied to her when she asked how it was. She lied to see that beautiful smile again, to gain her favor. But the smile didn't make her feel the same way it had the first time. So, the next time, she told the truth.

Anastacia admitted that this world was an empty half-life, half-death, and she would rather be damned to eternal nothingness than this. She meant it politely, didn't say it with any anger or malice, but it didn't soften the reaction to her words.

The woman was angry. She left and had not returned.

Her skin began to feel warm even though the air hadn't changed, and she finally moved, discarding the fruit on the ground. Her feet walked toward the river that surrounded Elysium, a calm and sweet thing. She knew she was not to cross it, though she thought she could if she tried.

Anastacia didn't want to, she reminded herself. The woman had told her so. *You do not want to see what is on the other side, Anastacia. It is ugly and it is painful.*

There was no reason to leave. This place was perfect, peaceful, wonderful.

And still, her feet led her to the same place every time she allowed herself to wander. To the shallowest part of the bank, to the place she could almost see the other side.

She knew she didn't want to cross. She didn't want to.

She did not want to.

Or perhaps, it was only that she wasn't supposed to. Because every time she came to the bank, she went a little farther in the river. A little farther away. Or perhaps, a little farther *toward*.

She swallowed hard, her fists clenching. She was surprised at the feeling of an item clutched within her grip, certain she had discarded the uneaten fruit. Anastacia glanced down as she unfurled her palm.

There was a necklace clutched within it.

She pinched her eyes shut and forced herself to release it, dropping it heavily into the soil before she moved her sandal to cover it with dirt. It wasn't the first time she found herself with something she wasn't supposed to have, but it always disappeared eventually. Back to its original owner, she assumed.

She jumped as a voice startled her. "What did you steal this time, little liar?"

She stumbled forward quickly, moving away instinctively as her feet gracefully avoided any stones, turning to look at the man who had surprised her.

Anastacia hadn't seen him here before. No, he didn't belong in a place like Elysium. He was far too dark to belong here, though she couldn't deny that the world suited him. Perhaps though, he was so beautiful that anything suited him.

He was in a dark cloak, one that seemed too heavy for the warm climate. The skin visible was olive, beautiful, smooth. He had a dusting of black hair on his jaw and lip line, and jet-black hair on his head.

She couldn't see the exact color of his eyes from this distance, but she had a feeling they would be just like his hair. So black that there would be no distinction from his iris to his pupil.

Her heart skipped, as if it could still do such a thing. As if it was reminding her she was alive. "What?" she asked.

He took a step forward and she took one back. "What did you take?" he asked as he cocked his head.

"Nothing," she answered naturally.

"Still so quick to steal, and even quicker to conceal the truth," he smiled. "I wonder what other traits have followed you to Elysium."

She didn't know. She didn't remember.

"Is that why you called me a liar?" she asked as she tilted her head.

His brow furrowed with confusion for a moment before a short laugh burst out of him. Then, a longer one. It was beautiful, the prettiest music she had ever heard.

"No, my thief. Although, that would be an apt description. I did not call you a liar, but a *lyre*. So mesmerizing, so charming. Such a pretty, tempting instrument that I would like to strum my fingers against. I was gifted with its music once before, and only you have made me feel the way I felt then."

Anastacia stayed silent, watching him warily, though she already knew that if he were to turn his back and move those predator eyes away from her, she would follow. She would step into his footprints, place her hands on the same trees he touched, would try his discarded food just to know their mouths had touched the same thing.

"You speak as though you know me, but I don't know you."

The man simply looked at her, drank her in. She could drown in him happily. Anastacia had felt so unsettled here, searching for something she could not name, but now that she had seen him she knew. It was him. He was the piece she was missing, the man who her soul was aching for, the reason she had almost thrown herself in the river every day since she arrived.

Whenever that was.

He sat, and she finally allowed herself to approach him. "Don't you know me?"

Anastacia sat beside him just out of reach. He was large, too broad to be fast. If he lunged for her, she could escape him at this distance.

She didn't answer, but he didn't let her get away with her passiveness. "*Don't you*?" he asked again.

And her mouth opened. "I don't dream here. I don't know if I sleep. I know that days pass, people are happy, and I am not one of them." Anastacia faced him. "I know that when my eyes settle for too long, I feel empty. My fingers itch, my feet and legs ache from being sedentary, and my soul hurts. My throat feels like someone has their fist around it and is squeezing slowly until I choke. I am a frog in boiling water, the heat increasing so gradually that I am burning alive before I have the chance to escape. I know that my mind doesn't remember you but my being does. I know that wherever you go, now that I have seen you, I will find you."

She had no reason to lie, her words flowing from her, likely too honest. Truthful enough that she expected him to run. Instead, his expression became immensely pleased. Even arrogantly so.

"Tell me about your time here," he requested.

Anastacia could not bring herself to tear her eyes away from him, although she had been looking for too long. She was worried that if she turned, he would disappear. "My time here is useless. There is only contentedness."

"Contentedness is not bad."

"Nor is it good," she said quickly. "There is only ease. Only happiness. Only laughter. Half of me is empty and I cannot bring myself to feel sad about it."

"And the necklace?"

"An accident," she waved it off.

"Have there been other accidents?"

She paused, eyeing him suspiciously from where he sat. "No."

It was a lie. She found herself with a collection of items more often than not. It was something rooted so deeply within her that while she didn't know why she took from others, it was as necessary as breathing. Perhaps even more so, because she didn't truly have to breathe in Elysium.

So enamored with watching him, she had leaned forward. Her weight was too offset to move well when he finally reached out and grabbed her arm, rolling them both until she was pinned beneath him.

As his cloaked chest settled against hers, his torso fitting in between her legs, she gasped out, "You are not supposed to be here." She didn't know where the words came from, but she knew they were the truth.

"I couldn't wait any longer," he said, his face close to her own. "A handful from the Lethe takes away memories for all eternity. I had to know that a drop wouldn't do the same."

Her mind was scrambling, throwing itself painfully against her skull.

"And I had to know you weren't happy here, without me. That even when you didn't remember me, you felt my absence like a missing limb."

"It is far worse than a missing limb," she admitted. "It is so painful that even in this perfect place, I wish to leave." Her fingers clutched at her forehead like she could unravel the mess within.

"It is because you are mine in every world. You gave yourself to me, Anastacia. And I did not return you. You were meant to come back to me by now."

He was speaking in riddles, in half-conversations that she didn't fully understand. "Did the woman send you to take me away?" It was the only explanation that made sense.

"The woman?"

"Yes. The one I told to send me to an empty place. Are you here to take me there?"

The man paused, his face growing stormy. He seemed to swell with emotion, his chest trembling as he attempted to contain the wrath within his skin. "An empty place?"

"I don't like it here," she said quietly.

Her heart was pounding against her chest as the man's jaw clenched. She waited as he worked out whatever was in his mind, whatever had set him off. Finally, he reached his hand up and tangled it in her hair. "There is no empty place for you," he said darkly. "No empty place, no damnation, no peace. There is nothing for you but the river and me. I told you once that there would be no one else for you and I meant it."

His words were possessive, sending shivers down her spine, her body squirming to move closer to him.

The world was quiet around them. No one had come to the river today, though even if they had, they wouldn't care that she was caught on the ground like a hare in a trap. They likely wouldn't even look twice. It was a forced happiness, a pretty cage. Anastacia hated looking at them because their eyes were glazed with eternal peace, not a care in the world. And she knew she looked just like them.

But not this man. This man had passion, he contained fury, he was a raging rapid wearing flesh.

As if he could tell her mind had begun to wander, back into whatever drug kept her trapped here, he rocked into her hard. His hips rolled up, and she felt it—the way his cock was hard like a spearhead, how it pierced her immediately like he had lined them up perfectly the entire time they were laying here, talking.

Anastacia immediately spread her knees apart wider, pushing her tunic up farther, but when he thrust again, she still felt fabric between them. She moved with frustration, glancing down to see what was in the way. The bottom half of his cloak lay crushed between them, the only barrier that kept their skin from touching.

She went to move the clothing, but the man growled and pressed himself against her harder, his mouth kissing hers until she could think of nothing else but how good he felt against her lips, how she had never kissed someone with a beard that tickled her face, the way her body wanted to take him within it.

When their lips separated, she was breathing hard despite the fact that she didn't need to. "You make me remember," she whispered.

"It's because I have kept all the pieces of you that you have ever given me," he replied, his voice sweet. "I do not mind giving them back for now, as long as you promise to return them after you no longer need them."

Anastacia smiled, reaching up to touch his face, the hair growing there. "You act like they are physical pieces."

"It feels like they are," he admitted. "Like treasures I cannot bear to part with."

She shook her head. "You don't need to part with anything. Your touch is enough to... to remind me there is more than I know. Something I have been looking for."

A grin stole over his face, eyes brightening at her words. "My touch?" His hand skimmed down the side of her face until it covered her throat lightly. "Tell me, is my hand enough?"

There was no doubt in her mind as she answered, the words coming from somewhere deep within her. "I will always take more when there is more to be had."

"For you, there will always be more," he said darkly, pushing himself deeper against the apex of her thighs, her skin shivering against the rough fabric.

She didn't remember sex, but she wasn't sure how she could forget such a thing. Not with him. He continued to thrust, small little movements that hardly penetrated her at all with his cock covered by the cloak. It wasn't enough.

"Please," Anastacia begged. She didn't know how long it had been since he arrived. Perhaps minutes, maybe years.

"Please what, little lyre? My charming woman, you are captivating like this. Begging, on the cusp of pain and pleasure, your face flushed and your body so sweet. Could you spend forever like this?"

She answered immediately. "Yes."

As if rewarding her, his hand moved his cloak aside. She almost orgasmed at the feeling of his bare length against her skin.

"Am I your happy eternity?"

"Yes, Ferryman." She didn't know why she called him that, but it fit him. The word came unbidden from somewhere deep that she didn't have access to yet, that was unraveling every moment that spent together.

"Call me by my name," he requested as he pushed his cock into her slowly, inch by inch. She tried to recall it, wanted to search, but her mind was running away from her at the feeling of him—the slow way he dragged along her body until he was fully seated. She expected him to move, to turn that passion into a frantic fucking, but he did the opposite and stilled. The only relief she got was from the little thrusts she made herself, tilting her hips back and forth slightly, pinned as she was.

The man smiled at her desperation. "My name, Anastacia. If you want my cock, you will scream my name. Beg me to give you what you need." But she didn't know his name. She could cry, for she knew she should. She *wanted* to feel his name on her tongue, see the way he looked when she said it. "Look at you, beautiful woman. Your body yearning for me, your soul cursed to live a half-life without me. You feel full now, though, don't you?"

And she did. As he sat there within her, his restraint far better than hers, it felt like she was whole. "How long will you do this to me?" she asked quickly as he sat still, her body begging for more.

"Until you remember my name. Until I have been inside of you for so long that you feel like my cock has always been here, that I am part of your body. That to be away from me is too painful to survive. I will be here until you remember."

She groaned with frustration, doing her best to encourage him with her wiggling, but his face didn't change. There were cracks in the back of her mind and she could feel them widening. They had been there for a long while now, but it was as if his presence was forcing her to pound against them.

"If you cost me this trial—"

He kissed her to stop her from speaking. "You have already asked to leave. The trial is over, little lyre. The rest of this is, I believe, a test. To see how badly you want to return to our life together."

She froze. Something about his words were off. There should not be a test, only trials. Only her agreed upon labors.

"Like how I threw you back into the river although you had already brought your souls across," he whispered. "It is something extra. Something the goddess tricked us both into."

"And what do I need to do to complete the test?"

She had stilled, her arousal discarded as she ran her mind through her time here, picking and prodding at memories that ached like a bruise.

"You must come back to me, Anastacia."

"I have been trying," she said even as she confused herself. It was as if someone else was speaking through her.

He pulled back and slammed into her hard. The feeling scattered her mind again, the slap of their bodies as they met once more. The curl of his cock hit her perfectly, teasingly. "Not trying hard enough," he criticized.

Anastacia's hands clawed briefly at his shoulders. "Do not pretend you know what it has been like here," she hissed.

"I know what it has been like without you," he responded, his teeth bared. "I know that I have never been so distracted in my existence, that time has never moved so slowly."

"Fuck me into remembering," Anastacia said quietly.

His eyes turned hooded and he flipped them over so that she was straddling him. His hands were tight on her thighs, keeping her from moving. "I was saving this, you know," he said.

"Saving what?"

"Fucking you without your memories. I have had time to think, while you have been gone. I promised myself the next time I took you, there would be no going back. That when I spill myself inside of you, it is because you are mine and *you know it.* That you are willing to carry my children in your belly, that you are ready for what this binding will mean." He forced her hips to roll, his fingers dipping into the divots of her stomach near her pelvis. "But now, I find that I do not want to wait. Do you know why, Anastacia?"

Her eyes fluttered at the feeling of him inside of her as she tilted herself backwards. Her peplos still covered her body and she wished it was gone, wished her skin was as bare as her soul felt. "Because I have known those things from the moment I saw you," she said.

He stilled as if surprised by her answer. She wondered what he was thinking, if he had been about to admit that he didn't care anymore whether she knew it or not. But she *did* know it. There wasn't even a question.

Her eyes locked onto his as she brought her body up slightly before riding him slowly, like she had been dreaming of since he arrived. "You keep looking for me to prove my dedication to you, Charon. But I have already told you that you have whatever is mine to give, and then some, because I will take whatever I don't have from others. You are the only deity I worship, Ferryman."

She thought she had seen him smile before, but it was nothing compared to the look that appeared on his face at her words, at his name.

"You remember?" he groaned out as she ground herself against him.

"Enough," she said. Certainly not all. But she remembered him, at least.

At her admission, he gripped her hard and turned them over once more so that her back was in the dirt. "There are so many ways I intend to fuck you, Anastacia. But today, I wish to see your face while you come apart on my cock. I want to see the look on it when I spill inside of you, when I brand you with my come."

He rocked forward quickly, unrestrained. Their coupling was frenzied, so impossibly beautiful and raw that she wanted to cry. She spiraled upwards with him, their words forgotten in their passion, until suddenly they were falling apart together.

He told the truth, stilling deep within her as he came and then sitting there so it wouldn't spill out.

Could she get pregnant with a deity's child? She supposed so, though it would move her timeline back. She would need to act fast to accomplish her goal before the baby quickened, if it took.

When they had both caught their breath, he leaned onto his forearms.

Memories were spilling slowly into her brain, filtering in easier the longer he touched her. "How long have I been here?"

"A month." Not as long as she had worried, then. A month wasn't bad. She had lost more time to sillier decisions. "How do you feel about cheating, little lyre?"

Her hand rose to touch the side of his face. "I think if you're not cheating, then you're not trying hard enough."

He grinned. "That's what I thought you would say."

And he took her hand and pressed it within his cloak, towards his lower back where her hands had not ventured. There, hidden, her hand hit smooth bone and intricate artwork. She didn't need to see it to know what it was.

Anastacia smiled.

CHAPTER TWENTY

A nger kept Anastacia from falling back into Elysium's lull. How long had Persephone and Hades planned to let her rot here after she had proven it wasn't what she wanted? She wondered what the cost of her failure would have been. If she had truly forgotten all she was and been happy here.

Would they have left her forever?

Caduceus in hand, she entered the river. Charon was gone, returned to his home, but she didn't need him for this journey. She knew this area of the underworld. Elysium was near Persephone's grove, after all.

She didn't go there yet, however. Anastacia didn't know when Persephone would return to find her missing, but with Charon gone and the goddess preoccupied, Anastacia had a moment alone. Truly alone.

And unwittingly, she had been handed a trail into Elysium. The very thing she needed, that she had been searching for. She scouted the river as she traveled it, but it was calm. If she was correct, this was a mixture of the Lethe and the Styx, an area of serene waters that were easy to swim across. Once she had memorized Elysium, she crossed to the other side of the river, memorizing the way to the grove.

She didn't need to go further within. She knew the way out by heart from there.

Anastacia traced her footsteps backwards to Elysium until she knew she could cover the distance quickly, and grinned. The month in Elysium was worth the delay if it had given her easy access to the blessed lands of eternity. It would have been difficult to find on her own, earned her too much suspicion if she did it under watchful eyes.

She didn't hide Caduceus as she walked through the underworld, though she was careful to avoid any lesser deities and immortals. She didn't mind being seen, but she didn't need to be detained.

It wasn't difficult to find Hades' home, the towering structure bigger than anything else and located in the center of the underworld. Plenty of other gods had rooms within, Hecate and Hermes, lesser deities and beings. The palace was large enough that it could likely fit every god and goddess in Olympus and still have room. Her eyes scanned the behemoth, looking for something specific. A room she wouldn't succeed without visiting.

The palace was a beautiful piece of art, spires twisting high into the sky, exposed columns keeping the structure open, even high up. Balconies had flora hanging off them, green stalks with intermittent flashes of color blooming within. It didn't take her long to note the rooms that looked most promising.

Some of the trellises were low, brushing the ground.

It made the guards useless. Cerberus might protect the palace doors, sentries spaced throughout the grounds and low windows, but they didn't see Anastacia as she wrapped her hand around a vine and tested it with her weight.

It held her easily as she placed her feet against the textured wall and began her ascent.

***

The gods weren't in the throne room yet, and Anastacia was pleased. She wasn't irreverent enough to sit in the seat, but she certainly perched herself against it, leaning her chin on the back. The throne was tall enough that she had to stand on her tiptoes, but it didn't matter. From the front, they wouldn't notice.

She draped her hands over it, Caduceus dangling obnoxiously from her fingertips, tapping against the stone of the seat as her free hand's fingers danced along it.

When the god and goddess of the underworld walked in with the three judges and Charon, they all paused. Only Charon's eyes looked pleased. She wasn't sure how long it had been since his visit. At least a few days.

Long enough that the apex of her thighs was no longer sore.

She met Persephone's beautiful eyes. "Have I passed your trial?"

Persephone did not smile, nor did she frown, her expression unreadable.

"I think I have proven myself to you, goddess. And if I have disappointed you in what you found, I am sorry. But I never disguised what I wanted."

"I had only hoped you might change your mind and see the truth," Persephone said as she inclined her head.

Anastacia shrugged as she stepped from behind the thrones. "Truth is subjective."

"Elysium will be lost to you forever," Persephone warned.

"I never wanted it anyway. Give me my soul."

Hades frowned, stepping in front of his wife. "You are quite a mouthy thing. Watch how you speak to my wife."

Anastacia waved Caduceus at him. "My apologies." To Persephone, "Give me my soul, *please.*"

The goddess stared at her before her eyes softened. "Hades, if you would."

He turned towards her. "Which soul am I giving you?" he asked, and Anastacia laughed incredulously as she glanced at the goddess.

"You didn't tell him?"

She shook her head with a small smile. "This deal was ours, and ours alone."

Anastacia could tell that Charon was listening intently, and she realized that all but Persephone had misunderstood her when she said she wanted *her* soul.

"My own," she clarified. "I want my own. I don't want to follow Hermes, I don't wish to drink from the Lethe and forget my life. I wish to continue living on my own terms, go where I wish to go."

"You must be dead for me to give you your soul," Hades corrected her, and Anastacia nodded.

"I am. My soul has been dead for over a century. I'm on stolen time, and I don't wish to steal it any longer."

It was the only reason the underworld had allowed her to stay for so long. It already knew she belonged to it, that she wasn't truly living even if she wasn't truly dead either.

Charon, if possible, looked even happier. A question finally answered and understood.

Hades stepped in front of her, and Anastacia did her best not to cower backwards. His presence was jarring, perhaps because it was so new to her. Persephone and Charon, she had watched from afar for years. Hermes, she had spent her childhood with.

Hades though, she had no sway with. Nothing other than the fact that he loved his wife, and his wife had a soft spot for her whether she wanted to admit it or not. That was why she had wanted Anastacia to understand what eternal life would mean, what she would be missing out on.

She had tried to give Anastacia a choice the way she had not been. But both women were born damned. Anastacia had no doubt Persephone would have ended up Hades' Queen no matter how it happened. Some things were meant to be, destined in fate.

The strings of the loom tied them together long before they knew about it.

Hades reached out and touched her forehead. His hand was surprisingly warm as he traced something on her skin.

"I have not felt Caduceus in years," he commented. "Hermes told me it was broken."

She shrugged. "The one he carries is."

"Broken, or never blessed to begin with?"

Anastacia smiled, her fingers skittering over the staff, reassuring her.

Hades let out a short laugh. "Charon, my friend, I think you will have your hands full with your thief. You had best watch her, lest she get into trouble."

"With my soul my own, there is not much that can be done to me," Anastacia said quietly.

Hades paused as if he hadn't considered that. He was making her a very difficult woman to punish by giving away the gods 'domain over her. Of course, there were still many other ways; the gods interfered with one another's lives all the time. But death would no longer have the same threat.

Then, he hummed. "I suppose it is a good thing that you respect my Ferryman and my wife then, isn't it?"

"Yes," she agreed.

"Does that mean I will be safe from your thieving?"

She nodded. "Yes."

It was a lie, and perhaps they both knew it. Hades didn't comment on it, though.

When Hades pulled his hand away from her, she felt no different. She thought there might be an unmooring, an invincible confidence, but there was nothing except the absence of his touch.

"It is done?"

He nodded once, assessing her carefully. "Your soul is your own."

"Thank you."

Her gaze swept towards Persephone and Charon. Persephone stared at Anastacia, perhaps looking for something more, another reason she had done such a thing, but she didn't ask. Likely, she knew Anastacia wouldn't answer. Instead, she joined her husband.

Anastacia didn't wait for a verbal dismissal. She walked carefully towards Charon, her head inclining to look at him the closer she got.

"Hello, stranger," she whispered.

His smile showed teeth. "Not any longer."

"Is there more work that must be done?" Anastacia asked as she let her fingers reach out to grip his lightly.

He pulled her into him, their chests bumping one another. "Not today."

"Then I think I would like to go home."

His gaze turned wary. "Which one? The one above, or the one below?"

"Can they not both be my home?"

He shook his head, picking up her hand until he could press his lips against her palm. "No."

It was his preference more than a rule, she knew. "Come with me," she asked. "Above."

"I—" he cut himself off, looking around as if someone would tell him no.

"You said that there was no more work to be done tonight. You will still be by the Acheron, still have access to the world below when you want it. There is no excuse."

She was not sure why he was hesitant, but he eventually nodded his head in agreement. "Okay. Do you need anything?"

Anastacia picked up her loose hand, revealing Caduceus within it. "I've got everything I need."

He raised an eyebrow. "You should be careful where you brandish that. Word will get to Hermes, and I don't think he will be pleased."

She laughed. She was counting on it.

Chapter Twenty-One

Charon could tell Ophelia wasn't happy with Anastacia's prolonged absence despite her reasoning. His lyre did her best to appease her friend, offering compliments and sweet thoughts, but Ophelia didn't fall for it.

Charon wouldn't have, either.

Anastacia was too skilled a liar for anything she said to be believed at first glance. Even now, he had spent the day trying to understand why, of all the souls in the underworld and above, she would choose her own.

After all, she had already stolen it without anyone knowing any different. Why go through the trouble of fighting for it after the fact? Anastacia had to have known that Charon wouldn't say anything about her death and resurrection to Hades.

She had been stealing souls for years and escaped attention for it. Not only that, but she had spoken with Charon about her detest for the gods' gaze, her reluctance at having them know her name. Anastacia had been anonymous.

No one had been looking for her or the other souls because no one realized they were missing.

But now, Anastacia had changed that. She had made both Hades and Persephone aware of her presence for a reason that didn't quite add up. There was very little gain by having her own soul. It meant nothing, other than she would not go to Elysium or Tartarus upon judgement. That she could stay with him.

But she could have done that anyway.

He knew there was something else, something more, but it was difficult to see what she was hiding within her mind. She kept her thoughts so close to her tongue, and even those she gave were layered. Her truths were half-lies, and her lies even more confusing.

Charon watched her speak with Ophelia as his gaze traveled towards their home. It was a beautiful place, close to where the Acheron met the sea. Dusk was approaching, the sun making its descent as Poseidon readied the water to swallow the rest of the light.

Already, stars scattered themselves across the sky. He didn't know the constellations, couldn't find the way the patterns connected, but it didn't matter. They were beautiful, whether he could read them or not. He had settled himself in the sand, his feet covered in the soft grains. It was easy for him to keep an eye on Anastacia without looking like he was doing it obsessively.

Although he was.

He had been without her for far too long. All he had known was that there was a chance she would spend eternity in Elysium, that she would willingly forget the life she left behind, forget him. It was unacceptable.

Persephone hadn't listened to his pleas for updates, instead telling him that this was her trial to beat. Little did he realize that already, Anastacia had won. He wondered how early she had asked Persephone to leave, if it was only a lingering pettiness that Anastacia had proven her so wrong, so quickly, that made the goddess keep her there.

When Persephone had forced his hand, declining to update Charon on how much longer she would keep Anastacia secluded in the land of the blessed, he went in himself. It was a place Charon didn't visit; he didn't care to see the souls who were already allowed past the river.

But for Anastacia, he didn't mind.

Seeing her there, that empty face, those lifeless eyes that lacked their usual clever spark, had torn him apart. He had been certain there was nothing of her left until he saw the glint of that beautiful necklace in her grasp.

It was the first breath he had taken since she left.

Anastacia settled next to him. "Is Ophelia going to stay in the house?" he asked.

She laughed, a light, pretty sound. "She will come out eventually, I'm sure. She is wary of you."

"Because she is a witch?"

"Because she doesn't trust you."

His brows raised. "She doesn't trust *me?*"

Anastacia waved her hand. "She doesn't understand how a man I have stolen so much from can stand to be around me, let alone be fond of me."

Charon hummed. "Then she doesn't understand the draw you have on others."

"I have never had a draw on people. That has always been Ophelia."

"Only because you don't allow people to see. It is your eyes that set you apart, but you are clever. You know how to hide those with hooded lids and distant stares."

Anastacia didn't answer, only looked thoughtfully at the sea.

"What are you going to do with your soul?"

Her head turned towards him slowly as though she was surprised. "I have already done what I planned to do. It is mine."

At his unamused look, she smiled. It was so innocent, so serene and peaceful, that he almost believed her. If it wasn't for the feeling niggling in the back of his mind, he might have let the thought go.

But he didn't, even though he didn't comment on it further.

Charon thought it might bother him, the constant guessing game of what she was thinking or doing. Instead, it made him feel... alive.

Like every day was special. The monotony of his existence had never bothered him before, and though it still didn't, Anastacia added something to it. Something he was unsure he could survive without.

"If you don't trust me enough, there is something Ophelia can do that would help."

Charon wasn't certain he wanted Ophelia or her magic anywhere near him, but he also knew the witch would never hurt Anastacia. "Like what?"

Anastacia placed her hand in the sand, allowing it to filter through her fingers. "Connect us so we can always find one another. A tether, of a sort."

Charon didn't even have to think about his answer. "Yes."

There was never anywhere he went that Anastacia would have to find him. His schedule and location had been the same, always. But the ability to locate Anastacia wherever *she* went was an opportunity he wouldn't miss.

He pictured Hades warning him that Anastacia would get into trouble, that she would somehow be Charon's responsibility. He didn't think he would be able to control her, but at least he would be able to find her.

She smiled, pleased with his quick agreement before she stood up and offered her hand. "Good, because she is readying the spell now."

Anastacia walked ahead of him, the sun hitting her perfectly. He found himself hoping the ritual was quick so he could have her all to himself once more. Ophelia reminded him of a barely domesticated animal, one that was waiting for Charon to move wrong so she could attack him.

While there was nothing she could do to damage him, he didn't think Anastacia would like it. He didn't know what he had done to make Ophelia so worried about him, other than his position in the underworld. However, he thought himself to be respectable. His role was important, it was treated with honor, it was given his dedication.

He ducked his head to step through their doorway, straightening once fully inside. Ophelia was standing at a work desk by the window, her hair falling to frame her face delicately. Its golden strands were highlighted in the setting sun, shadows beginning to stretch behind her.

Charon had seen other souls with her coloring, but the one he found her most similar to was Aphrodite. The blonde hair, the symmetric and beautiful face, the lithe body. One look at Ophelia, and the goddess either would have loved her, claimed her as her own and kept her to show off like a trophy, or she would have maimed her in a fit of jealousy.

That a mortal woman could look so close to godhood without their blessing was reason enough.

Ophelia didn't look at Charon or Anastacia, focused on the work at her fingertips. They were skilled as she plucked herbs apart, mixing and grinding ingredients down into a poultice.

"You are sure about this?" she finally asked.

"Yes," Anastacia confirmed before glancing at Charon.

"I will not be able to undo this, Ana. Once you are connected, he will be able to find you anywhere. You will not be able to simply turn it off." Ophelia turned her gaze onto Anastacia, her face severe. "You will not be able to run away when you need an escape, or go plan one of your ideas. We will never be able to get rid of him."

I will never be able to rescue you if you change your mind, is what Charon heard unsaid.

Anastacia walked towards her friend, placing a hand on Ophelia's shoulder. "Thank you, but I am the one who offered this to him. With or without this spell, I am tethered to him irrevocably. I would end up with him at the end of my days either way. I know him."

Ophelia's voice was weak as she raised a hand to Anastacia's cheek. "Do you?"

Anastacia covered it with her own. "Better than he knows me."

That didn't comfort Ophelia like Anastacia meant it to. Instead, her golden brows furrowed as she hissed, "And when he does know you? When he finds out how your mind works, how you trick and scheme, when he recognizes your blood and your plans? I love you, Ana. But that doesn't mean it is an easy thing to do."

Charon could tell that she didn't mean the words to come across as cruel, but the look in Anastacia's eyes promised she felt it that way. He took a step towards her, reaching out until his hand wound itself through her hair at the base of her neck. It was a gentle touch that gave him control over her. If Ophelia said one more word against either of them, they would leave. Spell or no spell.

"I haven't found it to be difficult at all, witch." He looked down at Ophelia, feeling his body flood with power that so often stayed dormant within him. Darkness began to leak across the floorboards, caressing Anastacia's feet and calves like a begging lover. He could feel the Acheron diverting, straining to jump onto the shore and come to them. If he pulled hard enough, it would.

"Whatever she does, whatever she is, she is mine first. The rest doesn't matter. Only that she returns to me, only that she knows there is no one else. I am not a god. I don't require her worship, her reverence, her unyielding devotion. But I certainly intend to earn those things. Perhaps you cannot understand. I don't think it is within mortals to grasp what the love of a deity is. But Anastacia will never be rid of me, in life, in death, in purgatory. The thief is mine, now. You asked her how I could not hold the things she has stolen against her, but I have."

At that, Anastacia's head moved even in his grip, her eyes turning to stare at him.

"Every soul she has taken from me is another crime that ties her to me. An eye for an eye, a soul for a soul. She might own hers now, but she *owes* me. And I intend to *take*."

Charon leaned forward and pressed a kiss to the side of Anastacia's temple, inhaling slowly. "Do the spell, Ophelia," she said.

Ophelia licked her lips before her jaw clenched, but she turned away and gathered the jar for them. She grabbed a piece of twine, running it through the thick liquid.

"Did you have to sacrifice something for this?" Anastacia asked.

"A bird," Ophelia answered.

Anastacia's face screwed up, but she said nothing else as Ophelia lifted the little rope and gestured for them to come closer. "Face one another and hold out your hands. Now, cross your wrists and grab one another's hands."

Charon stared down at their skin, the way her hands felt soft in his. He ran his thumb down the side of her wrist, wanting to press a kiss there but stopping himself from interrupting the spell.

Ophelia began looping the twine around their wrists, tying them together. It was longer than he thought, starting loose but then growing tighter and tighter with every pass until it was pressing a hard line into their skin. Ophelia was muttering something, her voice low.

He didn't focus on the words, instead giving all of his attention to Anastacia.

Anastacia, who stood there so sweetly and stared up at him without any reservation. Her hair looked closer to chestnut for a moment, a reddish highlight catching the sun as it made its final descent. He promised himself that they would continue to visit the world above, even if only so he could see her in it.

Watch her interact with the sunlight, see her against the ocean, watch her soak in the warm waters and eat fruit fresh off of trees and bushes. He wanted to taste juice on her skin, lick the heat off her neck, kiss the redness off of her cheeks when it got too warm. Charon wanted to watch her nipples pebble in winter, see the flesh on her arms texture from the cold, wanted to heat her with his body.

He could feel a tugging in his heart, an uncomfortable stretching as if it was straining to reach her. Charon had a brief moment of wondering if he should have asked further about what the spell entailed when he was distracted with a searing pain. He tightened his grip on Anastacia's hands, both of their fingers going white as he felt like a piece of him was torn away.

It was there and then gone, replaced as quickly as it came with something soothing. Something that felt different.

Where there had once been smooth completeness in his chest, there was now a small fissure. His eyes closed as he prodded at the feeling, his mind met with sharp and concise edges. It didn't feel like it would cut him, but it wasn't fully his soul anymore.

To Charon, his soul had always felt like a smooth stone lodged at the bottom of the river. Hard, unyielding, worn and shaped by years of water rolling over it. This piece felt like a chipped shard of clay, something shaped by hand, by painstaking year after year of putting it together. He could feel the imprints against it, like an artist had decorated it slowly, beautifully, hidden messages written on it that told a whole story if you had the entire piece of art.

His eyes opened as he looked into Anastacia, past her body, past what her soul appeared as to the naked eye.

And there she was, her soul within her, a piece of handmade clay and art with the base replaced by stone. A piece of him melded to the whole of her, the whole of him fixed with part of her.

He needed to read what was on her soul, needed to see what had been so important that she had crafted it without even meaning to. He had seen so many souls in his life that looked similar, that looked like pieces of jewelry or felt like a cool breeze, that dragged against his fingers like water or like a leafy branch.

Every one was unique, but Charon did not need to examine them all. There was no point; the judges would do it anyway when they found a soul's eternal resting place.

But Anastacia's was so intricately designed that he couldn't look away. The pleasure he felt at seeing himself so tightly ingrained inside of her was enough to make him tremble. He didn't feel empty, like he had lost a piece of himself.

No, he felt like he had gained something. He would give her the rest of his soul immediately if it meant he got hers in return.

The twine fell from their wrists slowly as Ophelia unwrapped it. She didn't smile as she dismissed herself. Charon didn't watch her go, too focused on the woman in front of him. The person who contained more of him than even the river did, now.

He grabbed her quickly, ripping her into his embrace. Already, his body was straining to reach her, weeping to be inside of her. What she had taken from him required he touch her, that he be within her body as he was her soul. Charon was frantic as their teeth clashed, nipping and kissing and breathless. She tasted like fruit and sea salt.

Anastacia wrapped her legs around him as he lifted her, his hands beneath her thighs. She wasn't wearing anything underneath her peplos, his cock bobbing against her as he walked them over towards the desk. She pushed aside everything on it, a loud clash as items scattered onto the ground.

Charon didn't look to see if anything broke, biting a mark into the crook of her neck before he pulled back and removed his own clothing, watching the way his head slotted so easily against her. He knew he was larger than would be comfortable, that he should be polite and use his fingers on her first, but her hips were already nudging him with encouragement.

Anastacia's eyes were wild, the black bleeding into brown as her pupils threatened to swallow whatever color was left. Her pretty lips were parted, and Charon couldn't help but place his hand on her face, dipping his thumb into her mouth. "Suck, little lyre."

His voice was rough with demand and lust. She obeyed him just as he lost what was left of his control and thrust inside her.

Their coupling was rough, as though their bodies were trying to claim back the pieces they had willingly given to one another, as if they could fuck hard enough that those sewed together parts of their soul would dislodge and return to their original places.

But even as Anastacia came apart on him, even as she called his name and squeezed every ounce of him into her body, he knew there was no undoing what they had given.

Already, she was settling into him, his body adjusting to the new strangeness within it.

"I think I have loved you for all of eternity," he whispered against her forehead after he kissed it. "I think I have been waiting for you since the dawn of time."

"Sometimes I agree," she admitted. "Other times I feel like no one created me other than you. That I was so lost and broken when I saw you on the riverbank that I designed myself for you. I don't know which idea I prefer more."

He smiled, and then laughed. "You were you, long before me. My romantic, clever thief. I didn't make those things. I may have helped you remember who you were, may have given you something to hang onto of yourself, but that was only because they were part of who you were before you died. I will not take credit for the strongest parts of you."

They cleaned themselves up slowly in contrast to their quick and frantic lovemaking, eyes watching one another. The sun was fully set outside. Anastacia led him into her room where they settled easily in her bed.

"Do you truly call me a lyre to compare me to Orpheus' music?"

"Yes," he admitted. Until then, he had never known what it was to truly mourn. How it felt to love, what it was to be willing to sacrifice everything for a chance to see a loved one again, to *save* a loved one.

Orpheus had descended into the gloom of the underworld, down steps not meant for the living, a staircase that only one other had attempted. And that one other had been a demigod; brave, arrogant, heroic.

Orpheus had only his lyre clutched in his shaking hands, his fear so potent that Charon could smell it in his sweat. Charon had stood on his bank, head tilted as he watched this... average looking man approach. His body was nothing special, but his soul was magic. A visual melody, light chords covered with heavy grief. And he had asked Charon for an audience with Hades.

To win back his wife. A soul that Charon had taken across his river already, her coin stowed safely in his skiff. He still remembered the weight of that coin, how it felt impossibly heavier after Orpheus failed.

But he had not known the man would fail when he pulled out his lyre. When he played a song so heartbreaking, so forlorn, that Charon could deny him nothing. Charon had never felt loss. There had been nothing in his life possible for him to have taken. He loved nothing but his home, and that was permanent.

But even when Charon had nothing to compare it to, he knew from that song what it was like when Orpheus lost Eurydice. The grief overwhelmed him at the sound, and he bowed his head to the musician, allowing him access to Hades.

And then Orpheus failed his only task.

But even knowing how it ended, Charon would cherish the gift Orpheus gave him when he had played his lyre at the riverbank. Even years after, he swore he heard the music rushing down the tunnels, into the underworld. He wondered if Eurydice could hear it in Elysium, if she knew it was for her somewhere in her forgetful soul.

He was glad when Orpheus died. He hoped they had found one another again. After hearing Orpheus' music, he didn't know how they could not.

"It was the most beautiful thing I had ever heard," Charon finally said again. "Orpheus faced me with only an instrument in his hands, and he convinced me before he even finished his song. I hoped for him to be successful, that he would bring Eurydice with him and they could live their lives happily on Gaia until the fates cut their strings again. But it was not meant to be. He failed."

Anastacia was silent for a moment. Then, "He didn't fail."

Charon squeezed her, unsure if she was aware how his endeavor had ended. "He turned around when it was a condition of his not to. He wasn't permitted to see her face until they were out of the underworld, Anastacia. Eurydice returned to Elysium and Orpheus was forced to finish his life without her."

"Yes, I know," she admitted, bringing a frown to his face.

She smiled at his expression, patting his hand to explain. "But he still didn't fail. How lucky were they both, to get one last moment with one another? A look when they knew it was the final time? Eurydice knew that Orpheus came for her, that he traveled to the depths of the underworld for a slim chance at getting her back. She got time to stare at the back of his head, perhaps at the curls at the nape of his neck, at the freckle that she had memorized since the moment she saw him. Maybe she was able to trace the muscles of his back through his tunic, see the way his calves flexed as he walked, watch the way his footprints stepped steadily on the ground. They got to be in one another's presence again. Perhaps she always knew he would turn around to check if she was following. Maybe it was doomed from the start. But Eurydice knew she was loved."

Anastacia paused and then sat up to look him in the eyes.

"To love someone is to turn around. Orpheus only checked to see if she was there, if she was okay, because he loved her. If he did not love her enough to turn around, then he wouldn't have loved her enough to try and save her."

"You believe you would have turned around?" Charon asked gently, but Anastacia only laughed and flung herself next to him once more.

"No. I never would have asked for the god's help in the first place."

They only spoke for a few more minutes, but Charon waited to hear her breathing even out and feel her body relax before he allowed sleep to take him. It felt good to have her back in his arms. He wondered if Eurydice had cherished that time with Orpheus, if she had felt the same way about him that he felt about Anastacia.

He had always seen Orpheus' descent as a tragedy, a mistake, a cruel strike of fate. That Eurydice would stumble so close to the top, or that Orpheus had questioned if she was truly there and peeked behind him. But perhaps the failure was not on Orpheus at all. Perhaps it was only love.

He fell asleep wishing he could ask.

CHAPTER TWENTY-TWO

Anastacia had a moment of insecurity as she stared at Charon's sleeping body.

She didn't like to attribute much of her life to luck. Luck meant that she had left things up to chance, and leaving things up to chance meant there was the possibility of something going wrong. But she had no choice.

Anastacia was lucky that the tunic she wore in Elysium was long enough to cover most of her sandals. She was lucky that no one had inspected them closely, that they hadn't noticed a few stumbles when she used them incorrectly and on accident.

And she was lucky that Hermes kept extra pairs of shoes in his rooms at Hades' palace, and that she had located them before the gods returned to the throne room.

If he went to get them now, he would find her old leather footwear in their place, average and plain. These were far better material, and far more worthy.

The wings at her ankles were white like Caduceus. Beautiful, soft things. Tiny, smaller than she expected could hold her weight. But she knew she needed a way to reach Mount Olympus, and this had been her quickest and most reliable option.

After all, she had spent her childhood standing on Hermes' feet while he flew them around, low to the ground. If he had chosen to stay with her and her mother, perhaps she would have fonder feelings towards the memories. Now, she was only pleased that she would be able to use them against him. That Anastacia had now stolen two precious items of his.

She hoped he found her dirty, ragged shoes that she had replaced them with. Hoped he knew they were hers after he heard about the way she flaunted Caduceus in the underworld.

She walked backwards quietly, unsure of how the new bond between her and Charon would feel as the distance between them grew. It didn't hurt, but she felt the way it stretched. There was no doubt in her mind that if she turned around now, her feet would gravitate toward him naturally.

Anastacia only hoped he slept for long enough that he wouldn't interfere.

Charon was too large, too imposing, too obvious to join her. There was nothing discreet about the Ferryman. Not only would he be difficult to hide, but he couldn't possibly blend in on Mount Olympus. If anything, he would specifically draw attention.

Anastacia clicked her heels together and then ran forward, letting the wings carry her up until she was soaring through the air. She dipped too far forward, awkward for a moment, her body having forgotten how to compensate for the strange mode of travel, but it wasn't long until she was pushing herself forward easily.

She stayed above unpopulated areas, traveling over foliage and deserted mountainsides rather than going over roads. It was slightly harder to keep her bearings in the night with no sun to guide her, but she recognized a few constellations to the west. So long as she followed them, she knew she would find Mount Olympus.

Her eyelids ached for sleep. Anastacia didn't remember the last time she had gotten true rest, that which was not from the empty nothingness of Elysium. She had pushed through her exhaustion in her rush to complete her tasks before Hermes found her, and although she wanted nothing more than to spend the night in Charon's arms, she knew her window was closing.

Her first sight of Mount Olympus was lackluster. Clouds had moved in while she traveled, blocking the stars from her view. The moonlight hardly penetrated through, leaving the ground and mountainside heavily shadowed. She swallowed her disappointment.

While Anastacia wished she could see Olympus in its prime—surrounded by moonlight and bright stars, beautiful arches glinting, the gods in their glory—she knew this was better. For her, anyway.

For darkness loved Anastacia.

Her best work was done within it, shadows clinging to her body like a needy child, begging her to disappear within them.

No gods or other beings walked the mountainside. She descended quietly, close enough to Zeus' palace that she wouldn't have to travel far. The final climb to the summit was steep, difficult enough that in the dark, her fingers slipped off some of the ill-chosen handholds.

But this was the only way in for one like her. They would not take kindly to her request if she spoke to the gods formally, and she had heard about Zeus' wrath. *He* was a god she wanted to avoid at all costs. She was neither pretty enough to catch his attention, nor kind enough to prostate herself for forgiveness if she offended him.

A piece of rock crumbled under her foot and she cursed as her knee cracked against the mountain side. Blood trickled its way steadily down her shin, pooling in her sandal. Anastacia forced herself to ignore it. It wasn't seriously injured, but *she* would be if she was caught sneaking in to Mount Olympus.

When her hands finally touched the smooth surface of the pantheon, her breath rushed out of her in relief. She hoisted herself up, taking only a moment to rip off a piece of fabric from her peplos and wipe the blood from her leg and foot before tying it securely around the wound.

She didn't want to leave a trail to where she was going. After all, if she did this correctly, no one would know she had even been there. At least, none of the gods who would punish her for it.

Anastacia racked her brain as she oriented herself. She had studied Heracles and his writings, both what was truth and what was rumor. She had learned of his labors, of the cruelties the gods put him through to test him. Of what he had lost and what he had gained.

She wondered sometimes if his godhood had been worth his family. If immortality here, at the seat of the gods, at the summit of the world, was worth being apart from them for eternity. Did he yearn for them, even still?

Or had godhood and immortality taken away the parts of him that had lived before?

She didn't think that was likely. After all, she had died too, and she was still very much the same. Did he stay because he felt some attachment to the gods and thought them his friends, was he honored to be among them?

Or was he trapped?

It didn't matter either way. She had only studied his texts to learn about *how* he became a god, not whether he liked it or not.

Her steps were silent against the stone floor. She preferred to be barefoot but couldn't risk taking off the winged sandals in case she needed to escape quickly. She passed pillar after pillar, the arches and architecture so large that the gods must have believed themselves to be twenty feet tall.

Her breathing was calm despite her nerves. Stories warned her that Zeus always watched, that he was some omnipotent being who rewarded those who were good and punished those who were bad. Anastacia didn't believe that. If he could see her, he would have stopped her by now.

Her ears were tuned to the world around her, listening for the tiny scuff of a foot, a voice carried on the wind. She knew that Zeus' throne was deep within the pantheon, and that was where he turned Heracles into a god and granted him immortality. The legends were convoluted, mixed. Some said Zeus simply willed it, and so it was. But Anastacia didn't believe that, either. Like Achilles dipped in the Styx, immortality was possible, but it was a ritual like any other.

She had her soul, she had her god blood, and she had consumed water from the Styx before she left the underworld. All that was left was to drink out of Zeus' cup, the nectar of the gods.

And then she would have completed what she and Ophelia had hoped for so long.

They would be able to make a true difference in the lives of mortals.

A low voice forced her to vault behind one of the columns, pressing herself to the side within the shadows. She wasn't able to see which god passed her, but they didn't notice her presence. Perhaps they were so used to this seemingly impenetrable place that they didn't feel the need to search.

It took her significantly longer than she hoped to locate the throne room, but there was overwhelming relief when she made it and saw Zeus' cup by his overly large chair, perched like a prize. This would be the riskiest portion; there was nowhere to hide, nothing to do but approach quickly.

After she took a deep breath and fortified herself, she sprinted. Anastacia's heart was beating as though it wanted to leap from her chest, her eyes alert as she scanned the room, her ears waiting for an alarm to be called.

But she reached it without problem, bringing the liquid to her lips and drinking before she could question herself. She had just long enough to contemplate taking the pretty goblet with her before the flavor hit her tongue.

It was the most beautiful thing she had ever tasted, so complex that there was nothing to compare it to. It was—

Pain.

Anastacia's hands instinctively set down the cup as quietly as she could before they rushed to her throat, doing her best to keep herself silent. Self-preservation won out against the need to scream, to rip her skin open with her fingernails and tear the nectar out from her body as she convulsed.

It was cruel, the way her jaw still tingled with the delicious drink even as it boiled her chest and stomach alive. Anastacia took a staggered breath, dragging herself behind the throne as if it would keep her hidden for long. As if her pained gasps wouldn't notify the gods that she was here. Her jaw ached as she clenched her teeth together, her teeth grinding in her ears even as the sound of blood rushing tried to drown it out.

Her limbs shook with adrenaline, seizing as her blood spread through them and set the rest of her body on fire.

Was something wrong? Had she doomed herself, reached too far, like Icarus when he flew too close to the sun? Should she have taken what she was given with grace instead of begging for more?

Her skin felt like parchment, like it was splitting open as she writhed on the floor. Even when she had drowned, she had not felt such panic. Such pain. She knew that drowning would eventually end, that she would die and it would finish.

This had no expiration. It felt like she had been there for hours, as if time had left her suspended for her new eternity. She had sacrificed Elysium for this. Never again would she see Charon, kiss his lips, hear his voice. She would not even be granted the peace of forgetting, of living in content quiet. She thought she might take anything over this.

Slowly, though, like all things, the feeling began to fade. Her eyes were able to focus, her gaze spinning lazily for a moment before it settled on the ceiling.

Everything felt heavy as if she were made of marble. Anastacia questioned if this was still her body or if she had been remade completely. Perhaps this was not mentioned in Heracles' tales because if mortals and demigods knew what it felt like to be remade, they would never hope to reach such heights.

Her throat burned from holding in her screams. Her fingers ached and her nails were broken from where they had scrabbled against the ground. Her muscles felt tense, her joints sore, her body raw.

Still, she shoved herself up to her elbows slowly, resting until she could move to her hands and knees. Anastacia couldn't stay here; it wasn't safe. Perhaps Zeus would overlook the missing nectar, but not if she was still hidden behind his throne.

Her hands trembled as she dragged herself slowly back to the entrance, praying to the only god that could help her now, the one that she was counting on even when she didn't want to.

Anastacia moved as quickly as she could, though even that felt like a snails pace. She didn't bother going the way she came, instead moving behind the throne room and to the edge of Mount Olympus. It was impassable, the side too sheer to attempt even on her best day. Perhaps that was why they didn't bother to enclose the space.

She rolled over and let the cool stone soak into her back, let it calm her racing heart as she waited. Her skin felt overly sensitive, different than before. Each individual piece of rock felt unique against her skin.

The sky slowly began to lighten, and she began to question if her plan had truly worked or not. There were so many moving parts she had counted on; Hermes hearing about his staff in her possession and being angry enough to chase after her for it, Charon waking and knowing where she was.

The two of them finding one another in order to make it to her in time.

She swallowed hard as the stars began to fade into the sky. Anastacia had become certain she was going to have to take her chances throwing herself off the side of Mount Olympus and hope her sandals would carry her limp body when she heard the noise of feet against the ground.

Anastacia hadn't heard anyone walking to her prior to that one step, as if they had been floating on air before they landed, and she knew what that meant. Who had come for her.

Her head fell to the side as she looked at Hermes.

Gods, he was angry. She could see the fury in his face, in the narrowing of his eyes and the tenseness of his jaw.

"Don't crack your teeth," she commented tiredly.

She shifted just enough to feel the staff's length against her side, to reassure her it was still there.

He assessed her with his lip curled. "You have something of mine."

"I have many things of yours," she said. It didn't come out as clever as she intended, her words dripping with exhaustion. "Your wings, your staff, your blood."

Even tired, she saw the moment of shock and disbelief register before it was hidden once more. She expected him to comment on her remark, but his eyes darted around the throne room as if he knew there wasn't time to pry for the explanation he wanted.

"The Ferryman sent me to retrieve you. He is not happy."

She didn't think he would be. In fact, she imagined she would need to do quite a bit of groveling and explaining to earn his forgiveness.

"Take me to him," she requested.

He knelt down next to her, his eyes assessing. "Why should I?"

"Because he is your friend." She didn't bother mentioning she was his daughter, and that should be reason enough. It was clear that Hermes didn't feel their relation mattered, not towards her and not toward Epiphanios. She wondered if there were any children he favored, if the two of them were simply unlucky or if Hermes was always a bad father.

Perhaps all of the gods were.

"I have done worse things to my friends," he said as he rocked his head back and forth, as though contemplating. "I could lie and say I couldn't find you."

"That seems like something you would do," she agreed sadly as she nodded.

He had the gall to look affronted. It was only then that his gaze caught on her face.

He gasped, his hand darting out to grip her chin. Hermes couldn't hide the tremor that rippled through him, the slight opening of his mouth as he moved her face slightly back and forth. His eyes were wide as he leaned forward, closer.

They hadn't been this close since she was a little girl, but she hadn't felt his attention so keenly, even then. As an adult, she now recognized that as a child, he had not truly paid her mind. She was no more than entertainment to him, a fleeting toy he loved and then forgot about.

If he had loved her, he would not have been able to leave her as he had. Without word, without visitation, without care. If he had loved her, he would have recognized her face, even with the time that had passed upon it.

Still, she didn't rip herself away from him. She needed his help, and if she could garner even an ounce of pity, she would do her best.

Though, it was not pity that decorated his face as he asked, "What have you done?

A slow smile made its way over her mouth, and she couldn't help but revel in her answer even as she knew they needed to leave. "Taken what the world wouldn't give me. Some people must claw and scream for what they should have earned. Are you proud of me, Hermes, father, thief god?" She laughed. "It doesn't matter anymore. *I* am proud of me." Her head thumped down on the ground with exhaustion after the short tirade.

His head shook slightly from side to side, quickly. It was the only time she had ever seen him panicked. "And what of the cost?"

"I have paid it," she said. "Take me home to my Ferryman."

"Why should I?" he asked again, quieter this time. Kinder. She could read in his tone that he had already made up his mind.

Maybe he wanted to hear her say it again, that he was her father and she his daughter. Or maybe that was only Anastacia's heart still yearning for him to want something more from him, even as she hated to admit it.

Either way, she didn't give him that satisfaction; either that of hearing her admit it, or that of letting him see how much it still mattered to *her*.

"Because I will return Caduceus to you."

"And my sandals," he added.

She inclined her head. "And your sandals."

He picked her up easily as though she were a baby, cradling her in his arms. She had a brief moment to wonder if he ever held her like this when she was born. Her memories of playing with him, of clinging to his back while he flew or jumping into his arms when he visited, were never so intimate.

Anastacia made sure to avert her eyes from his face. She would rather focus on their impending fall, their flight from Mount Olympus, than stare at Hermes.

Voices echoed nearby and that was the final encouragement Hermes needed to make his decision. He stepped off the marble floor, their weight falling immediately before Hermes took a step and began flying through the air.

It was much faster than she had traveled, his skill clear in his movements and control. The landscape jumped beneath them, passing in only moments what had taken her hours. Perhaps it was his gift that helped him speed through the air, something that his blood contained that hers only had parts of.

He only slowed when her tiny village appeared, the pretty costal area lighting up with the first rays of sunlight. It was a sight of which she had never seen, whether because she was watching from so high in the air or because her eyes had changed with godhood.

Godhood.

She couldn't comprehend it; she was no longer mortal. Between the pain her body had experienced and the anxiety of her plan, she hadn't had time to come to terms with it.

Not only was her soul her own, but now she was immortal. No longer a demigod who would have to come to terms with some type of death one day, but a goddess.

Better than that, a goddess that no one knew about. A goddess of *anything*.

Hermes brought her to her home without a word. Anastacia glanced up at him, noting the simmering anger, disapproval, and confusion there. She didn't feel regret in her chest at what she had made him complicit in, didn't worry that she had upset him.

No, Hermes would forget about her transgression as he had always forgotten about her.

But the man standing below, waiting for their feet to touch the ground... him, she found it in her to feel regret for.

Ophelia peeked out from the doorway of their home, but at the sight of Anastacia, she disappeared within. She knew what Anastacia's return meant for them, that it was good news. She wouldn't berate her the same way Charon wanted to.

During the flight, she had gained some of her strength back, though her legs were still weak as Hermes set her on the ground. Charon didn't wait to see if she could support herself, approaching her quickly and allowing her to lean against him.

"Thank you," he told Hermes in dismissal.

Hermes crossed his arms. "I will not leave until I get what I was promised."

Charon's head turned slowly towards Anastacia, and she rolled her eyes. She bent, her body protesting, and slipped out of one sandal and then the other, kicking each one toward the god. She didn't have the energy to pick them up and hand them to him gracefully, though she wasn't sure she would have done so even if she did.

He glanced down at them distastefully, and she wondered what he had more issue with; that her feet had been within them, or that he had to bend to pick them up.

"And?"

She swallowed hard. She knew he wouldn't forget the staff, but she had still hoped he might. It felt like hers more than it was his, now. After all, he hadn't even noticed it missing. He didn't pay attention to it the way she did, know the way each groove felt against his skin, the exact shade of bone that even with her practice and craftmanship, she hadn't been able to perfectly imitate.

It was only a symbol of peace to Hermes, but to Anastacia, it was a symbol of her childhood, of her goals, of the plans she and Ophelia had put into action after a hundred years. It was only a blip in the entirety of Hermes life, but she had loved Caduceus.

Still, she reached into her belt and gripped it hard, her fingers as white as the bone when she held it out for Hermes to take. She remembered the other times he had done this, taken the staff from her when she had stolen it from him, the way it felt leaving her fingers. Then, it was not the staff she was holding onto, but her father.

Still, they both always left.

He took it from her cautiously, as if to make sure that it truly was his staff in his hands once more. Then, he pulled out the fake one, the staff she had spent years perfecting until it looked the same, only without the same gift within it.

"How did you get it so perfect?" he asked, a small measure of wonder in his voice as he examined the two side by side.

"You don't remember me, but I remember you," she said simply.

His eyes didn't leave the staff. "I suppose it is the curse of parents, that such meaningless words and actions are perceived so greatly by their children."

"A curse, a gift," she shrugged. "It could have been a beautiful thing if you were a better father."

"Gods are not meant to be fathers," he said offhandedly, setting down the imitation staff and bending down to pick up the sandals, tucking them under his arm.

"Aren't they?"

His eyes rose to hers slowly. She wondered if he saw what she did; the way they stood the same height, how their noses were the same shape and their hair was the same shade. "I will not apologize for what I am."

"I would not accept it, even if you did." She didn't say it harshly, did not mean to insult or bruise. It was simply the truth.

Charon cleared his throat. "You have what you wanted, Hermes. Excuse us."

In a show of power Charon often didn't demonstrate, he whisked them away into the underworld. The riverbank looked the same way it always did, the symphony of the water against the shore one she recognized as she did her own heartbeat. She sighed a breath of relief at the knowledge that she was safe once more.

When below had started feeling more of her home than Gaia did, she wasn't sure, but it settled in her bones anyway.

"Charon—" she started, but he interrupted her quickly, before she could speak. It was just as well; she didn't know what she was going to say.

"What have you done?" he asked angrily.

"I'm sorry," she said lightly, apologetically, reaching over to touch his face. He pulled away violently, abruptly. He didn't let her go though, as if he knew she would collapse without his help.

Charon shoved the door to his home open with his shoulder, setting her down in the bed gently despite the tension in his muscles. He backed up immediately, and Anastacia attempted to put her feet on the ground to approach him again, loathe at the distance he had placed between them.

"Do not move," he ordered her.

She froze, obeying.

Charon paced back and forth in the room, his face turning toward her every few steps as if something would change, as if he was trying to convince himself that his eyes were lying.

She kept her mouth shut and her hands folded in her lap, wishing he would only let her explain. Perhaps this time, with her plans finished, she would be able to bring herself to tell the truth; to spill the secrets she cradled against her chest like riches.

It was true that she hadn't only come to the underworld for him, but he *knew* that. She didn't understand why, then, there was betrayal etched into his skin, harbored by his shoulders, in the way his calves were strung like he couldn't decide if he was going to run or not.

Run from her?

"You are a goddess," he finally ground out.

"Yes," she admitted.

"And you were a demigod, before."

"Yes," she said again.

"Hermes' daughter."

She realized he was talking to himself more than he was to her, and stopped responding.

"So it *was* all a lie. Your reason for entrancing me, for pretending to care for me. It was for godhood, because you were not content being mortal. Even after I explained what the gods were, you did not care."

"It was not a lie. I told you I was in the underworld for other reasons, that I wanted things I couldn't tell you about."

"You did not imply you wanted to be a *god*," he said angrily, frustrated, as if he had made a picture of herself that he could handle and now found out that it was a fake. He had painted it wrong, chiseled her in a distorted image.

"You knew what I was when you met me," she argued. "You are the one who has claimed you are unchanging. Did you expect me to be the same?"

"I expect you to respect me the way I respect you! To respect the way we have changed to become one. I expect not to be left behind and made to look a fool every time you do something impulsive."

She couldn't stop her jaw from clenching. "I have never done anything impulsively, without countless hours of thought put into my decisions. Perhaps deities and gods have that luxury, but mortals do not."

"That makes it worse, thief. That means you could have told me. Instead, you left me asleep in our bed, happy in the lie that you were there with me. But congratulations, Anastacia. You have gotten what you wanted, no? Godhood, power, a fool wrapped around your finger?"

"My quest for godhood had nothing to do with my desire for you," she said, forcing herself up on shaky legs. "The two things can exist at the same time, independent of one another. Godhood was my plan, you were the unexpected benefit that came with it."

"I would have come to you, godhood or not."

She sighed, exasperated. "*Not everything is about you, Ferryman.*"

His jaw clenched as his body flinched backwards, his hand coming up to cover his chest involuntarily. He glanced down at it as though surprised, in pain. A deity who had spent his entire existence without discomfort, now understanding what it meant to feel something ugly.

Not as empathy, not as an evoked feeling from an imagined wrong, but a true pain. She tried to search her brain looking for a way to fix the words that had forced that look onto his face, the moment she forced him to stagger, but Anastacia didn't understand how she had upset him so.

"Please, Charon. You must try to see my side of things."

"How could I, when you have not explained them to me? Should I trust your lying words always?"

"My intentions have always been true."

"Then tell me of your *intentions,* Anastacia. Tell me your lies."

And she bowed her head, and did.

She told him about growing up on Hermes' knee, the agony of watching him abandon her time after time, a child's hope that she would be enough for him to return, failing her as he went longer and longer between visits until he disappeared.

The way she had practiced her tricks and skills to impress him, how she did not understand that his gaze never watched her; not really. His eyes tracked her mother, and she had simply been an accidental result.

How her anger consumed her at her death, the fact he had forgotten her face, her name, how she realized then that mortals meant nothing to the gods. After all, if a child could not convince her father to love her, could anyone? She knew then that she would spend the rest of her existence doing whatever she could to assist those like her.

Her god blood was nothing but a drop, nothing but a piece of her that she hated to nurture. She didn't want to be like her father, but she knew that if she played her game correctly, she could do something worth it.

Anastacia told him how she and Ophelia had planned to steal souls, bring those who fought hard back to life, but that they couldn't find a way into the underworld until she died and made her own escape route. That she fell in love with him during that time was no secret, but she explained it again anyway to help him remember.

"I did not have to fall in love with you to do those things, Ferryman. But yes, I knew that I wanted you. I knew that I would do whatever it took to steal you for myself. It is up to you, as to whether you believe that to be manipulation or dedication, I suppose."

She couldn't look at him as she rubbed her peplos between her fingertips.

"Ophelia and I wanted to make a difference, Charon. Not for everyone. I understand death is something necessary, something inescapable. But there are times when it can be held off, when a soul is not ready and is willing to fight to stay. I will give them that honor, that chance. I will steal them from your bank, I will guide them from Hermes, I will give them *time* when they have earned it. But I could not do that as only a mortal. I had no power, no respect, no say."

Charon scoffed. "You think you can be a god with a mortal's soft heart? They will eat you alive."

"They will not know about me. A goddess of resurrection, a soul thief no longer," she said softly. "A goddess with a mortal's soul and a deity's heart. If he will still have me," she added.

He turned his back on her, his shoulders rising and falling.

She waited for him to correct her, to admit that she had pushed him too far. He had accepted her when he thought it was only luck that brought him together, but what would he say now?

Now that he knew she had manipulated every aspect of their interactions after she met him?

When he turned to face her, it was with dark eyes and flat lips. "Whatever you contain, whatever you are, I will never give you up."

Anastacia felt like crumbling into herself at his tone. "You do not sound happy."

"Because I am not. My want to understand you, the compulsive need to put you before myself, is something I don't appreciate when I am angry with you."

"Then don't be angry with me," she begged. "I came back to you, as I always meant to."

He sighed, running a hand through his hair. "I am not angry that you are a goddess, Anastacia. I am angry that you didn't tell me your plans, that I was left to discover them with Hermes. Your *father.*"

"In name only," she mumbled.

"Is it too much to ask that we be on the same side, little thief?"

She walked forward and placed her hand on his cheek, feeling the smooth skin beneath it. "We will never be on the same side, my love. Would you allow me to take souls from your bank?"

She could tell he wanted to say yes, that his mouth opened to affirm their teamwork, and she saw the moment the word got caught in his throat.

"They belong to me," he said. "To the underworld. I couldn't give them back to you. It is against everything I am." He frowned as he spoke, but she didn't berate him for it. She knew that this would always be between the two of them; that neither would win in their battle of will and purpose.

"I will do my best to reach them before Hermes, so that it does not come in between us more than it already does. But I will always take them from you, my Ferryman. I may do it under your nose, behind your back, or while you sleep, but I will not stop. Does that bother you?"

They stared at one another, their chests moving silently in the empty air. Finally, he shook his head.

"No. I have always known what you were and why you were here. If you are willing to lie to me about it, I am willing to pretend I believe you. So, will you stop stealing my souls? Will being a goddess, being my partner, my wife, be enough for you?"

"Yes," she promised with a smile.

And they both acted like they believed her.

CHAPTER TWENTY-THREE

Charon stared at his thief, his lyre, this woman who had plotted and planned and stolen him. Beneath his anger was admiration at her cleverness, her determination. The way she had played him so thoroughly, even though he had expected it, had intended to counteract it. He had no doubt that eternity could pass them together, and he would never stop finding new secrets.

Godhood suited her. It hadn't made her more beautiful, but it had enhanced her features. Her honey eyes were more golden, her hair with sun kissed accents. Her skin glowed, her face and body changed just slightly to become more... perfect.

Charon couldn't say he had a preference for either form.

After all, the look on her face was the same; the kindness and innocence that she displayed, the cunning gaze and astute mind hidden within, only flashes betraying her. It was *that* which had caught his attention.

"You will not run from me again?"

"No," she said.

"I do not believe you," he admitted. "But I will always find you, now." He wrapped his hands around her wrists, still so small compared to his own hands. Fragile, like bird bones, though now that she was a goddess, they would not crush so easily in his grip. He wondered if she would bruise the same way, if he could still suck marks into her skin and leave handprints with his touch. "But I will show you what happens when you leave me, so that you know what awaits when you return."

He placed his hand lightly around her throat, pushing her towards his bed until she was splayed upon it, her short hair fanning her face like a siren in water. "You will learn to stay still, Anastacia," he said as he turned to grab a span of rope.

She eyed it carefully, watching as he curled it around his hand, the way his veins became more prominent as he gripped it hard.

Charon unfurled it slowly, letting her see the intention in his face, in the way his body moved. "Your hand, my lyre."

She reached towards him, her hand so delicate as he grasped it in his. For all her work, all of her maneuverings, they were still soft; without his same calluses. He wrapped the rope around it tight, tighter than was likely needed, but she was a thief. He had no doubt that if he gave her room to escape, she would do it.

He had never thought he would use his knowledge of knots in such a way, had never considered it in the past, but he did so now, tying Anastacia's wrist to a corner of his bed.

He could see her throat bob as she swallowed hard, but he didn't allow her time to change her mind, to question him. He grabbed her other hand quickly, before she could offer it to him, and looped the length around it as well, securing it easily. The position forced him to lean over her body, and she leaned up the best she could to place her lips against his neck, her tongue tasting the artery there.

He hissed, jolting away, his cock filling at the simple touch.

Charon bared his teeth at her, wrangling himself back into submission. He was making a point, this memory both a warning and a fantasy he hadn't known he possessed until this very moment. He backed away from her, watching for the moment she realized that there was nothing she could do to escape the situation he had placed her in.

How her arms were stretched so tightly that there was no leverage for her muscles to pull, the way her hands were tied so that she could not maneuver her wrists out of them. Anastacia had just begun to pull herself up when Charon grabbed her foot, a smirk working its way on to his face while he secured it to the end of his bed.

There was enough rope that he could move her as he willed, could loosen it and situate her differently on the bed.

He planned to take advantage.

Charon grabbed a carving tool from his desk, bringing it to the fabric in between her legs. "I don't have another peplos here," she said, portraying calm though she could not hide the tinge of panic in her voice as she raised her head to watch him.

"Then walk naked," he commented as he brought the sharp edge to her tunic, ripping it through the cloth slowly, the threads tearing like butter beneath the blade.

When he got to her core, he let the tip rest against the skin of her thigh. "Did you know, now that you are a goddess, that you cannot die from a normal blade?"

He could hear the way her heart had worked itself into a frenzy, the way her blood was surging through her veins with a mixture of uncertainty and arousal. She might not fear him, but she feared what he would do to her.

He moved the sharp edge to her center. "Better use that pretty skill of yours and stay still, my thief," he said as he ever so lightly pressed it against her clit.

She was smart. Even at the slight indent he was certain she felt, she didn't flinch, didn't tilt her hips up or away.

He moved himself so that he stood in between her spread legs, so he could see the way that she looked tied and unable to cause trouble. He found he liked it. She couldn't see his hand with the fabric blocking her gaze, and he swiftly turned the blade around until he could push the handle inside of her, sheathing it.

She gasped, unable to contain her flinch then, perhaps as she waited for pain that never came; it was a small handle, and he could see the way her arousal glistened around it already.

"My beautiful lyre, be careful not to close those pretty thighs."

He released the blade, grabbing onto both pieces of loose fabric and ripping it up her body easily, tearing the rest of it apart until she lay bare beneath him. Charon sighed, leaning forward to tweak her nipple and watch it pebble.

Her eyes widened as her breath hitched. Those full lips parted around her tongue as she licked it quickly. "Charon—"

"I don't want to hear you speak," he said. "I don't care to listen to your lies right now, Anastacia. Let your body tell me its truth. I may not always know when you mean your words, but your body? I can read that like a story."

He placed his thumb on her clit, rolling it beneath his finger slowly, lightly, as he grabbed the blade handle and began thrusting it ever so slightly. It wasn't enough friction, he knew, but he didn't want her to reach completion. No, he wanted her sobbing, begging, a mess beneath his hands.

He wanted her to feel as he did.

When her legs began to tremble and her hips started to twitch uncontrollably, he leaned down and pressed his tongue against her, torturing himself for just a moment, just a taste. He blew air onto the wetness he left behind before abandoning his spot and shedding his own tunic.

His cock was full and angry, weeping at the sight before him. "I have so many plans for this mouth, Anastacia. You never should have made yourself a goddess." He placed his hand against her neck once more, moving his thumb sweetly over her trachea. "Did you know gods can hold their breath much longer without losing consciousness? It is extraordinarily uncomfortable, the act of breathing instinctive among us all. But it would take so much more time without air to kill you. A shame, for I liked knowing you were breathing my air that time we coupled in the Acheron."

He paused, tilting his head as he moved his thumb to her bottom lip, watching the way she took it into her mouth without complaint and sucked on it.

"Though, I think I may like this more."

He dragged his bed away from the wall and into the center of the room so he had access to her on all sides. Then, he loosened her restraints enough to pull her to the top of the bed, leaving her head ever so slightly hanging off the side.

"How are you feeling, little lyre?" he asked.

She swallowed hard and met his eyes. "Like you could do anything to me and I would beg you for more."

"Do you need something thicker inside of you yet? Clench for me, feel the handle before you answer."

"No. I want the first thing to stretch me to be your cock," she said in return as he watched her pelvis contract.

He smiled. "You will regret waiting. It is a long time before you will be allowed any relief."

"And you would deny yourself, too?"

"No, *I* am not being punished. And you have given us eternity; I am no longer fighting with time to see who gets you longer."

He walked back toward her head, which she finally allowed to relax. Her pretty doe eyes stared up at him from the bed, her body naked and waiting, stretched out before him. Her hair hung slightly off the edge of the bed and he pushed a strand out of her face before pulling her so that she was tilted perfectly, her throat stretched and bared to him.

"This will look so beautiful bulging with my cock."

She sucked in a breath as though surprised, but he only pressed the head of his length to her lips. He waited, hiding the tremble that wanted to shake through him at the look upon her face, the way her eyes watched his shaft, how her tongue darted out to lick a line up his skin.

After another moment, she opened her mouth wide and allowed him to press into her mouth slowly. He knew she wasn't ready to take all of him, that with her lack of experience, he couldn't expect her to take his cock as deeply as he wanted her to, and yet he couldn't help himself.

Every thrust forward inched him further down her mouth, only pulling out to allow her snatches of air even though she didn't need it yet. Not anymore.

Her chest began heaving on the inhales he allowed her, her breasts shaking as he fucked his anger out on her face. When he began to feel the tingling in his spine, the warning that he wouldn't last much longer, he pulled out and watched the way her drool followed, dripping around her cheeks and onto the floor.

His look was loving even if his words were not. "You will not breathe again until I spill myself down your throat. Do you understand?"

Her pupils were blown wide, so large that her eyes were a pit of black, but she nodded eagerly and opened her mouth once more.

Charon was not so gentle this time, pressing forward until finally, he could watch what he truly wanted; the way her throat moved with every thrust of his cock going down it, how when he placed his hand upon it, he could feel his shaft within.

He had promised himself he would not make her take all of him, but his intentions went out the window at how well she was doing. "Look at you," he said as his thumb caressed her throat. "Look at how good you are, feel what you do to me. Do I do the same to you?"

He reached forward as he slammed himself as deep as he could go, pulling the little dagger out of her and replacing it with his fingers.

She shook violently, her legs widening and hips arching up towards him. She was soaked on his fingers, arousal dripping out of her. He finished suddenly, pulling away from her to watch his cock empty over her body.

Anastacia's cheeks were flushed, her face and body a mess, and all he could think of was that he was not through with her. That he would never be through with her.

Charon walked around her body, trailing his fingers against her skin. "How are you feeling, my lyre?"

"Please, Charon. I need you."

"Then why do you keep trying to take yourself away from me?" he asked as he bent before her, leaning to press his lips against the inside of her thigh. "Why do you insist on putting yourself in danger?"

"I'm not, my Ferryman. I never will. We are bound, now and forever. I was sure that you were mine long before you even knew my name. There was never a choice. I would have done whatever it took to keep you."

Her words brought a fierce satisfaction into his chest, a primal feeling of completion. She chose him, enamored him, there was no one else for either of them.

"I should deny you on principle," he said as he licked a line up her core before he slid his fingers inside of her once more. "But lucky for you, I find my patience has thinned."

He curled his hand, loving the way her body responded, the way she writhed. "How does it feel to fuck a goddess, do you think? Different than a mortal? Or will your body still clutch me like I am the air it needs to breathe?"

He explored her with his hands and mouth until his cock was straining again. He knew neither of them would last much longer, that he wanted to watch her come apart on him while his hands ran across her torso.

Charon pulled away before she could orgasm on his mouth, enjoying what his denial did to them both. "Perhaps you *should* misbehave more often, little thief. I find I like this mode of punishment. Do you?"

"No," she gasped out. Then, "Yes."

He teased them both for long as he could take, waiting until enough time had passed that he couldn't be sure if it had been minutes, hours, or days. There was nothing but Anastacia, the smell of her, the taste of her skin, the feeling of her body wrapped around him.

By the time he lined his cock up with her and pushed in, it was only a moment of hard thrusting and plucking fingers until they were both coming apart on one another.

Anastacia had tears streaming down her face and Charon had so much tension in his muscles from holding himself back that he couldn't help himself from resting his head against her stomach, kissing her multiple times while he caught his breath.

"I love you," he said softly as he pulled away and began untying her. Her wrists and ankles were red from where she had strained, but not so much that they would not heal within minutes.

He rolled her over to her stomach and began rubbing her back, her arms, her legs, waiting until she relaxed into their bed and he could lie next to her. Her body had softened, healing itself easily, removing the marks he loved so much. Then he let his fingers rise to her hair, brushing the strands slowly, scratching easily against her scalp. She groaned happily, her eyes fluttering shut.

Charon wrapped his thief in his arms, tucking her in close. "If you are a goddess of those on the brink of death, then what would you have the world know of you? What should I tell them of my lovely, clever, disobedient thief?"

She turned her head towards him, her eyes heavy with sleep as she pried them open. "The world doesn't need to know anything at all. I don't need their prayers or their worship, don't need them to know I have claimed you. What is between us, is between us alone. Is that enough for you?"

"As long as I have you, it will always be enough. I don't care if we disappear from myth, from legend, if no one believes in me until they have reached my river and I have taken their coin. If you do not want mortals to know about you, then I will make sure they never do."

He supposed he did not mind that he would not have to share her with the rest of the world, above or below. Hermes knew about her godhood, and perhaps Hades and Persephone would discover it in time, but Charon wasn't worried about them.

They were the ones closest to them both, and had their own reasons to protect her.

Hermes' daughter, he thought. It fit her, explained so much he had first overlooked.

"I should warn you," she spoke, her breath warm against the skin on his neck. "I have somewhere to be in the morning. I will not be long, though."

He shut his eyes, bringing his hand up to run it through the strands of her hair. "Should I ask?"

"No."

And so he forced his mouth shut, marveled at the woman in his arms, and they didn't speak for the rest of the night.

CHAPTER TWENTY-FOUR

Anastacia waited for Charon to leave for the Acheron before she snuck away quietly, following the path she had memorized back to Elysium. No one saw her as she darted from shadow to shadow, no trace left behind. She no longer had Caduceus, but it didn't matter.

The underworld recognized her as its own. It wouldn't betray her. Besides, she didn't believe Hermes nor Hades would remember her trials.

Or think that she would have lied during them.

She waded through the shallowest area of the river, the water lapping at her kindly. It was cool on her hands as she trailed them over the surface.

When she stepped into Elysium, the smell of flowers greeted her, soft as though someone had crushed them in the distance and they had floated over on a nonexistent breeze.

Anastacia didn't bother to hide. Those who resided in this place wouldn't recognize, nor remember, her. They nodded politely as she traveled between them, listening and waiting to find the only man she had returned for.

She was glad Charon hadn't asked further about her plans. Anastacia thought she might have told him if he pressed, and wasn't sure what his duty would require of him; if he would push her to do the right thing, to admit to her lies, or if he would be content with the outcome.

He *had* helped her during her Elysium trial, after all. Though, she wasn't certain he would be so forgiving about her promise to another man. Her brother, yes, but only by half. Gods had done stranger things.

Anastacia finally caught sight of the man in question, a content smile on his face as his eyes gazed into the distance. He looked healthy, his muscles strong and his skin darkened. His hair was thick and brown, no longer shedding from sickness.

His demeanor was so happy and carefree that for a moment, she thought he had caved. That he had changed his mind, dipped his hands into the Lethe, and drank for real.

But then, as if he could feel her intense stare, his head turned until his eyes found hers.

And she recognized that look within them, that clever glint, mischievous and full of promise. It was one she had seen Hermes wear.

One she had worn herself.

"You came," he mouthed silently.

She inclined her head. "I promised."

Her promises didn't always mean something, of course. But she had known that her word to Epiphanios did. It was the only way she had convinced him to come with her.

He was always going to end up in Elysium. He couldn't outrun the gods forever. But with the help of a goddess, he could certainly sneak away later.

After all, her task had only been to get Epiphanios into the underworld. They said nothing about her freeing him afterwards.

He abandoned the others he was with, walking leisurely until he reached her, hands swinging like he hadn't a care in the world. "Hello, Anastacia. Have you come to retrieve me, finally?"

"If you are still ready to return," she said lightly.

"I have a life to live," he shrugged. "A person to be."

She accepted that without question, turning back the way she came. "Then I will take you to meet my friend. She has been storing your body, awaiting your return. I will escort you there, but then I must leave."

"You won't stay above?" he frowned.

"I will be there sometimes. Long enough to see my friends, at least." She smiled at him. "Long enough to make sure that the mortals who fight hardest for life are given another chance at it."

They didn't speak as she led him to Persephone's garden, to her hidden tunnels, and up until she reached the exit to the underworld.

She followed in the pathway she had created year after year, seeing the footprints that seemed to be part of the ground they were pressed so deeply into the soil. In hundreds of years, would mortals find this place and wonder whose sandals touched this area, so high up in the mountains?

Would they stumble into her entrance? Traverse their way within, searching for the rumored underworld? Could they navigate the tunnels and trails it had taken her a century to perfect?

Anastacia liked to believe they could. After all, mortals had so much more curiosity than the gods gave them credit for. One day, they would be like the gods themselves, overthrowing their own titans. Would Anastacia be spared, recognized as one of them, or would they get rid of her with the others?

Or perhaps, they would not overthrow the gods at all. Maybe they would simply forget them. Leave them to rot like statues in gardens, covered in vines and crawled on by children who didn't know better.

Anastacia didn't think either of those things would be bad outcomes. Humanity would always come out on top, creating ways when there were none previously. Man was water over a stone; fleeting and useless as one drop, but capable of greatness when together. They would find their way, with or without the gods.

Epiphanios didn't speak as he followed, as though worried if he broke the silence, it would break their pact too. As if he worried the gods were watching them.

But Anastacia had been doing this for too long. She no longer felt the same paranoia, the itch between her shoulder blades. The gods didn't care for her, nor him; not now that they believed him cowed.

Not now that—

She inhaled and paused, her foot setting down carefully on the soft ground, just slightly spongy beneath her sandal. Epiphanios copied her movement, two thieves mirroring one another in their position. They were still far enough from civilization that no one should be nearby, and yet Anastacia *felt* it.

They were not alone.

And mortals may not be able to see Epiphanios, but the gods could.

Without her instructing him, he moved further into the foliage, crouching low to the ground. Anastacia swallowed her heart and did the one thing she was most concerned about; she looked up.

Hermes sat perched on a tree, one leg bent as he rested his arms around it, his chin on his knee. He watched them keenly, his free foot swinging as though he were humming a tune.

Anastacia said nothing, waiting. Eventually, Epiphanios joined her, realizing they were both already caught. There was no point in hiding any longer.

Was Hermes angry? About the staff, the shoes, her godhood? About her sneaking in and stealing Epiphanios from his final resting place? He had been, yesterday. He had looked furious.

But whatever it was, it had fled him overnight. Instead, he peered down at his two children, his eyes darting between them. Perhaps seeing himself in their bodies, or maybe their mothers—if he even remembered what they looked like, who they were.

Hermes laughed then, so suddenly that both Anastacia and Epiphanios flinched, the instinct to run like a child from an angry father. But Hermes only continued chuckling, finally laying down on a branch that didn't seem like it should be able to hold his weight, let alone that he should find balance on.

"I wondered how you convinced Epiphanios to walk into Death's arms so easily. Why he listened to you. If it was something I could have done differently, if you had bested me. But you did not best me at all, did you?" Hermes shook his head. "No, it was *my* blood running through your veins that gave you such a clever idea. *My* children. Look at you both."

Neither of them bothered to correct him, to add that Hermes had nothing to do with their raising. After all, perhaps in a strange way, he had—his absence burrowing into their skin, making them want to be like him so that they might be worthy of his attention.

Perhaps his absence had raised them more than his presence would have.

But it made no difference now.

Hermes simply stayed there, looking at the sky and chuckling every few seconds. Anastacia finally tested their luck and began walking once more, Epiphanios stepping carefully behind her.

They did not turn around to see if Hermes watched.

CHAPTER TWENTY-FIVE

O phelia cut her hand open over her half-brother's chest at noon. The sun was shining upon Epiphanios's body when his eyes fluttered open, his chest rising as he coughed violently to rid it of the dust that had settled in his throat during his soul's absence.

His body was healed, healthy enough to contain him for a long time. His muscles were still atrophied from years of sickness, but he was rather handsome once more; or perhaps Anastacia had only seen him sickly, so he looked much better.

She didn't miss the way his eyes darted towards Ophelia, his mouth hanging just slightly open at the way the sunlight caressed her blonde hair, the way she looked like a golden goddess in her own right. Anastacia had godhood running through her veins, infusing her skin and eyes, and she still couldn't hold a candle to Ophelia.

Anastacia pulled her friend aside, their hands clasped as they gave Epiphanios time to adjust to his body once more.

"Thank you," Anastacia said as they stood together, watching the ocean.

"Always. Thank *you*. I am excited to teach mortals how to keep the heart beating, even when the soul has fled, and even more so to watch you bring their loved ones back from the brink. I am only sorry you had to sacrifice so much to do so."

Anastacia shrugged. "I don't think I have sacrificed anything at all. I have only gained. I am happy, Ophelia. I belong."

Her friend couldn't understand. She had always belonged, never questioned her place in the world. Her heart had always been full and her words had always held weight. Anastacia wasn't angry about the difference of their impact, but it was the truth, nonetheless.

"Godhood looks good on you," Ophelia finally said.

And Anastacia smiled.

She didn't think it was godhood at all that had changed her, but Charon. The deity she already itched to return to, the one she felt like a dock in a river, the string that connected them to one another pulling taught at their distance even now.

Anastacia stayed long enough to ensure Epiphanios was settled in and to visit with Ophelia. But then, she said goodbye.

She ran as fast as her feet would take her, following the pathway up the mountain and to the cave. She didn't need to look beyond it to the ocean any longer, her skin itching to be back in the world below.

At every point she ran, she felt a memory. A flower for Persephone that had fallen, the place where she had set down the amphora she and Charon had shared, the spot he had noticed her for the first time.

She paused there, on the ledge, and felt her soul settle in her chest as she found him resting at his dock, taking the coin of the people waiting there. His eyes rose to her easily, like he had felt her arrive.

She smiled, turned, and continued the walk home.

To the Acheron.

To her Ferryman.

To Charon.

ACKNOWLEDGEMENTS

There are so many of my friends and family who have turned this book into what it is today. Your encouragement has meant the world to me. I have always loved Charon in every retelling, but he's often a side character. I loved getting a chance to watch him become the MMC I always pictured him being!

First, to my readers! I hope you loved Charon as much as I do, and that Anastacia stole your heart the same way she did mine. Every time you pick up one of my books it makes me feel like a million bucks!

To my husband, thank you for telling me to follow my dreams. You were the first person to ask me what I could do, what I *wanted* to do, when I started staying home. I'm glad to have this opportunity.

To our children, I can't explain how much you mean to me. You are the reason I write, the reason I want this to work so badly, and I am so glad to get this time with you. I hope you grow knowing how much you mean to me and you get the chance to follow your dream the way I am.

To my parents, who had to deal with me reading all the time when I was younger, had to buy me book after book, thank you.

To my siblings, Sam and Jason, I love you. I will always write about sibling love in books because of you.

To my author and book community. Louise, Tanya, and Elizabeth, I'm looking at you specifically (though all of you are wonderful). You guys inspire me, you're in this with me, and I will always support you the same way you support me. Let's go get published together.

ABOUT THE AUTHOR

Allie Grey is a fantasy, romantasy, and romance author who loves to write both open and closed door novels. In her free time, she can be found playing with her dogs and horses, raising her kids, or with her family. She has always dreamed of being an author and has been writing since a young age. Follow along on social media (authoralliegrey) for updates, or just to see her yap.

ALSO BY

Fantasy:

The Lady of House Garvoni

The Lady of Lies

Romance/Thriller

Don't Look Away